"Paul Trembling scores a winn̲ mystery, which has more e̲ beautiful game itself."

AMY MYERS, author of th̲ Neil Drury and Tom Wasp crime series

"Trembling turns ordinary people inside out, dead or alive, and you recognize all of them, even the murderers. The biggest twist is in the reader's heart when you understand the human failings that led to murder.

Trembling's inside knowledge of people adds as much authenticity to his Local crime series as his insider knowledge of CSI procedures. Even when the crime scene has been cleaned up by the villain, Trembling knows exactly where that last trace would be found. Ultimately, he shows that the biggest crime is how people treat each other. Murder is just the fallout."

JEAN GILL, author of *The Troubadours Quartet*

"A compelling mystery told with an extraordinary insight into the heights and depths of human nature. Paul Trembling has a gift for making heroes out of ordinary people."

FIONA VEITCH SMITH, author of *The Death Beat*

Books by Paul Trembling

Local Poet
Local Artist
Local Legend
Local Killer (coming in November 2020)

PAUL TREMBLING

LOCAL LEGEND

DEATH BONDED THEM.
LIFE DIVIDED THEM.

LION FICTION

Published by
Lion Hudson Limited
Wilkinson House, Jordan Hill Business Park
Banbury Road, Oxford OX2 8DR, England
www.lionhudson.com

ISBN 978 1 78264 277 0

e-ISBN 978 1 78264 278 7

First edition 2019

A catalogue record for this book is available from the British Library

Printed and bound in the UK, July 2019, LH26

I too have lost a brother: this book is dedicated to his memory. No matter how much time passes, Philip, you are never forgotten and always missed.

CHAPTER 1

"I'm not saying that sport is corrupt. But money and corruption go together like nuts and bolts. And there's a lot of money in sport."

Adi Varney, quoted in *Adi Varney – A True Legend* **by Graham Deeson**

A lot of things start at weddings. A new life for the happy couple, obviously. New relationships among the guests, quite frequently. A fight, sometimes.

For me, June and Rob's wedding was the beginning of the end to a very long story.

I picked my place card out of the detritus of the meal, and ran my thumb over the name. Nice clear font, slightly embossed printing, and they'd spelled my name right.

"GRAHAM DEESON".

Perhaps a bit more businesslike than was right for a wedding, but on the whole I approved. Having some good contacts in the area, I'd been asked to recommend a printer who'd do a quality job at a reasonable price: I was glad to see that they hadn't let me down.

I picked up the card next to mine, and checked that as well.

"SANDRA DEESON".

It had a smudge of something on it, which I carefully wiped off. And finally admitted to myself that I was bored. Weddings are OK, up to a point. I like the ceremony and I'm always ready for a free meal. But I've never been one for parties. Not the loud and crowded sort, anyway. My idea of a social occasion is a quiet meal in a good restaurant with a few friends, and the reception was well past that point.

It had taken a while, since Rob's mates – mostly van drivers – had been wary of June's colleagues, who were all coppers. However, with a bit of alcohol to remove inhibitions, they realized that police officers were basically just people, and the party took off.

The live band helped. A local group – pretty good, actually, but they were really hammering it out, and it wasn't doing my ears much good.

But now the wedding photographer was on the prowl, looking for less formal but more revealing images of people celebrating. I don't look good in photos. Even when I was younger, my lugubrious features had always made me appear miserable, however hard I smiled. Now, with thinning grey hair and sagging jowls it looked as if I had something to be miserable about.

Time to make a move.

I turned to my wife, who was deep in conversation with a young woman I had been introduced to earlier. David Macrae's wife, I recalled. I hadn't realized that the Detective Inspector was married – apparently she'd just moved down from Scotland, and was giving Sandy the full details.

"Sandy – I'm going for a walk, get some fresh air," I told her. She nodded, looked around. "Where's Sam?"

"Over there by the buffet table, talking to that CSI girl. Alison, is it? Discussing something technical about photography." Our son had spent a good many years wandering the globe and in the process had discovered an interest.

I glanced over to the far side of the room, checking he hadn't moved, but his dark blond hair was still where I'd last seen it, along with a paler-blonde ponytail. Sam had been fortunate enough to inherit his hair colour and good looks from his mother: I often wondered what he'd got from me.

Sandra peered through the crowd until she'd identified Sam, and nodded again. There was still a part of her that was afraid he'd take off again and disappear back into the world. I was almost certain he would. "OK, love." She returned to her conversation.

I weaved between the tables, picking up odd scraps of conversation on the way. Old habits. I've had a lot of useful leads that way.

"… I kid you not, this bloke must have been seven foot tall…"

"… If you know you can't handle them, why do you keep on…"

"… I bet you've arrested every one of my mates!"

That one sounded interesting, but I moved on, found an exit, and stepped out into a cool summer evening.

The Stag is a bit of an architectural disaster. It started off as an unremarkable village inn. Then it had a big single-storey dining area added on and became a gastropub. The development of a major road network nearby suggested other possibilities to the owners, and they built a two-storey extension and made it into a hotel – or motel. Do we still use that word? Finally, as an afterthought, they put in a semi-permanent marquee at the back and advertised it as a "function room", which was where I'd just escaped from.

It wasn't the place I'd want to begin married life, but it wasn't my choice. Apparently, Rob and June had some history with the place, first date or something. And at least the catering had been OK. Especially the gateaux. I'm very fond of gateaux.

There was a wide terrace along the back of the gastro section of the pub, opened up for eating during the day but closed now it was dark. The restaurant itself was crowded and doing good business, but I ignored that, preferring the relative quiet of the lawn on the other side. It ran down to a stand of trees and some picturesque ruins a few hundred feet away. They had made a nice backdrop for the photographs earlier. I suspected that they had been placed there for just that purpose. I wondered if there were builders who specialized in fake ruins.

The original pub building at the end of the terrace was now a separate bar for guests in the hotel section, which stretched off beyond it – a drab and featureless concrete slab that should never have been given planning permission in my opinion. But nobody had asked me.

I glanced into the bar as I strolled past. It was crammed full of rustic charm – horse brasses, quaintly rusting farm implements, and, of course, a stag's head. Not nearly as crowded as the restaurant, just a few people sitting here and there, nursing drinks.

And sitting on a bar stool was Adi Varney.

I nearly missed seeing him altogether. He was with two other people, half hidden by a tall, thin man in a suit. But just as I glanced that way, he was leaning back, glass to his lips, and I saw him in profile.

I stopped. And stared.

Of course it wasn't him. It couldn't be him. Not back in England, back home again. Not after all these years.

But it looked like him, just like him, and a big bubble of joy burst out of me and even while I was still not believing it in my head, my body was at the window, banging on it and shouting, "Adi! Adi! Hey – Adi – it's me!"

A middle-aged woman sitting nearby jumped, and splashed her drink. She gave me a furious look which I barely noticed.

Adi didn't respond, perhaps didn't hear me. They'd put some thick double glazing in the old windows, and the bar was on the other side of the room. He just sat there, cradling a drink and looking at something in his hand. A mobile, probably.

The thin man looked round as I continued to bang on the window. He touched Adi's shoulder and said something. Adi glanced up and saw me.

He looked puzzled. Frowning. Looked right at me – and looked away again.

Not a flicker of recognition. As if he didn't know me at all.

I stood, staring through the window, not understanding. *It must be the light,* I thought. *There's a reflection on the glass or something. He can't see who it is.*

I moved along to another window, a bit closer to where Adi was, and tried again. A bit more carefully this time. No frenzied banging, just a gentle tap. Less gentle, though, as he continued to ignore me.

The other man with him looked around, and frowned at me. Not a puzzled frown. More of a warning, a "back off" sort of frown. He was a big bloke, wide shoulders straining at a black leather jacket. He looked as though he was used to telling people to back off.

The thin one, an older man, was saying something to Adi. Who shrugged and stood up, finishing his drink.

They all headed for the door, without a glance back in my direction.

I looked around for a way in, saw a fire door at the far end of the old pub. Of course, it was locked from the outside. I hammered on it with the heel of my hand with no effect.

Beyond the original buildings was the long concrete block of the hotel accommodation. I started running. They hadn't bothered landscaping this end of the site – it was all rough ground and scraggly bushes. Hard going for anybody, let alone someone with all my recent health problems. I was panting hard by the time I rounded the end of the building – at which point it occurred to me that it would have been quicker to go back into the marquee and out the front.

Too late. It was further to go back now, and there was at least a path this side, running down towards the hotel entrance.

I burst into the lobby, and the young man at reception jumped up in alarm – as well he might, when a panting, sweating, balding middle-aged man suddenly charged through the front door and ran at him.

"Sir? Do you need an ambulance?" It was a reasonable question, under the circumstances.

"N... N..." I gasped, and waved my hands ineffectually. "No!" I finally managed to get out, as he picked up a phone. "I'm OK." Pause and gasp again. "Really. Thank you. I'm fine."

The lad didn't appear convinced, but he put down the phone and gave me a wary look. "Was there something else I could do for you, sir?"

"Yes. I've just seen someone. In your bar. An old friend. Adi Varney?"

"Adi Varney?" He frowned, then his eyebrows shot up. "You don't mean *the* Adi Varney? Adi Varney the footballer?"

"Yes, that Adi Varney!" Was there another one? "He's in the bar – was a few minutes ago, anyway."

The receptionist shook his head, regretfully. "No, sir. You must be mistaken. That bar's for hotel guests only, and I'm pretty sure that Adi Varney isn't one of them. More's the pity – I'd love to be able to call my dad and tell him we've had Adi staying here!"

I took a longer look at him. He couldn't have been more than twenty, so he wouldn't have been around when Adi was in his heyday. But his dad would have been.

"You a Vale supporter, then?"

His face lit up. "Third generation! Used to be there for every home game – me, me dad, and me grandpa!" In his enthusiasm, a bit of local accent began to creep in. "Me ma as well, sometimes. Me dad can't get out much nowadays, so I don't go so often. And they're not doing too well just now, are they – not like the old days."

"That's a fact. Only just escaped relegation last season – and to be honest, that was better than they deserved."

We shared the sad look of loyal fans who've been let down by their club.

"You wouldn't mind just having a look at the guest list, would you? Make sure that Adi's definitely not on there?"

He shrugged. "Couldn't do any harm, I suppose." He turned to the computer, punched some keys, and studied the screen. "No, sorry. Twenty-three guests currently, none of them a Varney. But I can't see someone like him coming here in any case. He'd be at a five-star place somewhere."

The lad had a point. Adi had always been ready to enjoy whatever money could buy him. I scratched my chin, baffled.

"OK, so perhaps he came in as someone's guest? Visiting someone who is staying here?"

"Perhaps. But I've been on all evening, and I'm pretty sure that he didn't come through here."

"But if he'd been here earlier?"

"Maybe, but if Adi Varney was in the hotel, someone would be bound to recognize him and the word would get around."

That was a thought. The bartender must have seen him.

"Could I go through to the bar and ask in there? Just to put my mind at rest?"

He hesitated. "I'm not supposed to let anyone through apart from guests…"

"Just for a few moments. I'll just look, ask a few questions – no trouble, I promise."

"OK then. For a Vale supporter!"

He nodded to a door just past the reception desk.

"Thanks." I slipped through quickly, in case he changed his mind.

The bar had filled up a little since I'd looked in from the other side – there was another entrance that came directly from the guest rooms. The one that Adi and his companions had been heading for, I decided, as I looked around and got my bearings. They certainly weren't here now. The woman I'd caused to spill her drink was, though – fortunately engrossed

CHAPTER 1

in something on her mobile. I stayed well clear of her as I made my way to the bar.

The barman looked up as I approached and took on a wary expression. He had obviously seen me banging on the window.

I held up my hands. "Sorry about earlier. I didn't mean to cause any trouble. It was just that I thought I saw an old friend in here – someone I haven't been in touch with for years – and I was trying to get his attention."

He relaxed slightly at my explanation. "Yes, sir. I understand." He had a definite transatlantic twang.

"His name is Adi Varney."

He returned a polite but essentially blank look. "I don't know the name, sir."

"Adi Varney the football player. England international, top league goalscorer…"

"I guess you mean football as in soccer? Sorry, sir, I'm not much of a sports fan."

"Over from the States?" I hazarded a guess.

"Yes, sir. Taking a little time out from law school."

"OK, so you wouldn't know about Adi Varney. But he's a really big name round here. Ask your colleague out in reception."

The barman picked up a cloth and began wiping down the bar. Every barman does that while they're having a conversation.

"So he's like the local superstar? And a friend of yours as well?"

"That's right. We were born in the same hospital, grew up on the same street. And Adi played for the local team for his entire career. So in these parts he's a really big deal – nearest thing we've got to a superhero! But I haven't seen

15

him in years – not since he went out to the US. California. Are you from that way?"

He shook his head. "Boston. Never been further west than Chicago. I guess it must have been a surprise, seeing him after all this time?"

"You can say that again! Listen, he was sitting just about here. Do you remember? Reddish brown hair, little moustache, a sort of roundish face?"

"Yeah, I remember him. Didn't hear his name, though."

"Is he staying here at the hotel?"

"I couldn't say for sure. The guy with him is though, because he had the tab put on his room."

"The man with the black jacket?"

"No. I didn't know him either. It was Mr Lonza who was signing for everything."

"Lonza?" It wasn't a name that was familiar to me.

"Sure. Rocco Lonza. Hey, you think you were surprised to see your friend here? Well, it was one heck of a surprise to see Lonza, I can tell you! Never expected a guy like him to turn up in a place like this."

I still had no idea whom he was talking about, but he seemed happy to talk and I was happy to let him. Hotel staff are often a bit tight-lipped about their guests – but bar staff are the best bet for a bit of information. Especially when they are essentially just passing through.

"You know him, then?" I prompted.

"Not personally, but over in the States he's real big in business. *Some* sorts of business." He put a distinct emphasis on "some", and gave me a knowing look. "Sort of like your guy is in soccer, I guess: if you know the game, you know the name."

"What sort of business? Sports, perhaps?"

"Sure, sports. Lot of other things as well. He's one of these wheeler-dealer guys, always got a whole lot of things going on at once, you know?"

He glanced around, then leaned forward and spoke more quietly. "Word is, though, that a lot of those deals are – what's the word you use over here? Dodgy?"

"You mean dodgy as in borderline illegal?"

"That's right. That sort of dodgy. Not that he's ever been convicted or anything, so don't repeat it. But they say he's connected."

"Connected?"

"Yeah! You know. Like he's connected with the Mob."

The Mob. Gangsters, organized crime, Godfathers. I looked at him, incredulous. That sort of stuff happens in films. Not in commonplace little hotel bars in England.

"You're kidding me. The Mob? Really?"

He nodded vigorously. "That's what I've heard. All that money he does his dealing with – it's Mafia money, and he's their top laundry guy."

I stared at him, then shook my head. "Well, I must be wrong then. I mean – the Mafia? That wouldn't be Adi. Couldn't be. Sorry, my mistake."

I went back out through reception, nodding to the Vale fan, who was still behind the counter.

"Any luck?" he asked.

"No, it wasn't him. Just looked very much like him, that's all."

He shook his head, sorrowfully. "Pity. It would have been something, to have Adi Varney here."

"It would indeed," I agreed. "Thanks for your help, anyway."

I headed back to the marquee and the wedding reception, amazed yet again by the affection that local people still had for Adi, even after all these years. I wished it had been him. There was so much I wanted – needed – to say. But I was now quite sure that it couldn't have been. Adi, mixed up with the Mafia? One hundred per cent not.

Well, ninety-nine per cent not, anyway.

That odd one per cent was going to get me into trouble.

CHAPTER 2

"They say it's not about winning or losing, but about playing the game. B***s! It's all about winning!"

Adi Varney, quoted in *Adi Varney – A True Legend* **by Graham Deeson**

Sandy agreed with me. "That couldn't have been Adi," she said firmly. "Goodness knows he had his faults, but the Mafia? Definitely not him."

Once my excitement had died down, my natural British embarrassment at a case of mistaken identity had kicked in and I felt a strong need to apologize to someone. Lacking any suitable candidates for my remorse, I had turned to the family and told Sandra and Sam about it as we drove home.

As I drove home, to be precise, since I was the designated driver for the evening and consequently hadn't had a sip of anything stronger than fruit juice. Apart from the champagne toasts, of course. Not that Sandra was a heavy drinker, but she'd managed about three glasses of wine (by her admission). And, slightly to my surprise, Sam didn't seem to have had much more than that, even though he was now sitting in the back with his eyes closed.

But not asleep, it seemed. "Yes, but it's been what – seven years since you last saw him? People can change in seven years."

Sandy shook her head. "Not that much. Not Adi. Don't forget that this was the man who supported half the charities in town. I can't believe that he'd get mixed up with crime. And in any case, if he was back in the UK he'd have got in touch with you, Graham."

I shook my head. "Perhaps not. We had a bit of a falling out, just before he left."

"I know. But 'a bit of a falling out' doesn't count for much against a lifetime of friendship. You two were so close I sometimes felt jealous!"

I chuckled. "Hey, we were just good friends – nothing for you to worry about!"

What I didn't say was that it had been more than just 'a bit of a falling out'. A lot more.

"Do you remember him, Sam?" I asked, shifting the conversation.

"Who – Uncle Adi? Yes, sort of. He used to be round ours a lot when I was a kid. What I most remember about him was that walking stick he used, with the brass dog's head. He used to make growling noises and push it at me, and I'd pretend to run away."

"Walking stick! Of course!" I thumped the steering wheel hard, and the car swerved slightly.

"Careful, Graham!" Sandy looked at me in alarm. "What do you think you're doing?"

"Sorry. It's OK, I just realized. That couldn't have been Adi in the bar. He didn't have his walking stick!"

"Well, it's a good thing the roads aren't busy. Try not to have another revelation, or we'll end up in the ditch!"

"He might have had surgery, got his leg fixed so he didn't need the stick?" Sam suggested. "Was he limping at all?"

I thought about it, running the scene through my mind. "Yes. Perhaps. I only got a brief glimpse of him walking, when he left the bar, but he may have had a slight limp. But it would have had to have been some pretty good surgery for him to manage without the stick. That leg was badly damaged – he did well to get about on it at all."

"Collision with a goalpost, wasn't it?"

"That's right. At Wembley, of all places. An international against Sweden – just a friendly, and England were winning 3–1, but of course Adi was still pushing for another goal. There was a corner, the goalie fumbled a catch – bit of a scramble round the goalmouth and then the ball was running loose, across the front of goal. Adi got to it just before it went out of play, somehow managed to slot it in from a ridiculous angle, but then he couldn't stop himself. Full tilt into the goalpost, rammed it with his knee."

"Ouch! That must have hurt."

"Shattered his kneecap. That was 1995 – a month after you were born. He was only thirty-two then, could have had years left on the field, but it was the end of his playing career. Absolute tragedy."

"And just for a friendly that they were winning anyway?"

I nodded. We'd reached the end of our road. I signalled and made the turn. "Yes. Bitterly ironic. But also so typical of Adi. He'd never approach a game, any game, with the attitude that it wasn't important. *Winning* was important, and not just winning but crushing the other team if possible. Off the pitch he was charming. Considerate, even. Well, he could be, at any rate. But get him out there, in the game, and he was never anything less than totally focused, utterly committed to coming out on top."

I pulled into our drive and switched the car off. "You know, when I went to see him in hospital after that game, the first thing he said was, '4–1, mate! We hammered them! And I got that last one in, didn't I?' He knew that his leg was completely smashed up, that he was finished as a player – but the last kick of his career had been a goal, in a winning game. That was important to him."

"Almost better than being able to play again," Sam said. Not asking. Understanding.

"Almost."

"Sounds crazy."

"He was crazy," said Sandra. "In some ways. Football ways."

"That's what made him great," I suggested.

Sandy opened her door. "Well, in any case, I think we can agree that whoever you saw, it wasn't him. Let's get inside. I don't want to sit on the drive and talk football all night. Had enough of that in the past!"

We went round the back and in through the kitchen. The front door had been out of action for a while last year, and we'd got into the habit of using the back. The damage was all made good now, but we still avoided using the front entrance.

Brodie hauled himself out of his basket and came to meet us with a wagging tail and a head thrust out for fussing. That was another reason for not using the front door. If Brodie heard anyone there he'd hide in his basket and howl. Dogs have good memories for important things, such as people setting fire to the house.

The memory made me run my hands over my head. Most of my hair had grown back, but I had a permanent bald patch at the front now. It wasn't noticeable as long as I kept the rest cut short, or so I liked to think.

"I'm glad to get this thing off at last," said Sandra, removing her blonde wig. "It really starts to itch after a while. I'm sure it's not supposed to, but it does."

I felt a now familiar twist in my gut as I looked at her. Plastic surgery had done all it could, and it was a lot, but she would never have her own hair again: there was too much scar tissue on her head. She had been through a far worse fire than I had, and had suffered accordingly. That deep-down pain I felt wasn't just from seeing what she had suffered; it was from remembering how close I'd been to losing her altogether.

"Perhaps it's just psychological, Mum. It's all in – on! – your head!".

"It's a pity that you didn't pick up a sense of humour on your travels, Sam!" she retorted – but with a smile. It was good to see that banter going on between them. When he'd first come back home, Sandra had been painfully cautious in everything she said or did, afraid that with the slightest wrong word she would lose him again. It had taken a while for us to get used to being a family once more.

"Oh, I picked up several senses of humour! Want to hear a joke in Chinese?"

"No thanks! I'm going straight up to bed. I'm shattered." She yawned, to prove the point. "Coming, love?"

I shook my head. "No, I'm not quite ready yet. My head's buzzing over this Adi thing. I'll be up in a bit."

"OK. Don't wake me when you do! Goodnight."

I went through into the converted garage we used as an office, fired up my laptop, and clicked on the "Adi" shortcut.

"Is this the book you've been working on, then? The Adi Varney bio?" Sam came in with two mugs, and set one down next to me while peering over my shoulder. "Thought you might like a cuppa."

"Thanks." I took a cautious sip. I'm fussy about my tea – it has to be just the right strength and just the right amount of milk. Usually I make my own, but Sam had it spot on in the first week he was home. "It's not really a book, not yet. Just a dumping ground for all the background information I've accumulated, plus some sample chapters, random memories, quotes, notes, etc."

"I'd have thought you'd got further than that, Dad! You've been working on this for a while."

I nodded. "A few years. Or all my life, perhaps! It's the structure I can't get right. I've got so much information about Adi that I can't work out how to organize it."

"Wood and trees?"

"Something like that."

"What are you going to call it? Have you got that far at least?"

I chuckled, and opened up the "Titles" file. "What do you think?"

"Ah. Still thinking about that, then." There were at least twenty possibilities listed. "What's the shortlist?"

"That is the shortlist! What do you think? I want something that's catchy but informative."

"Well, not 'The Adi Varney Story', for a start. Sounds like a made-for-TV bio of someone nobody ever heard of. And 'The Truth About Adi' – no, that's a newspaper exposé headline. 'The Legend of The Vale' – that works better. I like that word 'legend', but only the locals will know what 'The Vale' is. Otherwise, it sounds like a fantasy novel."

I nodded. "It's a work in progress, and I value the input. But what I wanted to do just now was to look at the photos, try to work out why I was so sure that it was Adi I saw."

I brought up the image files and opened the first one.

"This is the earliest picture I have of him. Earliest one of me, for that matter."

A slightly blurry black-and-white shot, the main subject was two ten-year-old boys and a football. One of them – the one with his foot on the ball – had a long, thin face and a frown. His companion was a bit shorter, with a roundish face, reddish hair, and a cheeky smile. Slightly behind the other boys was a younger lad, looking up at them with an earnest expression.

"I remember you showed me this before. Scruffy little urchins!" commented Sam.

"Show some respect," I admonished. "That's your old man there with the ball."

"And Adi with you? Shouldn't he have the ball?"

"Oh, he didn't mind me having it for the photo. Because it was my dad with the camera, after all. And Adi could take it off me any time he wanted, which we both knew. In fact, he'd probably just said so, which is why I'm frowning and he's grinning. Dad was mad at me for spoiling the picture with 'a face like a wet weekend'!"

"He should have taken another one, then."

"Do you have any idea of the price of film in those days? You lads nowadays, with your fancy digital gear, shooting off a dozen shots of the same thing, you've no idea! It was an Instamatic, Dad had only just got it, and he made that first film last six months!"

"And the kid photobombing you? That's Uncle David, isn't it?"

I didn't answer immediately. Just looked at the little fellow.

"Yes. The only photograph we have of him. He died not long afterwards."

"Oh, yeah, of course. That's…" He put his hand on my shoulder. "Sorry, Dad."

"It was a long time ago. Let's see something more up to date!"

I flicked through images of Adi in his playing days, and got on to his post-injury career. A head and shoulders profile of him, frowning. Taken with a zoom lens, nothing else in shot, but I knew he'd been in the home-team dugout when it was taken. "That's the day he became manager of The Vale… heck, he does look just like the person I saw!"

"It's still ten years ago," Sam pointed out. "What's the most recent image you have?"

I scrolled through the thumbnails. "How about this? It's a clip from local TV news, just after the last game Adi went to as manager. The last Vale game he ever went to, as far as I know. He'd just announced his resignation – right out of the blue in a post-game press conference. The TV crew followed him out."

I opened the file, and the video began running. A shaky, confused shot as the cameraman followed the female reporter through a car park. Ahead of them, a figure came into view. Walking with the aid of a stick.

"I see what you mean about the limp," said Sam. "It really was bad, wasn't it?"

They caught up with him as he reached his car, a bright red Jag. He half turned, looked at them over his shoulder, and I hit the pause button.

You could still see the child in the man. He had the same round face. The red hair was now a few shades darker and speckled with white, but complemented by a moustache in the same colour. But there was no smile now. Instead, he looked angry.

"Smartened himself up a bit, since he was a kid."

I shifted my attention from his face to his clothing, and felt suddenly chilled.

"Dad?"

"That jacket he's wearing. There's a story to it."

I sat back and rubbed my eyes. "When Adi was recovering from his injury – well, it was obvious he'd never play again, but The Vale couldn't lose him. So they made him assistant manager. Then, when old Danny Travis retired, he naturally became manager.

"As assistant manager, Adi turned up to games in his tracksuit. Which looked a bit out of place next to Danny, who was always very smartly turned out. Beau Dan, they called him. Dan the Dandy.

"So on his last day as manager, Danny produced this tweed jacket."

"That tweed jacket?" Sam asked, indicating the picture on the screen.

"The very same. Real Harris tweed, top brand, best part of two hundred quid's worth, I'd say. 'Here,' said Danny. 'I think this is you, Adi.'

"And everyone around stopped what they were doing, to see how Adi would react. Him and Danny hadn't always seen eye-to-eye; there had been some strong words exchanged behind the scenes now and then. And Adi never liked being told what to do. So it could have gone downhill fast from that point.

"But Dan had chosen his moment well. Just after the game – which we won, by the way – with a lot of people present, and reporters… me, for one! Adi looked round, taking note of who was there and who was watching, which was just about everybody. Then he smiled, and took the jacket. Shook Danny's hand, made an impromptu speech about hoping to maintain the values that Danny had established for the club, on and off the pitch, and how this jacket would help. Applause, cheers, photos, etc.

"Adi wore that jacket to every single game he attended as manager."

"Good thing that tweed's hard wearing, then!"

"Probably why Dan chose it." I ran the video a few frames forward. Adi turned and faced the camera full-on. "You see that button? The top one?"

Against the brown fabric, it was clear that the top button was lighter than the one beneath it.

"One Saturday, when there was a particularly big game on – Cup tie, against Chelsea, I think – Adi was running late and found that there was a button missing off the jacket. His wife was out, but Adi bustled around, found the needles and threads, and a box of buttons. Couldn't find one that matched for colour, but he got the closest in size and shape, and put that on. With enough thread to tie up a battleship, his wife told me afterwards, but he decided it was good enough and of course, refused to have it changed. So that became part of his image, something else that was distinctively Adi."

"So why did you look so shocked when you saw it?"

"Because I suddenly realized – the person in the bar was wearing *that* jacket."

"Wow." Sam leaned forward, staring intently at the picture. "Could you see the button?"

I frowned, trying to remember the details. "I don't think so. I can't remember if I did or not."

"It might not be the exact same jacket, then. But if it was so well known, it wouldn't be difficult to copy." He thought for a moment. "Still, if it's not Adi, then it's someone who looks like him and is dressed like him. Why? What for? That's the real question, isn't it?"

I shrugged. At the back of my mind was a lingering hope that perhaps it really was Adi after all. Adi with a miraculously healed leg. Was it really more far-fetched than an Adi lookalike wearing an Adi jacket sitting in a bar back here in the UK?

Perhaps.

"Could it be a sort of Adi Varney fan-club thing? You know, like all those big conventions they have where people dress up as their favourite character?" Sam rubbed his thumbnail against his lips as he thought about it -- which is something I often do myself. I was ridiculously pleased to see him copying my idiosyncrasies.

"AdiCon? I don't think so! That's not a football fan sort of thing. Not at The Vale, anyhow. Wearing a shirt with their favourite player's number on is as far as it goes."

"OK. So perhaps it's something for TV? A documentary or a drama about him?"

I thought it over. "Better. But then where were the rest of the film crew? And in any case, if there was anything like that in the wind, I'd have heard about it. In fact, I'd probably have been consulted on it."

"So what happened to the real Adi, then? I remember something about him going over to the States."

"Yes. Just a week or two after his resignation, he turned up in California. Big press conference, talking about a new team that he was building from scratch. 'California Strike All-Stars' or something like that. It was going to be huge, not just in the USA, but internationally."

"Was it?"

"No. Never really got off the ground. Oh, there was a lot of excitement for a while. Adi was all over the place, talking up the new team and the new project. He recruited a few players from here and there – Hans Van Hoorn, the Dutch international, José Santos from Brazil by way of Inter Milan – big names, if a bit past their top performance, but he had them parading round in the new kit. It took a while, but he got a team together, played a few exhibition games, looked to be doing OK. Better than OK, perhaps – they took on Real Madrid and beat them at one point! Just a friendly, of course, but it looked like this was really going to happen. And then…"

"And then?" Sam prompted after a moment.

"And then nothing. It all went quiet. No more team, no more Adi. Not a whisper."

"Until now!"

"Until now," I agreed. "Except that it wasn't Adi, of course."

"But who was it, eh? That's the question…" Sam yawned and stood up. "I'm going to bed. I can't stay up all night like you tough old guys." He patted me on the shoulder. "You'll have to dig around, though, and get to the bottom of it. Can't leave a story like that alone, can you?"

"Come off it, Sam. I was the sports hack on the local rag – not an investigative reporter!"

"Time for a new career, then! G'night, Dad."

I stayed up a bit longer, clicking through the photographs, remembering. Sam was right, I realized. I'd have to dig around.

*

Sunday morning. Which meant church for me and Sandy. Sam had shown no interest since he'd come back, and we didn't press him.

To be honest, I didn't have a lot of interest that morning. Bleary-eyed from lack of sleep, I slumped in the pew and let readings and prayers and sermon wash over me, while such part of my mind as was functioning was consumed with thoughts of Adi, and what I'd seen in the hotel bar. Without Sandy's nudging, I might not even have stood up for the hymns.

Afterwards, there was the usual coffee and biscuits in the church hall. I spotted someone on the other side of the room, and made my way over.

"Hi, Karen," I said, and she turned to me with a smile. Dark hair, still worn long, no grey showing, though her face was lined. Warm brown eyes, warm smile. Still a very attractive woman, she'd been stunning on her wedding day, when I'd stood as Adi's best man. Since then, though, many lines had been graven into her skin.

"Graham! Didn't stay too long at the wedding then?"

For a moment the two weddings – the one yesterday and the one thirty years before – mingled in my mind. Four lives, all full of hope for the future. Two still hoping.

"I'm long past the all night partying age! How are you doing? And the girls?"

"Fine, thanks. Sara's busy with her career, Jaqui's busy with little Patrick, and Adrienne is somewhere around…" Karen glanced across the room, then shrugged. "Off on youth group business, I expect. How about you and Sandy? And Sam?"

"We're fine, thanks." Formalities over, I hesitated over my next words. Karen tilted her head, with an expectant look.

"Come on, Graham, cough it up. Not like you to be short of words!"

"OK. It was just that I was wondering if you'd heard anything from Adi recently."

There was no overt reaction, but suddenly Karen went very still. I mentally kicked myself for not finding a more sensitive approach.

"Sorry."

"No. It's OK, Graham. I – it's just that, hearing his name even… it brings back things. I brace myself. If you know what I mean."

"Yes. Of course."

"And no, I haven't. Not recently. Not for a long time. Why – have you?"

She kept her tone neutral, but there was a look in her eye which suggested that she desperately hoped I had.

Or perhaps that I hadn't. I couldn't be sure which. Either way, I was likely to make things worse, but it was too late to back out now.

"Not heard from him, no. But I saw somebody yesterday who looked just like him. Couldn't have been him, though!" I added that hastily as I saw something like hope flicker across her face. "He was walking without a stick. Without a limp, even."

"You had a good look at him, then?" There was a sharp edge in her voice. "Did you speak to him?"

"I saw him through a window. Didn't get to speak to him, exactly. I waved and shouted, and he looked at me but it was clear he didn't recognize me. Then he walked away."

"But if it was through a window, he might not have seen you properly. Perhaps that's why he didn't recognize you?" It was definitely hope in Karen's face and in her voice, despite all I'd said to avoid arousing it, and I mentally kicked myself again.

"I think he saw me well enough. Everybody else in there did. They were all wondering who the nutter was!" I tried to wave it off as a joke. But it hurt to see something die a little inside her as she accepted my explanation.

I was expecting her to ask why I'd bothered to ask her about hearing from Adi, if I was so sure it wasn't him, and was trying to come up with an answer that wouldn't sound too feeble, but we were joined by a slender red-haired teenager.

"Hi, Uncle Graham," she said. I'd always been Uncle Graham to Adi's girls, just as he'd been Uncle Adi to Sam. "Mum, can we go now?"

"Hi, Adrienne," I said.

"Yes, I suppose so." Karen fished in her bag, pulled out some car keys. "Go and get in. I'll be along in a moment."

We watched her head off towards the door.

"She's really got Adi's hair colour," I said.

"And other things as well. She's brilliant at sports. The only one of the girls who took after him in that way."

"She's – what? Sixteen now?"

Karen nodded. "Going on twenty-one! Listen, Graham – I'd appreciate it if you wouldn't mention this person you saw when she's around. Or anything about Adi, really. It's – well, I just don't want to stir things up. You understand."

"Of course. Sorry I mentioned it."

She smiled gently. Perhaps a little painfully. "It's OK. I know you miss him too. Perhaps more than I do, even, in some ways – you were his friend for ever, weren't you?"

"I don't know. It seemed that way. But..."

She patted my hand. "People change, Graham. Adi changed. I think it had been coming a long time, but it was a shock when it happened. When it became obvious. Well, I'd better go. See you next Sunday, if not before."

"See you, Karen."

She turned to go, then turned back again. "About that limp... You know, when Adi first left, when he was still keeping in touch, he said something about getting some special treatment. Something only available over there. Made a joke about how he'd be playing again. I don't suppose it would be that good, though, even if it ever happened."

I watched her leave the room. I'd wanted to ask her about the jacket, if Adi had taken it with him, but under the circumstances I hadn't dared mention it. To give her even the slightest thread of hope would have been too cruel. I wished I'd realized that sooner.

*

After lunch I slipped away into the office and set about searching online for all and any possible treatments for severe leg injuries. I was almost convinced that Adi's leg would be impossible to repair, even with the most cutting-edge medical technology available – but once again there was that nagging one per cent uncertainty.

After a couple of hours, Sandra came looking for me.

"Come on," she said. "It's a lovely afternoon: the dog needs a walk, I need some company, and you need some fresh air!"

I stretched and yawned. "Right. As you usually are. I wasn't getting anywhere with this anyhow. I'll get my boots."

Half an hour later, out on our favourite walk across the fields and into the woods, Sandra wondered aloud what I'd been doing. My explanation led, inevitably, to my conversation with Karen, and a serious telling-off.

"You actually said that to Karen? You asked her about Adi! Graham – you…" Sandra fell silent, either because she couldn't find words to express herself (unlikely) or because the words she was coming up with weren't the sort that she liked to use.

"Sorry. I didn't think it through," I confessed, humbly.

"You didn't think at all! Of all the idiotic, insensitive… and pointless! We'd already agreed that it couldn't have been Adi you saw. Why bring it up at all? And with Karen, of all people! Have you forgotten how it was for her when he left? Do you really think it was worth raking that up? And suppose Adrienne had overheard?"

"I know, I know. I just thought that – if there had been any word, any hint of him coming back to the UK…"

"If there was, Karen would probably have been the last person to find out! Don't you remember how she learned about that woman he'd met over there? Not from Adi! He was still sending messages about bringing her and the girls over to join him – still keeping her hopes alive – and then there's pictures on the internet of Adi with his arms round that – person – and her hands all over him!"

I made to speak again, but she held up a hand. "Don't say anything more! I don't want to hear about any more of your speculations!"

She'd left her wig behind, preferring a sun hat on bright days. Now she tore it off, flung it at me, and strode on ahead, shouting for Brodie to get his nose out of a cowpat and keep up.

I sighed, watching her scarred head recede into the distance. Once again I'd asked the wrong questions at the wrong time – always a possibility for a reporter – but now I didn't even have the mediocre excuse of following a story. Just as well I hadn't mentioned the jacket. It would have been pointless anyway. Even if Adi hadn't taken it with him, it would have been easy enough to reproduce it.

Which of course left the question of why anyone would have gone to such lengths to imitate him. I still didn't have a good answer to that, either.

Brodie came running back to round me up. I obediently followed on, keeping at a safe distance.

It wasn't until we were back home that Sandra was finally talking to me again.

"So what did you discover on the internet? Could his leg have been repaired?"

"Nothing conclusive. There's a lot of information about how to deal with a broken bone or a torn ligament, but Adi had multiple injuries. There's no website that I could find that dealt with all those things at once. Plenty of people making big claims about acupuncture, or stem cell treatment, or all sorts of other things, but nothing that could be tied down to a definite answer for someone with that amount of damage. Apart from what the doctors said at the time, of course, which was that he was lucky to be able to keep his leg at all."

"So, once again, it wasn't Adi!"

"Probably not," I agreed. "But, in that case – who was it?"

"I've no idea. But why did you think Karen would know anything?"

Obviously, I had no answer to that.

"Just don't ask her again, OK?" She touched my cheek. "Look, I know you want to find out for sure and lay this to rest – but don't involve Karen. She's been hurt enough."

"Right. Of course. But I may ask around a bit in other places. Discreetly."

She smiled. "I know you will." She paused for a moment. "Does Karen know about you and Adi – and David?"

Somehow, even after all this time, I can't hear my brother's name without feeling something. I'm not even sure what it is, any more. Guilt, regret, a space left empty many years ago and never entirely filled.

But it's very deep, and I don't think it shows. Not even to Sandy.

"I expect she knows what happened. It was no secret, after all. I never talked to her about it though. Perhaps Adi did."

"Yes, she probably knows. And if so, she probably understands why Adi's so important to you. Just don't forget that you're not the only person who was close to him."

I nodded. "I'll keep it in mind. Right then – I'll put the kettle on, shall I?" Nothing like a cup of tea for putting life into perspective, I thought.

But, even while my hands were going through the familiar routine of filling the kettle and measuring out tea (not teabags, not for someone who wants the proper flavour),

I couldn't help wondering how much Karen did know about the past. Adi might not have told her about David.

After all, even Sandy didn't know everything.

CHAPTER 3

"The only history that matters is the history
you make yourself."

**Adi Varney, pre-match talk – quoted by
several Vale players on different occasions**

I slept in on Monday morning. Since I became semi-retired,
I've been doing that more and more. It wasn't that I had
nothing to do – there were several freelance projects I had on
the go, at various stages of completion – but the deadlines
were mostly my own.

I quite liked it. However, the downside was that Sandy
was out and gone by the time I finally wandered downstairs.
Sam, however, was still there, eating egg and bacon straight
out of the frying pan – a habit his mother had had no success
at all in breaking.

"Morning, Dad. Kettle's just boiled."

"Mng. Thnks." I started fumbling with cups and teapot.
"So where were you yesterday?" I muttered.

"New job – bar work at Studio Cool. Didn't get in till
about two. Maybe later... hope I didn't disturb you?"

I grunted a grumpy negative. What right did he have to
be so bright and chirpy when I could barely put one thought
in front of another? "What happened to the warehouse job?"

"Dumped that. Rubbish pay for the hours, and boring as well. This is more fun and I get to sleep in."

I poured the tea and sipped at my cup, hoping the caffeine and sugar would kick in quickly. "How many jobs has that been now?"

Sam shrugged. "Who's counting?"

He'd worked his way around the world by doing any job that was going. A few weeks fruit picking, a month as a waiter, a bit of bicycle maintenance, and so on. With his natural charm and ability to turn his hand to almost anything, he'd managed very well. What's more, he'd acquired an extensive (if informal) education along the way. I was only slightly worried by the fact that he hadn't changed his lifestyle even though he was now supposedly settled back at home. Another reason why I didn't think it would last.

"And," he continued, "it means that I'm free to come with you."

"With me? Where? Doing what?"

"Wherever you're going to next, to track down this fake Adi."

I finished my tea and gave him a long look. He smiled back and gave me a dose of the same Sam magic that had taken him all over the globe. It worked on me as well, and had done ever since he was a baby.

Still, I put up a show of resistance. "Who says I'm going to track him down?"

"Mum does. She said, 'Keep an eye on your father and don't let him make a nuisance of himself. Again.' And she said especially that you weren't to go near Karen Varney."

"I have no intention of talking to Karen again, and I already told your mother that!"

His grin broadened. "But you are planning to look into this Adi thing." It wasn't a question.

I shrugged. "I thought I might go to some places, talk to a few people."

"Ah-ha! What places? What people?"

"The places I'd expect Adi to go to if he was back, and the people at those places."

Sam stood up. "Sounds good to me. When do we start?"

"When I've had some breakfast, and you've done the washing-up." I nodded at his pan.

"Sure. No problem." He tossed the pan into the sink and started a tap running. "This is looking like a fun day: I get to watch my old man doing his investigative reporter thing!"

Part of Sam's talent is his ability to say the things that people like to hear, and what father doesn't want to show off his talents to his kids? So I overlooked the "old man", especially since it happened to be true, and rummaged in the cupboard for cereal.

"So what's the first place we try?" he continued, adding washing-up liquid to the water.

"Adi's home."

He paused in his scrubbing. "But Mum said you had to stay away from Aunty Karen!"

I nodded. "And I will. But Karen's house was only where Adi lived. His real home was the Castle."

*

The good thing about eating out of the frying pan is that it reduces the amount of washing-up. We were on our way fifteen minutes later, with the cereal sitting heavily in my stomach. It's only a short drive, so another ten minutes saw us pulling into the car park in front of Delford Vale Football Club's stadium – aka 'The Castle'.

Sam got out and leaned on the door, looking up at it. "I see how it got its name," he said, indicating the false battlements running along the top.

I shook my head. "It was 'The Castle' long before that was built. When I used to come here as a lad, the main stand was just a rusty metal shed, with a wooden lean-to for a ticket office. But we still called it 'The Castle'."

"Really? I remember coming here as a kid, and when everyone called it that, I assumed it was an actual castle. I didn't know better until I went to a real castle on a school trip! So why is it called that? Come to think of it, why is it 'Delford Vale United' when we're nowhere near Delford and there's no vale in sight?"

"I'm pretty sure I told you all that."

"Yes, sure, but it would have been a few years ago, wouldn't it? I may have forgotten the details…"

"Or you weren't listening in the first place! You were more interested in getting ice cream, or a hot dog. Or both."

"That I do remember!"

I sighed. So much for my attempts to pass wisdom down the generations. Well, perhaps I had a second chance now. "Come this way, and all your questions will be answered."

I led him towards the stand, but instead of going into the club shop or the bar and restaurant (unsurprisingly named "Adi's") next to it, we went round to the side, to a small door labelled "No Unauthorized Entry".

"Are we authorized, then?" Sam asked.

I entered a number into the keypad next to the door, and it clicked open. "They haven't changed the access code, so yes."

We took a flight of stairs up to the first floor, and entered into a large room full of display cases and cabinets, lined with photographs and team banners. The Vale colours – yellow and purple – were everywhere: on flags and scarves and ribbons and signed shirts of different styles.

"Trophy room," I explained. "And club museum."

"Wow. Impressive. Reminds me of your office, only more so."

"Yeah, well, I'm not much of a collector. All I've got are a few things Adi or other players gave me over the years – just a few signed balls, some photos. And Adi's shirt from his first FA cup final."

"And the cricket bat."

"Yes, that's probably the only thing that isn't football related. Not signed by Adi, of course!"

A woman popped her head out from behind a cabinet containing signed footballs. "Excuse me, we are closed at the moment. Can I help you with something?" She did a double take. "Oh – Graham! Sorry, I didn't realize it was you." She came towards us, smiling. "And who's this young man you've brought with you?"

"This is Sam, whom you may remember as a cute little lad who was always charming you out of sweets. Sam, perhaps you remember Angie? She's the curator and resident expert in all things to do with The Vale."

Under thick chestnut hair, Angie's skin was starting to look a little worn, I thought. But then she must have been in her forties, I reminded myself.

"Sam? Really? Well look at you all growed up!"

Sam shook hands. "Sorry, I don't remember you, Angie. Though I think I remember the sweets?"

"You should – you had enough of them! I hear you've been off seeing the world. Nice to see you back again."

"Sam was asking about how The Vale and the Castle came by their names. I'm sure I must have told him, but he either wasn't listening or forgot it all when he went globetrotting."

"Oh, well you've come to the right place for answers! Come and look at this."

She marched off to the far end of the room. Here the photographs were black and white, or even sepia, and the club colours more faded.

"1902," she announced. "Castle Vale Football Club, quarter-finalists in the FA Cup, where they were beaten 2–0 by Nottingham Forest. A huge achievement for what was just a local team. Mostly farm lads from the villages along Castle Vale, which was a couple of miles south of the town, back then. It's mostly housing estates and industrial parks now." She indicated a grainy picture that showed two rows of serious-looking young men in long black shorts and striped shirts, most of them with impressive moustaches.

"They were dirt-poor, had to have a whip-round in the local pubs for the money to travel to the venue. But they had magic in their feet."

She pointed to another picture. "This was them in 1903. Didn't do so well in the Cup that year – came up against a top team early on – but see that silverware on the ground in front of them? Mid-Counties Challenge Trophy. They barely conceded a goal that season. They won it again in 1904, along with some other county and regional competitions.

"But in the meantime, there was another local side that wasn't doing so well."

The third photo showed a team in white shorts and hooped shirts. They were flanked by a portly gentleman in a top hat, and the moustaches were even more luxuriant.

"Delford Mills FC. Unlike Castle Vale, they had a bit of money behind them. Sir Randall Delford, owner of the Mills, was a bit of a sports enthusiast. Very athletic in his youth, apparently, and liked the idea of having his own team. So he bought some suitable land on the edge of town, had a pitch laid out, built a stand, and recruited some likely lads from his factories.

"The only problem was, they weren't that good. Well, to be fair, they weren't terrible. They did win a few matches, here and there. But they had nothing like the talent of Castle Vale, who comprehensively beat them every time they met. The Mills' best performance was when they got to the final of the Mid-Counties in 1904: The Vale beat them 5–0.

"Now, Sir Randall might have tried to rectify that by recruiting the Vale players for his team, but he was a canny man, and he was thinking about the business side of things. He realized that The Vale had already made a name for itself, had attracted a lot of local support, and he wanted to keep that.

"So instead, he proposed a merger of the two clubs. Delford would get the players, the players would get a new ground, some proper kit, and they'd get paid as well. The new club would be fully professional and what's more, they'd have a good chance of getting into the Football League. Sir Randall had heard rumours that the league – just two divisions in those days – was going to be expanded to twenty teams in each division, and he wanted to be in on that."

Sam laughed. "So Delford Vale United! Obviously. That way Sir Randall keeps the name and gets the publicity."

"To be fair, he was making a big investment as well," Angie pointed out. "He bought the land that we're on now, had a new ground laid out, with a proper stand and terraces…"

"Stand for the gentry, open terraces for the commoners!" I explained.

"… and changing rooms for the players, even! Facilities they'd never dreamed of before."

"The Vale supporters hadn't dreamed of turnstiles either. Sixpence to get in was a bit steep when a farm labourer – like most of them that had been following The Vale – only earned a few shillings a week." I grinned at her: it was an old argument between us.

"But they were joining the League, Graham. It wasn't just a kick-about on some farmer's field any more. This was the big time, and Sir Randall wanted the new team to be true professionals. He paid the players well, and they didn't have to provide their own kit any more, either."

Angie pointed to the back wall, which was entirely taken up with football kits, neatly laid out behind glass. The first in the collection was clearly the oldest – long black shorts and a long-sleeved shirt in greyish-white, with vertical stripes in a sort of dark grey with lilac tones.

"Is it original? Only it's faded a bit," Sam said.

"Oh, yes, this was one of the shirts worn in that first season. Back then they didn't have the colour-fast dyes we have now, and they boil-washed the kit after every match. But originally those stripes were purple, reflecting the colours of Sir Randall's family crest, and purple has stayed The Vale's colour ever since."

"And the ground became 'The Castle'?"

"A bit of a local joke, at first. They called it 'Randall's Castle'. But the 'Castle' bit stuck."

CHAPTER 3

"How did they do?"

"Not bad at first." Angie waved her hand at the team photographs, the tattered tickets and programmes, the signed footballs. "They won promotion in the 1908–09 season, and held their own in Division One. They never managed to collect any silverware, but they always seemed on the edge of it, and the locals packed the ground for every home game." She threw a glance at me. "In spite of the ticket prices."

"They were new fans, though," I pointed out. "Not the farming folk that had supported the original Vale. These were mostly town people, with a bit more money in their pocket. But Randall did OK out of it."

She shrugged. "He was a businessman."

"That he was," I agreed, conceding the point. Angie, I suspected, always liked the romance of a noble title and loved the connection with The Vale. My socialist leanings made me suspicious of anything resembling wealth or privilege. But arguing over people long gone to dust seemed pointless.

"Not bad *at first*, you said?" Sam asked. "What happened next?"

"The war happened. The Great War, as they called it then."

One end of the room was dominated by a large picture of the War Memorial, taken on Remembrance Day in 2005 – the hundredth anniversary of the club's founding. I remembered it well. I'd been there. In the picture, Adi was laying a wreath.

Angie looked at it wistfully. "Three of the names on there were Vale players. But many of those who came back never played again. Some were wounded, some had their lungs damaged by gas, some were just too traumatized. Oh, they recruited new players and The Vale went on. But it was never the same. The old magic was gone. For the next sixty years, the team just hung on. A good season was when they stayed around the middle of the League: a bad one was when they went down."

I nodded. "That's what we grew up with, me and Adi and every other local kid. The Vale was almost a joke: we still supported them, still went to the matches, but nobody expected much from them. In fact everybody thought that they'd disappear altogether in a season or two."

"Everybody but Adi," Angie said.

"That's right. Adi always thought differently. Even when we were kids, kicking a tennis ball around the school playground, he knew that The Vale would make a comeback. And that he'd lead it. Of course, a lot of schoolboys daydream about being football stars. But Adi never had any doubts. He was going to play for The Vale, he was going to win the FA Cup, the Championship, and every other trophy going. And... he did."

Angie nodded. "All that silverware –" she waved her hand at the display cases that dominated the room "– all that came with Adi Varney. Two FA Cups, three Championships, League Cup, the UEFA Cup, European Cup, Cup Winners' Cup..."

"Twice," I put in.

"... Cup Winners' Cup twice," she agreed, "and twenty-three England caps as well! Would have been a lot more, if it hadn't been for that goalpost hacking him down."

"Not that it stopped him collecting silverware," I added. "Some of those trophies are from his days as manager."

"Sixty years The Vale waited for the magic to come back," Angie continued. "Then it all came at once, in one man."

"Not just one man, surely?" Sam saw the look we both gave him. "Come on, he had the rest of the team as well!"

"He did," I conceded. "And yes, there were some good players. Great players, even. But Adi – he was the inspiration, the motivation, the drive…"

"The magic," Angie repeated. "And now he's gone, we're sliding back down again." She looked suddenly despondent. "And I still don't understand why he just suddenly walked away from us. Do you, Graham?"

I shrugged, shook my head.

"You were his best friend, though," Angie persisted. "If anyone knows why he went, it's you."

There was a look in her eyes that I couldn't meet. "Adi was his own man," I said, turning away. "Look at this, Sam." I walked over to a framed newspaper clipping. The paper was faded to yellow, the photograph was grainy, but it was clearly Adi in Vale kit, ball at his feet. The headline was clear as well, big, bold, triumphant letters: "NEW SIGNING SCORES HAT-TRICK". "Adi's first game for The Vale, and I missed it! I don't think I missed many, but I really wish I'd made it for that one."

Angie sighed, and shook her head. "I'm sorry, Graham. I know he hurt you too, leaving like that. I just thought he might have said something."

"Well, the thing is, Angie, I was wondering if you'd heard anything from him."

"Me? No. Not a word."

Her turn to look away, but not before I saw the glistening in her eyes. Nevertheless, I persisted.

"It's just that I thought I saw him the other day. Not that it was him!" I added hastily as I saw the look on her face. Who knew that hope could be so painful? "That is, I'm pretty sure it must have been just someone that looked like him.

But… I just thought that if it had been Adi, then he would have come here. To the Castle, that is. Or at least someone would have heard if he was back."

She shook her head. "No. I haven't heard anything like that. I don't think anyone has."

"Right. OK. As I said, it was just a lookalike. I can't imagine that Adi would come back and not come here. Can you?"

"No. But then I never imagined that he'd ever leave, either. Not after thirty years of total commitment, player and manager."

"Yes. Right." I glanced round at the trophies and mementoes. Without Adi, the room would have been more than half empty. "I thought I might go up to the bar, have a word with Johnnie, if he's in?"

She shrugged. "Yes, he's there. Go and ask him if you like. But I'd advise against it. We all took it hard when Adi left, but Johnnie said that if he ever saw Adi again, he'll kick away his stick and beat the… Well, Johnnie can be a bit basic in his language. Really, it's best not to bring the subject up."

"Yes. Right. Sounds wisest to let that go. I knew Johnnie was upset by it. I hadn't realized it was that bad."

"He can't let it go. He broods about it, and the more he broods, the angrier he gets. None of us can really understand it, that's the thing. If we knew why…" She shrugged.

"OK, we'll leave it then. Thanks, Angie. See you around."

"Sure. Anytime."

Sam and I walked back down the stairs and out to the car park in silence. "She was in love with him, wasn't she?" he asked as we reached the car.

Very perceptive. "Yes, I think so."

"Did anything happen between them?"

I shrugged. "I don't know. Not for sure. Perhaps. Probably. Adi... well, yes, he had... affairs. It wasn't the best side of him. But he was always very discreet, never let anything out in public. At least, not until he went to the States."

Sam got in and mulled it over as I started the engine. "Who's Johnnie, and why is he so mad at Adi?"

"Johnnie Muldoon. First-team goalie for most of the eighties. And Adi's next best friend after me, I think. Johnnie had to retire in 1989, heart condition, and Adi installed him as manager in the members-only bar up on the top floor. When Adi left, Johnnie took it very personally."

We left the Castle behind and headed back into town.

CHAPTER 4

"No one has given more to his town than Adi, but this may prove to be his most enduring legacy."

Declan Healy, speaking at the opening of a new sports hall at the Adi Varney Sports Centre

"So where next?" asked Sam.

"One more place to try. If Karen hasn't heard anything, and Angie hasn't either, then the only other person to ask is Declan."

"Declan?"

"Declan Healy. Another Vale player, but he retired in '82. Stayed on as assistant trainer for a couple of years, then Adi recruited him for another project."

We took a right, got onto Queensway, and headed south.

To our left was a vast scar in the landscape, acres and acres of crumbling, abandoned, and mostly burned-out buildings. As the road climbed we could see further, to the wasteland that had once been Delford Mills – almost cheek by jowl with the town centre. Even at this distance, we could see that it was busy, with bright green and yellow machinery crawling over it like an infestation of mechanical ants.

"What an eyesore," Sam commented. "About time they got round to doing something about it."

"It took a tragedy to get things moving," I commented, waving a hand at a swathe of fire-blackened ruins. "They think that a dozen people died in that."

Sam glanced at me and our eyes met. "And Mum was nearly one of them," he said.

"Yes."

It wasn't something to discuss. I hated coming this way.

We left the Queensway at the next roundabout, and doubled back through some side streets.

"Adi and me, we grew up not far from here," I commented. "Rough area then, all terraced housing, not these nice little semis. Not as bad as Delford, of course – they were the real slums!"

"Everybody has to have someone to look down on, eh Dad?"

I smiled ruefully. "Yes, I suppose it was a bit like that."

We turned off down a lane between the houses and came out onto a wide open space, laid out with playing fields and dominated by three big buildings. A large sign across the front of the middle one announced a welcome to the Adi Varney Sports Centre.

"Ah, I know this place." Sam got out and looked round with interest.

"You should. You spent enough time here as a kid. We were here as much as we were at home. Of course, we lived closer then."

"Adi's charity, isn't it?"

"One of them. He gave a lot to charities in this town, time and money, but this was his biggest project, his main thing after The Vale. We started it together, actually, back in the eighties. Adi'd had a bit of negative publicity from off the pitch – some scrapes he'd got into. He didn't like that. I encouraged him to do something a bit more positive, help his image, put something back into the local community. He wasn't keen at first, but I suggested a sports club, and he liked that idea. So we found this place – just empty wasteland then – and Adi bought it with his own money. Got it landscaped, put in some goalposts – went round local businesses and got them to cough up for a clubhouse…" I laughed. "Now look at it. Three pitches, skateboard park, sports hall, gym, and swimming pool – and all free for the local kids."

"Doesn't look very busy, though."

I frowned. He was right. The car park was almost empty, the lights were off in the buildings, and indeed the sports hall seemed to have a chain across its main doorway.

"I haven't been over here for a while," I admitted. "What with recent events. It is looking a bit run-down. Let's go over to the offices; see if Declan's in."

The central building housed the sports hall, the swimming pool, the squash courts, and a café, as well as the administrative offices. The front door was locked, however; the reception desk inside deserted. I led the way round to a side door, tried the bell, and then knocked.

There was movement inside, and after a moment's wait, the door opened and Declan looked out. And down – Declan's one of the tallest blokes I've ever met, at six foot seven and a half inches, and one of the best midfielders The Vale ever had. It was cancer that ended his career, and nearly ended him. They caught it in time to save his life, but after years of treatment he could never get back to the level of fitness needed at the top level, so Adi had put him in charge of the sports centre.

"Graham? Well, here's a thing! I wondered whenever you might be showing your face again!" Dec had lived in England since '85, but had never lost his strong Northern Irish accent. "And who's this with you?"

"Hello, Dec. This is my lad Sam – Sam, Declan Healy, the best man in the air that The Vale ever had!"

Declan laughed and shook Sam's hand. "I don't know about the best, but I had a few good games up at the Castle and elsewhere. Come on in, I'll have the kettle on."

He led the way back into an untidy office. The walls were decorated entirely with framed photos and faded cuttings from newspapers. Many of the photos had Adi in them somewhere – presenting trophies, opening buildings, posing with various sports teams. Most of the newspaper articles were written by me, and I was even in some of the pictures.

There were three desks, but only Declan to sit at them.

"Where's all the staff, Dec?" I asked. "Have you given Tracey and Sara a holiday?"

"Ah well, the thing is that Tracey retired last year, and Sara's only working part time just now." He busied himself with an electric kettle and an assortment of mugs, most of them with Vale logos and all of them chipped.

"Really? That must leave you a lot to do yourself."

He shrugged. "Not so much. Things aren't as busy as they used to be."

"I can see that. There's nobody else around, and everywhere's locked up."

Declan dumped teabags into mugs, then added milk and sugar in a slapdash fashion that left plenty of both outside the target area. I braced myself: some people can make a reasonable cup of tea, some can't, and Declan was definitely in the latter group.

He sloshed boiling water into the mugs and gave them all a token stir before handing them round.

"I remember this as well," said Sam, glancing round. "You used to bring me here sometimes when you had meetings."

"Back when I was a trustee. We had our meetings in here!" I smiled. "I'd send you off to play in the sports hall if it was open, or outside if the weather was good."

Sam grinned. "Oh, I could always get in the hall if I wanted to, open or not. Place was about as secure as a sieve. Any one of the local lads could tell you two or three ways of getting in – I could have told you half a dozen!"

Declan shook his head sadly. "We did try, but every time we sealed up one entrance, the lads found another! I gave up in the end, just locked away the valuables and let them have the run of the place."

"One time," Sam continued, "there wasn't much happening, and I got curious about what you might be up to. So I did a bit of exploring. I discovered that if you go right into the back of the equipment storage in the hall, there's a little door that lets you into the stationery storeroom behind the office. Comes out right behind the shelving, so hardly anyone knew it was there. But I could sneak up to the office door and spy on you through the keyhole!"

Declan laughed. "I'd forgotten about that door."

"Very sneaky, son. I don't suppose you learned anything of interest, though!"

"Only that meetings are boring. But I did have some fun joining all the paper clips together in a chain."

"That was you? We couldn't figure it out!" Declan shook his head. "I thought it must have happened in the factory. Wrote to the manufacturers to complain!"

"I only did it once!" Sam protested. "Or perhaps twice. Though I may have helped myself to a few bits and pieces, now and then."

"Please, enough confessions," I groaned. "I don't want to know what a delinquent I raised."

"Well, he seems to have turned out all right in spite of it, so he has. I hear you went globetrotting, Sam? You must have seen a few sights! Something more interesting than a trustees' meeting, anyway!"

I'd noticed that, in all the reminiscing, Declan had managed to avoid properly answering my question about the staff. I wondered if I should pursue the point, but I didn't want to get sidetracked.

"Yes, I've covered a bit of ground over the last few years." Sam flashed his grin.

"Ever make it over to Ireland?"

"Sure. I hitchhiked from Belfast down to Dublin once. Never got over to the west coast, though. I want to do that sometime."

I hadn't known that Sam had been in Ireland. I only had a sketchy idea of where he had been.

"You should certainly do that!" Declan enthused. "And don't forget to visit Derry either, finest city in all of Ireland!"

Declan, of course, was from there, though I don't think he'd been back in years.

"And how are you, Dec?" I asked.

"Oh, not so bad, Graham, to be sure." He sat back behind his desk. "A little older but no wiser! Glad to see you looking well, after all the troubles you've had. How is that fine young woman of yours?"

"Oh, Sandy's doing well – very well considering."

"It was a terrible thing, that fire. I could see it from here, like the whole town was ablaze! We were lucky, though. The wind took the smoke away from us. I couldn't believe it when I heard that Sandy had been caught in it." He shook his head. "Terrible thing," he said again.

I took a cautious sip of tea, and found it every bit as bad as I'd feared. If I left it long enough, I'd be able to drink it quickly. "Indeed it was, though things could have been worse. Anyhow, Declan, the reason I dropped by was, I wondered if you've heard anything from Adi lately."

He put down his mug, and stared thoughtfully at the ceiling. "Well, not really, Graham. Why are you asking? Have you?" He shot a hopeful look in my direction. More than hopeful – perhaps even a bit desperate.

"That's just it. I'm not sure. I saw someone a few days ago, and I thought it was him. Almost certain… but on reflection, I don't think it could have been. But I couldn't get to him to make sure. So I wondered if he'd been here. After all, if Adi was back I'd expect him to come round."

Declan was still staring at the ceiling. "Maybe. Maybe."

"Maybe?" I repeated back to him. "Come on, you know how important this place was to him. In the old days he was always dropping in to kick a ball round or do a few circuits in the gym."

Declan took his eyes off the ceiling to give me a sideways look. "Yes, well, we all know he liked to show off a bit." He raised a hand as if to ward off my objection. "I'm sorry, Graham. I know he was your friend. Mine as well, for that matter, but that was the truth of it. And after his accident, we hardly saw him. Unless the press were around for something special, then he'd put in an appearance. But apart from that…" He shrugged. "Perhaps you should talk to Karen."

"I did that first. She hasn't seen him or heard from him. And before you ask, I've been to the Castle as well, and he hasn't been there either. So this is my last shot. If he hasn't come here or at least contacted you, then it wasn't Adi I saw."

"Well, I can promise you that Adi hasn't contacted me himself, and certainly hasn't been here." Declan glanced at me, then looked away.

Declan was no better at prevaricating than he was at making tea. I'd been sensing the ambiguity in his answers since we'd started the conversation.

"So what *has* Adi done?" I kept my tone neutral, not pushing. Pushy questions shut people up. But gentle ones give them the opportunity to open up, if they want to. And I sensed that Declan wanted to.

"I don't know that he has done anything, exactly…"

"But?"

He sighed, and shook his head. "But if he's not behind it, then he must know about it."

I didn't have to say anything else. Just kept my eyes on him and pretended to sip my tea.

"Well, you've seen the state of the place, haven't you? We're practically closed down. No staff, you see, apart from a few volunteers. I'm just around to answer the phone and open the place up for a few hours in the evening. That's all we can manage lately."

"How come?"

"You know the arrangement we had. Of course you do, you helped set it up. All the land and most of the buildings are in Adi's name. He's the owner. The charity – the sports centre – has the use of them for a token rent. Or at least so we did, up to a couple of years ago. Then, out of the blue, we had this letter from some firm of lawyers, saying that they were acting on behalf of the owner and that the rent was going up."

"What? Adi started charging you rent? His own charity?"

"That's what I'm telling you. Well, the lawyers did. Terrible shock, so it was, but we managed to get the money together, dug into the reserves, and so on. But then a few months ago it went up again. A lot. Full commercial rates – for all this land, all these buildings."

I shook my head, aghast. "I didn't know. I hadn't a clue, Declan… why didn't you say something?"

"You had troubles of your own, Graham. With your heart attack and then all that business with Sandy… and in any case the lawyers invoked some confidentiality clause that I didn't even know existed. Nobody was allowed to know apart from myself and the trustees. I shouldn't even be telling *you* this. Though you were a trustee, of course, and I suppose you've got a right to know about it, really. But the lawyers didn't want it getting out. I asked if I could put out a special appeal for funds, tell our supporters why we needed extra help. They said no. I pointed out that if we didn't get any extra income, they wouldn't get the rent money. They said that if the charity defaulted, then the contract with Adi would be terminated and we would be evicted. I asked to speak to Adi directly. He wasn't available."

I sat and stared at him. "Eviction? They said that? But – can they?"

"They are doing. We're already behind with the payments. Last week they informed us that myself and the trustees would be held personally liable for any outstanding debts. We've been summoned to a meeting this afternoon, to discuss the issue."

Declan closed his eyes, rubbed his forehead. His hair, I noticed, had turned a lot thinner and greyer since I last saw him.

"See, Graham, I never kept much in reserve. I never saw the need to. What came in, I put back out. Wages, maintenance – if we had enough I sponsored promising kids for extra training, sent the more deprived ones on holiday, things like that. So now – we've nothing left. And if they insist on this personal liability thing…"

I stared at him, appalled. Declan didn't look back. He kept his hands over his eyes, and I realized that he was struggling to keep it together. Not surprising. Dec was a good man, a staunch Roman Catholic who had loved being able to combine his faith with his love of sport by running the sports centre – a place that had made a huge difference to many individuals and to the whole community. It had been Declan's life after he had to finish playing professionally.

"Personal liability?" I asked. "They said that?"

"They did. Along with a lot more legal language. We think – we hope – that if we agree to go quietly, sign over the remaining assets, and wind the charity up, then they won't chase us for any outstanding debts. They've sort of hinted at that, in among all the legalese. But it'll all come out at the meeting, I suppose."

"Wait a minute… let's think about this. What assets do you have? Have you got something you could bargain with?"

"Not really. Some office and sports equipment – most of it well used. Some memorabilia that might be of value to collectors. And there's the barn, of course."

"What's the barn?" Sam had been sitting quietly and listening hard.

"Oh, your dad knows the barn, don't you, Graham?" Declan gave me a wan smile.

I nodded. "It was the first building the charity had. Back when we first started this place, that was the only building here. Adi put in his own money to buy the land – it had been a sort of smallholding before – but the rest of us, the original trustees and a lot of the Vale players and supporters – we chipped in and bought the barn separately. Then we did it up ourselves as the first clubhouse. It had changing rooms and so on. Put a lot of graft into it, too. I painted most of the ceiling myself."

"You got just as much paint on yourself," said Declan. "And anyone who came near!" He mustered a smile at the memory, and I shared it with him.

"Yes, so DIY isn't my strong point. But the point is, the barn itself is the property of the charity. Isn't that worth something?"

"Not much. It's been used for storage for years, since we got all the new buildings, and it's not in a good state."

"You did it up once – couldn't you do that again?" Sam suggested. "Keep the charity going in a small way at least. Get the word round. I'm sure people would be glad to help out."

Declan took a deep breath and put his hands down. "Even if we kept the barn, they could deny access to it, since they own all the land round it. And like I said, we can't tell anyone, because of this confidentiality clause. They said that if word gets out, that's another thing we'll be held liable for. There will be 'serious legal and financial consequences for any unauthorized disclosure of any and all matters pertaining…' and so on."

"But it's bound to get out anyway, once you close down," Sam pointed out.

"Yes. Too late then. And you're probably thinking we could challenge that clause, but that would take time and money and lawyers, and we don't have any of them."

"Who's this coming from, Declan?" I managed a genuine swallow of the tea. "The lawyers, I mean. Adi always used to use Swann and Chapel, I recall."

"He did. But this is some new firm. New to me, anyhow…" Declan rummaged through the papers on his desk. "Here it is. Cornhall Lonza Hickon International. Big firm… the first letter we had from them they said they'd taken over all Adi's legal affairs."

I sat up so sharply that my cooling tea sloshed over my hand. "Lonza? Did you say Lonza?"

"That's right. Why? Does that mean something to you?"

"I heard the name recently. He was in the bar where I thought I'd seen Adi."

Declan frowned as he thought through the implications. "So if it was Adi – well, that confirms he's working with these lawyers. Working to destroy his own charity! I… I just can't understand that, Graham. This place – all we did here – it was part of his image. He was proud of that, proud of the standing it gave him in the community. Why would he decide to wreck it all?"

"Well – perhaps it wasn't Adi?" An idea was growing in my mind, separate facts beginning to link together. "Like I said, I didn't think it could have been, because he wasn't limping. And this Lonza, he's got a reputation – mixed up in some very dodgy business, apparently. So perhaps this is a scam. Perhaps he's trying to get control of this land and wants the charity out. And he uses this law firm to put pressure on you, then if he trots out an Adi lookalike to make it all seem legitimate…"

"Yes! That would be a classic con, wouldn't it?" said Sam. "They get you all wound up with these legal threats – then Adi turns up, tells you it's going to be OK, that of course you're not being held liable, and if you just sign it all over he'll see that it's sorted out and that you'll be back to normal business in no time! Except that of course it isn't Adi at all, and once you've signed you'll never see him again."

We both looked at Sam. I wanted to ask how he knew so much about con tricks, but Declan spoke first. "But why? I mean – why go to so much trouble to get control of the charity? What's some big-shot American law firm bothering with us for?"

I had the answer to that. It had been growing in the back of my mind for a while. "Not the charity, Dec. The land. You said that this really started just a few months ago?"

"The big rent demands did, yes."

"About the time when the government made a definite commitment to support the Delford Mills Project."

"Delford Mills?"

"Yes. Think about it, Declan. There's a huge amount of money, public and private, being poured into that. And it's lifting property prices all across town. Here you've got a significant chunk of prime real estate, most of it not built on. Imagine what that's going to be worth to a developer. Especially if they can get it for a song."

"It's Adi's land…"

"And someone pretending to be Adi is behind this whole thing. All they need to do is get the charity out, take full control of all the assets – and they've got a fortune just waiting to be made."

CHAPTER 5

"Adi will always follow a plan to the letter –
right up to the moment when he thinks of a
better one!"

Graham Deeson, in a discussion on
Match of the Day

Cornhall Lonza Hickon International had offices in the
centre of town. What a big international firm was doing
in our little backwater would have been a puzzling question,
if we hadn't already come up with an answer. I found some
parking on a side street a block away and checked the time.

"Nearly two," I said. "And we haven't had lunch yet. No
wonder I'm hungry. Ready for a bite to eat, Sam?"

"Do we have time?"

"Should have. Declan's meeting wasn't scheduled till
three-thirty, and he's got to talk to the trustees first."

"How do you think they'll take the news?"

"With shock, disbelief, and anger. Just like Declan."

It had been all I could do to persuade him not to storm
down to the lawyers' offices and have it out with them
immediately. Or possibly put a brick through their window.
Normally a gentle and God-fearing man, Declan had a temper
when aroused, and it had become very aroused indeed after

our conversation. But we'd managed to get him to agree to a more moderate plan.

He was going to talk to the trustees, and then we'd all meet in town to go over the situation. My suggestion was that they should wait until the lawyers brought out the fake Adi, and then confront them with their deception. There wasn't time to get proper legal advice, but I was pretty certain that they could threaten them with charges of fraud, or something like that. Enough to stop any evictions, at any rate. Sam and I would be in the vicinity, ready to come in and back them up when we got the call.

"If I'd known how exciting your life was, Dad, I'd have come home years ago! You're right, we'd better eat – can't fight crime on an empty stomach. Where do you usually go for lunch?"

"Let's walk down to the Victorian Market. Not the fanciest of places, but there's a little café there which does the best steak sandwich you can get in this town. The Dreadnought. And we can go past those offices on the way, have a look at the place."

"The Dreadnought? Like the battleship?"

"That's it. More recently, there was a nuclear submarine of that name. There is a connection – the owner is ex-Royal Navy. Gary Ward, known as 'Sharkey' for some obscure naval reason."

"And he was on the *Dreadnought*?"

"Well, no. But he was in Malta a lot, and in Malta there was a bar named 'The Dreadnought' – after the battleship, not the sub – and that's where Sharkey got the name for his establishment. Happy memories, apparently."

I'm fascinated by the history behind things, but Sam has a more pragmatic approach to life. "Should you be eating steak sandwiches?"

"Well, it might not be on the normal dietary list, but these are exceptional circumstances. So one won't do any harm – as long as you don't mention it at home, that is."

"You're paying, then!"

"Now I understand how you managed to go round the world without any money."

We walked out of the side street, and turned right onto Maiden Road, which passed for the business district locally. In architectural terms it was a bit of a nightmare – Victorian town houses repurposed as offices rubbed shoulders with gleaming modern steel and glass skyscrapers; monolithic piles of fifties brickwork overshadowed discreet little Georgian frontages. The rumour was that an entire new area of the Delford Mills development would be set aside for high-rise offices, leaving Maiden Road to find a new life for itself, perhaps as city housing.

Cornhall Lonza Hickon International had premises in one of the skyscrapers – an entire floor, it seemed. We stood outside and looked at the electronic display which listed all the occupants, complete with animated logos in many cases. Not Cornhall Lonza Hickon, though, which satisfied itself with just the name in a sober white font on a black background.

"Doesn't have a very high profile for such a big firm," Sam observed.

"No. Very discreet. Almost like they don't want to be noticed."

We peered through the glass front. A few people were moving about inside, doing whatever it was they were paid to do, and taking no notice of us. Apart from the uniformed security guard hanging about near the door, who was watching us watching. He met our gaze with a suspicious look, and fingered the radio on his belt.

"Let's move on; we're upsetting the locals."

We wandered on down the street.

Traffic here wasn't heavy, but parking spaces were at a premium. Just ahead of us a big limo was making hard work of squeezing into a gap behind a workman's Transit.

"He's not going to make it," said Sam, and sure enough there was a crash and a tinkle as the Transit lost a rear light cluster.

The workman appeared from nowhere, running out of a nearby building with a stream of colourful language floating in the air behind him. As we came up to the scene, he was hammering on the front passenger window and shouting threats.

The rear door opened, and out got Adi.

I stopped dead, staring.

It wasn't the real Adi, of course. He had Adi's jacket – I could see the odd button – and he was carrying Adi's stick, polished black wood with a brass dog's head for a handle. But he wasn't using it. No sign of a limp as he walked over to the pavement, looking nervously at the workman.

The front passenger was also getting out, and I recognized him as well. It was the big bloke I'd also seen in the bar, still wearing the leather jacket. He was squaring up to the workman, meeting aggression with aggression. The workman stepped back, but another man joined him and with that back-up, the verbal assault continued.

Fake Adi stepped away, up onto the pavement, making room for a third person to leave the car. Tall, thin, wearing a suit. I'd seen him in the bar at the Stag, so if the barman hadn't been mistaken, this had to be Lonza.

Both of them had their attention on the developing situation in front of them. Neither of them saw me approaching. Not until I was right in front of them.

I could have just walked by. I should have. We had our plan – there was no reason to change it, there was no value to letting them know we were on to them.

I didn't even think of it. I just walked up to the fake Adi. "Excuse me? I'd just like a word."

His eyes widened. This time he recognized me. He stepped back, glancing frantically at the car, at Lonza.

A third workman had arrived, and the security guard from the office block. Things were getting crowded, and a bit ugly. Lonza was getting involved in the argument, or trying to. With reinforcements at hand, the first workman was back on the offensive.

"I don't f… care who you are. You f… can't just f… smash my van and f…" He was making his point loud and clear, with generous use of profanity, and was about to lose his teeth if Leather Jacket had his way. But the security guard was also sticking his oar in.

Nobody was looking at us.

"I just need to ask you something. About Adi. My friend Adi."

Fake Adi stepped back from me again. A tactical error, as it took him further away from the car and his companions. I followed him.

"Please, I just want to talk to you for a moment." I stepped forward.

He turned and ran.

I followed.

Behind me the commotion increased, but I ignored it and concentrated on the figure ahead of me.

The receding figure. I was never very athletic, though being around sportspeople had encouraged me to stay in reasonable shape most of my life. But recently I'd let myself go a little, and the fake Adi was in better condition, with both legs in good working order. He was already a long way ahead as I lumbered in pursuit, and it became obvious that I wasn't going to catch up.

I glanced over my shoulder, looking for Sam, but he was still somewhere back in the small crowd that had developed round the van.

Ahead, the Victorian Market marked the place where Maiden Street joined the High Street. A round, four-storey edifice of red brick, it had been impressive in its day with elaborate stone decorations and six copper cupolas set around the roof.

But as you got closer you could see that the brickwork was crumbling, the stone had worn smooth, and the cupolas were long gone, with sheets of plastic draped over the stumps. It had been on the brink of being condemned for years.

Yet somehow it remained open. I could see Fake Adi passing the entrance, then coming up short at the end of the road. Ahead of him was the High Street, a dual carriageway with no pedestrian crossing at this point. To his left, there was a crossing over Maiden Street, but the lights had just changed, traffic was flowing out into the High Street, and I was still coming after him, however slowly.

He could go down the pavement alongside the High Street, but that was a long stretch of empty pavement, going nowhere he knew in a strange town. He needed to get back to his companions, back past me, and looking up he saw me, a bit closer now, and made his decision.

He ran into the Victorian Market.

If I'd been able to manage it, I would have laughed. He'd trapped himself.

The main entrance led through a dingy tunnel – once lined with market stalls, but now only with graffiti – into the open space at the centre of the building. There had been a fountain there once, but now it was just an expanse of grimy old cobblestones, surrounded by boarded-up shop fronts and topped only by torn netting that was supposed to keep birds out, but didn't. The few small businesses that still hung on were mostly huddled round the Maiden Street entrance, and all on the ground floor. The upper floors, ringed with wide internal balconies, had been closed off for years (though the flimsy barriers didn't keep out the druggies and tramps who often camped out there). Perhaps the fake Adi thought he could get out the other side, but there was no other exit – not open to the public, anyway.

There was, however, a closer entrance.

Between the back end of the Market and the next building ran an alleyway – wide at the ends, narrow in the middle due to the curving walls. Halfway down was the back way into the Dreadnought.

I turned down the alleyway and found the door already open, clipped back against the wall. I staggered through, gasping for breath. Inside, two or three blokes were sitting round chipped Formica tabletops eating unhealthy fry-ups. They looked up in surprise as I lumbered past and half collapsed against the counter. Sharkey Ward came in from the Market entrance and stared at me with alarm.

"Graham, mate – you OK?"

I managed a nod. Sharkey was unconvinced.

"Are you sure, because you look like…"

"Yes, I'm…" (gasp) "I'm fine," I managed to get out. "Just – out of – breath."

"You'd better sit down then, till you've got it back."

"No. Can't stop. Did you see someone run into the Market just now? From the Maiden Street entrance?" I was still wheezing like an ancient steam engine, but could at least form sentences now.

"Well, yes, actually. Ran right by here and up the stairs to the first floor. I would have stopped him – it's not safe up there – but he shot up them like a rabbit. Gone before I could get out."

"Right. OK. Is there any other way up? Or down?"

"Not any more. The other stairways are locked off. What's going on?"

I shook my head and forced myself upright again. "Later. If my lad Sam comes looking for me – twenties, blond – point him right, will you?"

I made my way out into the Market area, no longer attempting to run.

A third of the way round, stairs led up between two defunct establishments. I took them slowly. I had no choice in that; my legs were as wobbly as a trifle.

Halfway up the first flight, a flimsy wooden gate hung broken and useless. I pushed through it and carried on up. The first floor was blocked off with wire mesh fencing, recently repaired and still intact, so I went on up to the top. Here, the fencing was in a poorer state, pulled open and never restored. I stepped gingerly out onto the upper balcony. The ancient planks groaned alarmingly, but seemed sound enough despite Sharkey's warnings.

In its heyday, the Market had been *the* place to come and shop. Ladies and Gentlemen of Quality took tea around the fountain in the courtyard below, or browsed the shop fronts.

Some of the faded signs still visible might have dated from those times.

"Le Mouen and James Ltd, Haberdashers."

"Grey and Sons, Silversmiths."

"A. J. Feynton, Confectioner and Chocolatier."

Long-forgotten names. The Market's decline had probably begun at the same time as The Vale's, and for the same reason. The "Great War" had taken both men and money, and the hard years of the twenties and thirties had not helped matters.

A few new businesses had moved in, now and then. The next store front was marked "Atomic Video – VHS Rental".

I could remember it being open. New and cool. Now as dead and forgotten as its Victorian neighbours.

Between Atomic Video and Feynton's a narrow passageway disappeared into the shadows. Out of the wind that swirled in from the open roof, the dust had collected there, undisturbed. Until very recently. There were scuff marks, the outline of a shoe print.

I glanced back down at the courtyard, hoping Sam had caught up with me, but there was no sign of him. Listening carefully, I stepped into the passage.

I took out my mobile and switched on the torch app, which illuminated more shoe marks and a rough wooden door at the end of the passage. It had once been locked, but both door and frame were badly splintered where someone had forced it open.

Burglars, perhaps – but it was a long time since there had been anything worth stealing up here. More likely some down-and-out looking for a place to kip.

I eased the door open. Stairs ran up to the left, faint daylight filtered down. And a sound. Footsteps? Then a mobile phone rang.

I tried the steps. They creaked, but seemed to be holding, so I crept up.

Above me, the phone was answered.

"Yeah, I know. Look, I had to get outta there, OK?" A US accent. "No, of course I didn't talk to him! The guy never caught up to me. I ducked into this old building at the end of the street."

While he was talking I was climbing.

There were all sorts of rumours about the top floor. Local legend held that it had been a high-class brothel, an opium den, a gambling club – any and every form of Victorian vice had allegedly taken place above the shops. The truth was it had never been anything other than office and storage space.

Peering over the top of the steps I saw a curving corridor with closed doors along the inner side, and windows – mostly boarded up – opposite. Several boards had fallen or been pulled down, allowing enough light in to see Fake Adi about ten feet away, standing with his back to me as he continued his phone conversation.

"No. I'm up on the top floor. It's like, abandoned or something. I don't think anyone saw me come up."

There was a long pause, while he listened.

"Yeah, yeah sure. I'll do that. Look, perhaps I can find a fire escape or something? If I come down that way no one will know I was even here. You can tell Mr Lonza that we can go ahead, OK?"

As he spoke, Fake Adi was pushing at a window, one of the unboarded ones. It opened slowly, with great protest.

I finished climbing the stairs.

Fake Adi looked out of the window. "There's a sort of walkway here. I guess it's a fire escape. There's an alleyway below. You let me know when we're clear and I'll come down, OK? Yeah, yeah, sure."

He hung up, slipped his phone back into his pocket, picked up his stick which had been leaning against the wall, and swung his leg out over the windowsill.

"I wouldn't do that if I were you," I said.

The reaction was comical. Still halfway through the window he jerked round to stare back at me, open-mouthed, and nearly fell back inside. Instead he managed to grab hold of the window frame.

"Look, I just want to talk." I kept my tone low, reasonable. "That's all. Just for a moment."

He swore. Several times. "Get away from me!"

"Just come inside. I'm not going to do anything. I just need to ask you some questions."

Instead, he pulled himself all the way through the window.

"No – don't! It's not safe out there! I only want to ask you about Adi. Adi Varney – he was my friend. I just need to know what's happened to him."

I'd reached the window now. Fake Adi was barely two feet away, staring back at me.

The iron walkway had been a fire escape once. Not part of the original building, it had been added years later, when building regulations had finally caught up. But years later was still a long time ago, and it was in the same state as the rest of the Market. Actually, worse than most of the other parts. It was more rust than iron, and in some places not even that

– there were holes the size of a fist where it had been eaten away completely.

"It's not safe," I repeated. "Look at it. I don't even know if there's still a ladder down. That might have gone years ago. Even if there is, you can't trust it. Just come back in and talk to me, all right? I just want to know about my friend."

A calm reasonable voice, I kept reminding myself, even though my heart was rattling along, adrenaline fired, and a band seemed to be tightening round my chest. Just a few innocuous questions to get him talking.

"I'm sorry about your friend," he whispered. "Look, man, I'm sorry about him, OK? But it has nothing to do with me. I'm just doing a job. You understand?"

I nodded that yes of course I understood, and I was going to step back from the window, give him room to come in where we'd talk a bit more. But then his phone rang again. He reached for it, and glanced down into the alleyway below, and a look went across his face. Fear – that was the look – and it was all over his face as he looked back at me, and he didn't look anything at all like Adi then.

"I can't talk to you! I can't!"

He pulled out his phone, held it to his ear, and took two steps away from me, two steps along the walkway, then the rotten metal disintegrated under his feet and he fell, backwards and sideways and outwards, lurching against the guard rail, which snapped like a twig and he fell, screaming, into the air and down and out of my sight.

The screaming stopped with a dull thud. I stared, open-mouthed, at the hole in the walkway. Half its width had disappeared. I couldn't see the alleyway below, so I climbed out of the window. Responding to some foolish urge to see, to be sure, to help.

The walkway creaked and swayed under my feet. Directly below me a body was crumpled up against a big industrial-sized wheelie bin. There was a small pool of dark fluid under the head, and the back was twisted at an awkward angle. The stick lay nearby.

I looked along the alleyway. Down by the back door of the Dreadnought, the big man in the leather jacket was standing, looking at the body.

Then he looked up and saw me, and we stared at each other.

CHAPTER 6

"What's done is done. Move on. You can't
win by looking over your shoulder."
**Adi Varney, in an interview after losing
a match**

Under my feet, the metal walkway groaned and shifted.
The outer edge suddenly dropped several inches. I
lurched forward, grabbing on to the guard rail, which made
a little "tink" noise but held fast. For the moment. Rust was
flaking away under the pressure of my fingers.

Self-preservation overruled shock. I turned away from the
edge, stepped back to the window. Had my hands on the
sill when something snapped, a shock that I felt through my
feet and then the entire walkway came clear of the building,
swinging outwards under my weight.

Suddenly, I was hanging in mid-air. My hands still
gripping the windowsill, my feet on the swaying walkway,
and empty space in between.

Frantically, I tried to pull myself in. Managed to get an arm
over the sill, then both arms. But I couldn't get any higher. Every
time I tried to push myself up, the walkway swung out again.

I didn't have the strength to pull myself up. Too weak,
too heavy.

Come on! You fat old fool, Deeson! Come… on…

Adrenaline and verbal abuse helped to get me a few inches higher. High enough so that my feet lost contact with the walkway and scrabbled ineffectually at the brickwork. Relieved of my weight, the walkway swung gently back in towards the wall, catching the back of my heels and holding them in place.

Every ounce of strength I could muster only succeeded in raising myself – and the walkway – a fraction of an inch. I twisted my feet to try to get clear, but the walkway just swung in closer. I scrabbled frantically at the brickwork with my toes, but there was no purchase there, and the pain in my arms and shoulders was becoming too much, too much to cope with. My chest felt tight as I gasped for breath and a little part of my mind reminded me of the stents, those tiny little metal tubes that were allowing the blood to circulate round my heart, and how much pressure there must be going through them now…

I slipped back again. The ancient woodwork was crumbling under my grip; I could feel it disintegrating.

"Help…" I tried to shout, but there was no breath in me; it came out as a gasp. "Help!" I tried again. Slipped further back. Thought how bitterly ironic it would be if I ended up dead next to Adi after all these years. Except it wasn't Adi at all.

My hands were shaking with the strain. I thought of Sandy. I thought of Sam. I tried to pray.

"DAD!"

There were hands on me. Sam's hands. He got a grip under my shoulders and with one heave he had me back up on the windowsill, clear of the walkway, then another pull brought me inside. On the floor. Safe.

"Dad… what happened? Are you OK? What were you doing out there? Are you all right? DAD!"

All I wanted to do at that moment was to enjoy the solid floor under me and get my breath back, but Sam was insistent. I held up my hand to stop the flow.

"OK," I managed to get out. Out of breath, weak, shaking, and all too aware of how tight my chest felt. But OK. "Just – just give me… a moment."

"Right." He sat beside me, with a comforting hand on my shoulder. *Role reversal or what?* I thought.

My breathing slowed, and my chest eased as well. Not the stents failing, then, just adrenaline.

"I think I should get an ambulance, Dad. Have you checked over, at least." He had his mobile out and was dialling.

I didn't feel like arguing. I nodded. "Yes, ambulance. But not just for me."

Sam didn't catch that; he was already talking, giving details in a clear, concise voice that sounded like someone used to dealing with emergencies. I pulled on his sleeve and he broke the flow of questions and answers.

"Hold one moment, please… What's up, Dad? How are you feeling?"

"OK. Better." I was getting my breath back, but I didn't have a lot to spare. "Tell them someone fell off the building."

"What? Who?"

"Fake Adi." I nodded to the open window. "Down there."

"Right." He crossed to the window and looked down, while relaying the information. "Yes, that's right. I'm being told that someone fell from up here… it's three floors… no, I can't see anything, but my view's restricted. Yes, I'll do that as soon as I can, but my first concern is for my father…"

I managed to get myself upright, and went to look out of the window myself. The sight of the walkway swinging gently back and forth made my stomach churn. It looked as if the whole thing was about to drop into the alley below. But of more immediate significance was the fact that it completely blocked our view. I couldn't see where Fake Adi had fallen, or if Leather Jacket was with him.

Sam was still talking. "Yes, I'll stay on the line and keep you updated." He turned to me, held the phone against his chest to block the sound. "Sit down, Dad. They're on their way, but they said you shouldn't move."

"OK, but you need to get down there. Check on him. I don't think he could have survived, but if he's still alive…"

"I don't want to leave you."

"It's all right. I am feeling a lot better now, I promise. But you really should go and check on Adi. Fake Adi, that is."

He looked at me, doubtful, then glanced at the window. "OK then. I'll be back as soon as I can. Just take it easy, Dad."

"I will. Go out through the Dreadnought. There's a back entrance. It's quicker, it leads straight into the alley. He fell right below this window."

He nodded, and headed towards the stairs.

I knew I should probably sit down again and wait for help, but it seemed a pity to waste the energy I'd already expended on standing up. Besides, I needed to know what had happened to Fake Adi. So I followed Sam, though much more slowly. My legs still felt weak, but I ignored them, concentrating on retracing my steps.

Before I reached the ground floor, Sam was coming back up to meet me.

"Dad! You were supposed to stay there!"

I shook my head. "Never mind me. What about Fake Adi?"

"He's not there." Sam put an arm round me and started to help me down the remaining steps. "I tried to do what you said, but someone had shut the back door. Wedged it shut. So I had to go the long way round, and there was no body."

"No body?" I shook my head. "No Fake Adi? And what about Leather Jacket? I saw him down there as well."

"No, no sign of him either."

"No body and nobody?" I felt a ridiculous urge to giggle. Shock, I thought. Must have been. "Are you sure, Sam?"

"Certain. And Sharkey came round with me, to check the door. There was nothing."

"But – there was blood."

"Perhaps. But that alleyway is filthy, dirt and rubbish and who knows what... easy to overlook a bit of blood in that mess."

"I would have thought they'd have heard something."

"Sharkey's got the radio on, there are people chatting and some weird noises coming out of the kitchen – nobody noticed anything."

We'd reached the Dreadnought by now. Sam helped me into a chair and I slumped, head spinning. Sharkey was there as well.

"Graham – mate – you're white as a sheet!"

"Terrible cliché," I admonished him. "Never use it."

"He's in shock," Sam said.

He was right, I was in shock. Of course I was. I'd just seen Adi die. Not Adi though, not my best friend ever. I reminded myself of that. But it was starting to come back now, vivid mental images swirling round in my head.

"Got just the thing for that. Back in a tick." Sharkey disappeared.

"So what happened, Dad?" Sam asked gently.

I felt confused, the lights seemed very bright, much brighter than usual. I sat back and stared up at the wall. Faded photographs of battleships in Valletta harbour linked with the past. A very young-looking Sharkey Ward with a group of mates raised glasses to the camera outside the original Dreadnought bar. Superimposed over them I could still see Adi's face, falling away from me. Only not Adi. I sat back and shut my eyes, trying to sort through the memories. Adi's face stared at me, mouth open in a scream, water running from his hair…

"He nearly drowned," I muttered.

Sam was looking at me, puzzled. "Nearly drowned? How did that happen?"

"There was a wave…" I began, then shook my head. "No, no of course there wasn't. What am I talking about?" I rubbed my eyes, trying to force the images out of them. "Adi fell. No, not Adi. The pretend Adi. Fake Adi. He fell off the building. He was trying to get down the fire escape but it was rusted through and he fell. Then I went after him. You saw what happened then."

Sharkey returned with a mug of tea. A thick, dark brown liquid. Strong enough to walk on. Stronger than the fire escape. Not my usual blend, but right then it was probably just what I needed. I tried to stir in some sugar but my hands had started shaking. Sam took the spoon off me and finished the job.

I sipped it gratefully, trying to get my head in order. "I found him up on the top floor. He was talking to someone on his mobile. I tried to explain, to ask him about Adi – the real one – but he just kept backing away... then the walkway fell apart... Sam, did you say the back door was wedged shut?"

"Yes. There's a big wooden wedge that Sharkey uses to keep it open in hot weather – so he told me. Someone had shut the door and put the wedge in on the outside. Sharkey's a bit mad about it; that's supposed to be a fire escape." He frowned at me. "He's none too pleased with you either. He saw the walkway hanging up there, ready to fall at any moment, and he said something very nautical about it. He's afraid that if the council sees it they'll close the place down."

"They probably would."

"There's a mate of his coming round to sort it out, but I think he's expecting you to pay for it!"

I nodded. The tea was working wonders, and my thoughts were coming back into line. "Not unreasonable. Sam, what happened up the road, when I ran off after Fake Adi? I thought you'd be just behind me."

"I saw you take off, and the big fellow in the leather jacket was going to go after you, but that van driver grabbed hold of him and pulled him back. Very nearly got decked for it. He was slammed up against his own van and then his mates were piling in and it started to go seriously pear-shaped. But that tall guy in the suit..."

"Lonza."

"I suppose so. He got in there, stopped the van driver from getting thumped, and started telling everyone that he'd pay for everything... It calmed down a bit, so I started running after you, but you'd vanished. I got down to the end of the street, couldn't see you there, so I came back to the Market entrance. When I saw the sign for the Dreadnought

I went in and made enquiries. Sharkey told me where you'd gone so I went up as fast as I could."

"And I'm very glad you did. What about Leather Jacket?"

He shook his head. "Didn't see him. But I wouldn't have, if he followed me down the street and went straight into the alley."

"Fake Adi made a phone call, just before he fell. He was telling someone where he was. Leather Jacket must have been just outside the alley, because he saw Fake Adi fall." I nodded at the back door. "We were looking at each other."

"Ah. So you think he took the body?"

"They couldn't afford to have some random person who looks exactly like Adi Varney turn up dead, could they? So, as soon as he saw what had happened, he closed the back door, put the wedge in it to stop anyone coming out. Called Lonza to send the car down, got it backed up to the alley, dumped Fake Adi in the boot, and was gone before you could get down there. Not many pedestrians walking along this street, and drivers going past are all looking at the traffic lights. Who's going to see?"

"Right. Yes, I suppose that could happen. But why didn't you say so before? We could have got the police down here, had them looking for that car."

"Ah, yes. The police." I sat back and thought about it. "We could still do that – but I'm not sure if it's a good idea, Sam. I mean, just think about it. Once we start telling them part of the story, they'll want to know all of it."

Sam considered this. "They would want to know why you went chasing him up to the top floor in the first place."

"An area that I wasn't supposed to be in. Yes. And then I'd have to say that it was because he looked like Adi Varney."

"So you say that this body which disappeared belonged to a man who looks like someone who went to the USA years ago..."

"Who is involved in a scheme to sell off the charity that was founded by the man he looks like."

"And that's all maybe, perhaps, and only your word for it. OK, Dad. Perhaps calling the police isn't a good idea."

"Especially as I was technically trespassing up there anyway."

Sharkey, who had been not quite eavesdropping, but certainly hanging round close enough to pick up a few words, chose that moment to stick his oar in.

"Ah, about that matter of trespassing, Graham... obviously, I'm not going to say anything, mate, but it might be better if you didn't either? I mean, apart from any trouble you might have, this place is on a bit of a shoestring. The owners have as good as told us that they want to evict us and pull the whole place down, sell off the land for redevelopment. Especially with all the money that's supposed to be coming in to do up Delford Mills. They'd like to get some of that. Only thing that's stopping them is the Victorian Heritage thing. You know, local historians and such. They'd kick up a bit if anyone tried to bulldoze the place."

I nodded. "Not to worry, Sharkey. Nothing happened here. Except that I was walking by, saw something fall into the alleyway. Thought it might have been a person, but when I took a closer look, it was just a bit of the old fire escape. It's falling apart up there, but it's getting fixed – right?"

Sharkey nodded. "Mind you, that might be expensive."

"Well, of course I can chip in a bit to help with that. Preserving a bit of our heritage, after all. But the important thing to remember is that no one was up there and no one got hurt – right? I had a bit of a nasty shock, that's all. Bit of rust nearly hit me."

There were sirens in the distance. The ambulance was on its way.

Sharkey looked relieved. "Yeah, I think that must be what happened. Thanks, Graham. Anything else I can get you?"

"Another cup of tea? And a couple of your steak-and-egg sandwiches. I've been telling Sam how good they are."

"Coming up!" He headed back towards the kitchen area.

Sam gave me a sideways look. "For someone who's always believed in telling the truth, that's a heck of a whopper you just put together."

"I know. But sometimes the truth is too hard to believe. Or to explain."

"I find it hard to believe that you still want a steak-and-egg sandwich after what just happened."

"I don't. But if I'm sitting here eating and drinking, then the paramedics are more likely to believe it's a false alarm. I don't want them dragging me off to hospital… and by the way, no mention of my heart problems! Not to them, and not to your mother when we get home, OK?"

He shook his head. "And I thought there was nothing more I could learn from you, Dad."

That hurt. "Just learn to avoid my mistakes!"

The paramedics didn't stay long. We assured them that no one had fallen off the building, which was their main concern. They checked my vitals, confirmed that everything was within acceptable parameters, and made me promise to go to my GP if I had any symptoms. Then they left in a hurry, with more urgent jobs to get to.

Sam returned to his sandwich with a thoughtful look. "I was thinking... perhaps we should mention it to someone unofficially? You know some coppers, don't you? You could just run it past them. Maybe they could have a dig around, perhaps check out the car?"

I shook my head. "The police don't have as much freedom as people think. Without a confirmed crime, they can't go running searches or allocating resources. I did think of talking to David Macrae, perhaps asking him if Rocco Lonza had crossed his radar. But he's too good a policeman to just let it go at that. He'd need the whole story – and the thing is, Sam, we don't have the whole story. Just odd bits and a lot of suspicion."

He grinned at me. "Sure that's not the newspaperman talking, Dad? Wanting the whole story?"

"Could be. But do you know how policemen and editors are alike? Neither of them wants to be bothered with half a story. So I'm going with my instincts for now, well trained as they are. We'll keep it to ourselves for the moment."

"Right. But I was thinking it would be good for someone to go over that alleyway with an expert eye. Do a proper forensic examination. You did say there was blood there, right? Even if we can't do anything with it now, it would be good to get it sampled, just in case we can use it later, yes?"

I gave him a long look. "What are you thinking, Sam?"

"I could phone a friend."

"Which friend?"

"Alison Kepple. She's a CSI. We met at the wedding."

"Ah. Tall blonde girl. I didn't know you were friends."

"We got on well. Talked about cameras, mostly. But I could give her a call, see if she's free."

"OK, then," I said. "Just if she's free. She's probably busy, but I don't suppose it could hurt for her to look, at least. As long as it stays unofficial at this stage."

"I'll make that clear," he promised. "Give me a moment – my phone reception isn't too good in here."

He went outside, leaving me wondering if the reception was the issue or if it was more about me overhearing what he said. It depended on how good a friend Alison was. Ah, well, that was something for Sam to tell or not, when he wanted to.

In the meantime, I concentrated on the sandwich. To my surprise, I did indeed have an appetite. I couldn't quite believe that I was feeling hungry just after watching someone fall to their death. But then, I couldn't quite believe it at all. It wasn't something that had actually happened. It felt like something I'd seen on TV.

But it had happened. Right in front of my eyes.

I thought about Adi's face, screaming, falling away from me, and put the sandwich down again. When Sam came back he found me staring at the old pictures of battleships soaking up the Mediterranean sun, and trying to think only of the distant past.

*

Alison Kepple *was* free, as it turned out. Off duty, in fact. She turned up, forty minutes later, in a white Transit Connect with "Police – Scientific Support" on the side in large blue letters.

"Did you tell her to keep it unofficial?" I asked.

Sam shrugged. "She said she needed to bring a bit of kit with her."

Alison, in CSI uniform, got out of the van and came towards us. She was quite tall, attractive, but not pretty in any conventional sense. It was more about the strong lines in her face. And the way she looked at you – a disconcertingly direct gaze.

"Hello, Sam," she said, and looked at me. "Mr Deeson. You're not looking good."

Direct in her gaze and in her speech. To the point of being tactless – which is how Sandy had once described her. "I've had a bit of a shock," I explained.

"Yes. Sam said. Show me where the body was."

Not wasting time with formalities, then.

We went down the alleyway, till we were outside the Dreadnought. The fire escape door had been reopened, with a wedge put in to keep it that way.

"We think that the person who took the body must have shut the door and used the wedge to stop anyone coming out," Sam explained.

Alison nodded. She unclipped a torch from her belt and ran the beam along the bottom of the door.

"Nothing of forensic value there," she announced. She widened her search, examining the ground. "Very little chance of any footprints. Perhaps a partial tread mark on some of the rubbish, but not proof of anything. It's not a secure area; anybody could come along here for any reason."

"The body – well, when I saw it, it was over by that big rubbish bin." I pointed. "He fell from up there."

Looking up, it was easy to see the big hole in the fire-escape walkway. It was a long way up. I felt suddenly queasy and had to look away. I was regretting the sandwich.

"There must have been some blood," Sam added. "Perhaps that stain over there?"

The problem was, there were a lot of stains in the ancient tarmac. A lot of stains, a lot of rubbish, a lot of dirt over the cracked surface.

"No, I think it's probably that one." I indicated a dark area next to the wheelie bin. "There was a sort of – puddle – coming out of him."

I was trying very hard not to start shaking again. I didn't want the paramedics back.

Alison used her torch for a closer look. Most of what I presumed was blood had soaked into the dirt, but there were distinct reddish smears on some of the old polystyrene cups and bits of packaging that were strewn around.

"How was the body orientated?" she asked.

"He fell backwards," I said. Adi's face, screaming, falling away from me… "But when I saw the body, it was face down, I think."

She looked again. "That agrees with what I'm seeing here. The body fell backwards, struck the top of the bin, which flipped it over, so it landed face down, perhaps head first, on the ground just here. There would probably have been impact damage to the head and face, which would result in blood pooling just here. Perhaps internal bleeding as well. The smearing could have been caused when the body was moved, or by an attempt to wipe it up." She looked at me steadily. "But you do realize that while this is consistent with your story, it does not prove it. There are other reasons why someone might lose some blood here. I can't even say at this stage if it's human blood. Someone could have dumped a leaking bag from the kitchens down here while they opened the bin, and you'd get a similar effect."

"OK. What can we do with this?"

She looked round. "I can take some photos. Show the relative positioning of things, in case it becomes significant later. And I'll test this blood, just to confirm that that's what it is, and take a sample. I won't be able to do anything with it, you understand. Not without a crime number, or authorization from higher up. But I can put it into Property on a temporary basis, and it should be OK there for a week or so. If anything develops, then we'll be able to submit it for DNA, perhaps get a name. Or, if there's a suspect, we could check their clothing for blood traces and try to match those."

"What about up there?" I nodded at the walkway above us. "Where he fell from."

She peered up. "That looks dangerous. Has it been reported?"

"It's in hand," I assured her.

"OK, then. But rusty metal? Not promising. What other surfaces might he have touched?"

I thought back. "There was the window frame. Where he climbed out. But I went out of there as well."

"What condition was it in?"

I hadn't really been looking at the window frame. "Everything up there is in poor condition. A lot of old, flaking paintwork. But the floor was dusty, so there might be footprints."

"Yes, that's possible. Let me see the tread on your shoes."

I turned round and lifted a foot towards her, steadying myself on Sam.

"Herringbone with wavy edges. Distinctive enough. OK, I'll take a look. I want to get some images from up there in any case. I'll get my camera and get started. If you two could just guard the alleyway for a while, try to keep anyone else from coming by? It's not exactly a pristine scene anyway, but it'll help if we can keep it secure for a few minutes at least."

"How long?" asked Sam.

"No more than forty-five minutes," she said briskly. "Because after that I've got to be back at the station to start my proper shift. So I need to get on with it." She turned away and headed back to her van without another word.

"I don't think she means to be rude, Dad." Sam gave me a glance. "She just doesn't realize how it sounds."

I nodded. "I get that impression. Not a problem – she's doing us a big favour."

Her timing was quite precise. Forty-two minutes later, she was carrying her equipment back down the alleyway.

"Did he have anything in his hands when he fell?" she asked.

"He had a stick. That was on the ground next to him. It would have been quite obvious if it was still there."

"Anything else?"

I closed my eyes, reluctantly visualizing the scene. *Fake Adi, standing on the walkway. Talking to me. "Just doing a job," he said. And I thought he was going to come back in. But then his phone rang.*

"He had a mobile," I said. "Just before he fell, he was answering a call."

"Did you see what sort it was?"

"Not really. Small, black. I think."

"Something like this?" She held up a clear plastic evidence bag, containing a black mobile with a shattered screen.

"Yes, that could be it! Where did you find it?"

"Behind the wheelie bin. If it was in his hand when he fell, it could easily have ended up there when he hit. But, of

94

course, it could have been tossed over there yesterday, and have nothing to do with this incident." She frowned at the phone, not liking the ambiguity.

"So can you do anything with it?"

"Not really. It was in a pool of something that had dripped out of the bin, so no chance of DNA or fingerprints – even if there was a decent surface on it anyway, which there isn't, now that the screen's broken. If this was a real crime scene, I could send it up to the Technical Forensic Unit, and they might be able to get something useful off the SIM card. But not without a crime number, and even then there's a month's backlog for anything but high-priority cases."

"I could have a go at it," said Sam.

We both looked at him.

"Well, I worked in this place for a while, picked up a few tricks, that's all. I might be able to get something. Or not."

Alison tossed the bag at him. "I'd rather not have it sitting around in Property under my name anyway. A couple of blood swabs I can explain away if necessary, but if I pile too much junk up, someone might notice." She glanced at her watch. "I need to go."

She put her kit away, climbed into the van, and was gone without a goodbye.

"Not much for small talk, is she?" I said.

"No. But she's pretty good at her job." Sam held up the bagged mobile as evidence.

"No arguments there. Come on, we should get off home. I want to be back before your mum; it'll make the explanations easier."

"You're going to tell her then?"

"Much better than trying to hide it. Trust me, I speak from experience. She always knows."

CHAPTER 7

"I don't want excuses, I don't want
explanations, I don't want your honest
opinion! I want results, that's all!"

**Adi Varney, half-time team talk, as
quoted by Johnnie Muldoon**

Honesty may not always be the best policy, but it does give
one the chance to control the narrative. I was able to
avoid any mention of the steak sandwiches.

I also managed to downgrade my sprint along the street
to a "gentle jog" and the three flights of stairs I'd struggled up
to a "short climb", which didn't avoid a frown from Sandy.
However, there was no way of glossing over the fact that I'd
watched a man fall to his death.

"He fell? Three storeys?"

"Well, four actually," said Sam, not helping.

"And you saw it?"

I nodded. My wife has seen death. More than I have,
actually. She understands, and she understands me. I hadn't
realized how much until she put her arms round me, hugged
me tightly, then looked into my eyes and said: "Graham. It
wasn't Adi. It wasn't him. It was a terrible thing to see, but it
wasn't him. Have you got that?"

In my mind, it played out again. Adi's face, falling.

Not Adi, though. I focused on that thought. Overlaid the image in my head with the words. *Not Adi.*

I returned the hug. "Yes. Got it. Thank you."

"What happened then? Did you get the police?" Sandy continued to hold me. Sam took up the story, and explained about the paramedics, the missing body, and Alison's unofficial scene examination.

"That's bizarre," she said. "And you're sure that it was this Leather Jacket man who took the body away?"

"I can't see any other explanation."

Sandy stepped back, but kept hold of my arms. "You should have called the police."

"I wish I could have. But there are problems with it." I went over the reasoning again.

"You could have talked to someone unofficially. June perhaps – no, she's on her honeymoon. Or David Macrae?"

"A very busy man. I'd rather not risk squandering the goodwill we have with him. Not until we have a little more to go to him with, at least."

"A little more…" She narrowed her eyes. "Graham, you're not thinking of taking this further?"

Actually, I hadn't made a conscious decision. But as soon as she put it into words, I realized that I had no intention of leaving things as they were.

"Sandy, think about this. Think of the implications. That person wasn't Adi – but in that case, where is he? The real Adi. Because, the thing is, if they were resorting to using a double, that implies two things. One is that they couldn't get the real Adi to do it, and the other is they were confident that the real Adi wouldn't turn up to spoil the show. Either way, something must have happened to him. I can't just let that go, can I?"

She said nothing, just looked at me with eloquent tears shining in her eyes.

"Look, I understand your concerns. And I promise I won't do anything stupid. There isn't a lot I *can* do, actually, apart from ask around a bit. You know, check with some contacts, do a bit of background research, maybe find out a bit more about this Lonza and his company. Reporter stuff. Not detective stuff."

She didn't look convinced. "Graham… I can't lose you."

"I know. You won't." She was still looking at me in the same way, and slowly shaking her head. "What would you do? Would you just leave it alone?"

Which was a low blow, and I regretted it as soon as it was out of my mouth. Because we both knew the answer to that, and what it had cost.

She squeezed her eyes shut, but the tears were leaking out. "OK. OK. If you must. But just research. No chasing people round dangerous buildings. No chasing anyone."

I nodded. "No chasing."

She opened her eyes again, brushed at her face. "I know I sound like a hypocrite. But I was lucky, Graham. More than lucky. Perhaps I had divine protection or something. I don't know. But you know I would never have got into that if I'd realized how dangerous it was. You – you're talking about some sort of organized crime gangster. Someone who makes bodies disappear. Suppose that was you or Sam?"

Sandra has a special horror for bodies that disappear, or that are unidentified, unknown.

"I won't go anywhere near Lonza or his sidekick," I promised. "Internet searches, phone calls, that's all. If we go out of the house it'll be to walk the dog or get a pizza."

"No pizza!" she snapped, but with a faint smile. "You need to watch your health, Graham!"

"Yes. Of course. In fact, I'm going to have an early night tonight. I'll have a shower, come down for a bite to eat, then bed. OK?"

She nodded. "Off you go then."

I made my escape.

I spent a long time in the shower, and afterwards a long time sitting on the bed and staring into nothing. Reliving the events. I kept on seeing that moment when the rusty metal gave way, and Adi's face fell away from me, screaming.

It had helped to talk it over. I had read somewhere that we deal with trauma by putting it into words, where the events are defined, locked down, and confined to history. Then we can start putting it behind us, in the past, at an ever-increasing safe distance. I supposed that that was what I was doing.

Perhaps going over it again with Sandy would help the process along. I finally got dressed and went back downstairs.

Sandy and Sam were talking as I approached the lounge door.

"I should have stopped him running off like that," Sam was saying.

Talking about me, obviously, and I paused at the door. *Old reporter's instinct*, I told my conscience, and ignored the traditional danger attached to eavesdropping.

"I wish you had," said my wife.

"He caught me by surprise. This argument – it looked like it was going to get out of hand, and that had all my attention. I didn't even see him go. I just looked round and he was already halfway down the street. It was just so unlike him, Mum. Dad's never been the sort to act on impulse. He's a 'measure twice, cut once' sort of person. Suddenly chasing off like that, I just didn't expect it."

I suddenly realized that Sam was feeling guilty for not keeping me out of trouble. It felt weird to know that. Wasn't I supposed to keep him safe? When had our roles as father and son become reversed?

"I know, I know," Sandy was saying. "Don't blame yourself, Sam. He hasn't been himself lately."

Really? How so?

"How do you mean?" Sam asked my question for me.

"Oh, little things. Like the way he was badgering Karen Varney about Adi. It's not like him to be so insensitive. But it was thinking he'd seen Adi that set him off. He always was a bit strange where Adi was concerned."

Sam didn't say anything, but I could imagine the raised eyebrows and the little half-smile that said, "Come on. Don't leave it there, tell me more."

Sandra sighed. "They were a strange pair to be best friends. Very different people. And your dad used to get really frustrated with Adi. Like you said, Graham was never impulsive, always liked to think things through, whereas Adi was all instinct and action. Of course, his instincts were usually pretty good, especially with regards to football, but he dropped some monumental clangers sometimes as well. Graham said once that he never felt safe around Adi, always on edge."

Her voice dropped a bit, and I stepped closer to the doorway. "Between you and me, I was a little bit glad when

Adi left. Sorry for Karen and her girls, of course – but I couldn't help thinking that your dad was better off without him."

She'd never told me that. I'd never suspected that Sandy felt that way. I felt a curious sensation, as if the world had shifted slightly, was suddenly not quite the way I'd thought it was.

"But he wanted him to come back?"

"Oh, yes. He was very down when Adi left. Down in a way I'd never seen before. He just closed up, wouldn't talk about it. Not even to me, and he always talked everything over with me. But not this. Honestly, Sam, the thing that worries me most about this business is that it might bring all that back. And with his heart trouble now as well…"

"Dad keeps telling me that that's all OK since he had the stents put in."

"Yes, he says that. It's probably true. But once you've been through it, it's always at the back of your mind. It is with me, at any rate."

There was a long silence as we all thought about that.

Sam broke it. "There was another thing I wanted to ask you about, Mum. Just after it happened, Dad said something really weird. He was going on about a wave, and drowning. I don't remember exactly, but it wasn't anything to do with what actually happened. Do you know what he might have meant?"

"That is strange. I'm not sure. Except – well, you know about his younger brother David?"

"The one who died young?"

"Yes. Well, he drowned. In the canal."

"I never knew that."

"No. Not something your dad ever talked about. It was big news round here, of course – but that was a long time before I met him. I didn't even make the connection until after we were married, when his mother told me some of the family history. But the thing is, Graham was there when it happened. So was Adi. Perhaps the shock brought it back."

There was a quiet noise that I couldn't identify at first. Then Sam was saying, "OK, Mum. It's OK, he'll be fine," and I realized that she was sobbing.

I stood outside the door, shaken. I'd forgotten that moment of confusion. I didn't want to remember it now, but that was the price of eavesdropping, I supposed.

Instead, I went into the room and joined my wife and my son. We didn't talk – it wasn't a moment for explanations – but just then we needed each other.

*

Tired as I was, I didn't sleep well. There were no dreams that I could remember, but I woke up several times, with a feeling that something terrible had happened. Then remembering what had happened.

Eventually I must have dropped into a deeper sleep. When I woke up, it was to bright sunlight and Sam shaking me gently.

"What?" I muttered.

"Sorry, Dad, but Declan's on the phone. He really needs to speak to you."

"Declan?" Eyes only half open, I groped around the bedside table for my mobile, without success.

"You left it downstairs." Sam had correctly deduced the object of my search. "And it's dead. Battery, I suppose. Declan's on the landline."

We mostly used our mobiles nowadays. The landline handset downstairs was hardwired, practically an antique.

"OK." I rubbed my eyes. "Ask him to give me a minute. Or I'll call him back in half an hour."

"Yeah. I think that'd be better. I'll go and tell him."

"Um. Put the kettle on, please."

Sharkey's naval-strength brew had left my mouth with what felt like a coating of paint. Probably battleship grey. I spent five minutes cleaning my teeth and splashing water over my head, fifteen minutes preparing a more sophisticated blend of tea, and the remaining ten minutes of my thirty minutes' grace drinking it. Actually, Declan was five minutes early by my account, but I was feeling slightly human again.

"Graham? What the heck's going on?" He didn't waste any time on greetings, and from his tone was only barely restraining himself from much stronger language. "I've been trying to call your mobile."

"Yes, sorry, it's on charge. What's happened?"

"That's what I want to know! That meeting yesterday – cancelled at the last minute, so it was, and whenever I asked what was going on, they just hung up on me. Then another call this morning, telling me that we had ten days to clear all outstanding debts or they would commence proceedings to seize all assets. They repeated that the trustees were personally liable for any shortfall in the value. I asked them if we could meet to discuss things, and they said – some posh arse of a lawyer said – that they had decided there was no purpose to a meeting, that their position was clear and would be confirmed in writing in due course. When I tried to argue, he hung up again."

"Oh. I see."

"Well I don't! What happened to this fake Adi you said they were going to bring out? Did you have anything to do with this?"

Fake Adi. Mouth open in a scream as he fell away from me. I closed my eyes and shook my head to try to dispel the image.

"I... might have, Dec. That is – yes, probably I did."

"So...?"

I took another sip of tea. "There was an incident," I began, and proceeded with a summary of yesterday's events.

There was a long pause when I'd finished. Maybe a few muttered words, but all in all, Declan's restraint was impressive. "This Fake Adi – he's dead then?"

"Yes."

"And the body's disappeared?"

"Yes."

"Then they can't use him to pressure us into a quiet agreement. But we can't expose the scam, either. So we're back where we started, and they're going ahead anyway. I don't think we're any better off, Graham."

"No. We're not."

"Worse if anything."

"Yes. I'm sorry, Declan."

"What were you thinking, Graham? We had a plan! We had a chance of getting out of this." He didn't sound as angry as he should have done. More tired.

"I know. I wasn't thinking; that's the truth of it. I just acted on impulse. Went with my gut. I'm sorry."

"Not like you, Graham. Not like you at all."

Just what Sam had been saying last night.

"It was a mistake, yes. And I apologize. But listen, Declan – it's still a scam. I mean, if they were bringing out this fake Adi it's proof that the real Adi isn't behind it. So they don't actually have the authority to do this. If you challenge them, they'll fold. That's why they needed a fake Adi in the first place, to stop you doing that. Dig in, tell them you're taking legal advice, threaten to go public – whatever. Kick up a fuss and they'll back off."

"I don't know, Graham. They might not have Adi, but they've got the paperwork and the lawyers, so they have, and I don't know if I can fight that. Not if they can take me for everything I've got. The other trustees feel the same."

I shook my head, a useless gesture over the phone. "OK, I understand that. But don't give up just yet. We've got ten days, right? And they haven't sent the paperwork either. So get back to them, in writing perhaps, and tell them that without the paperwork you can't consider their demands. Tell them that you're taking legal advice. Tell them that you don't accept the deadline; that you insist on a face-to-face meeting… Tell them that you want confirmation from Adi in person, or you'll go public, and never mind their confidentiality clause! That'll scare them. They don't want any publicity on this or they wouldn't have bothered with that clause in the first place. My guess is that they know they're on dodgy ground, and can't afford to have too much exposure."

"I don't know, Graham. I mean – I hear what you're saying, to be sure, but – you're not the one with their head on the block."

"Yes. Of course. But just hang on in there, all right? Don't concede anything yet, that's all I'm asking. I'm going to dig around a bit, quietly of course. See what I can find that'll give us an edge."

Declan's silence wasn't a good answer. I hadn't convinced him.

"Dec, that charity has been your life since you finished playing. And you know how much it's meant to the kids round there. What it's done for them."

Still no reply.

"And it's Adi's legacy. The real Adi, that is. We don't know what's happened to him, but you know what it meant to him. We can't just let that go."

Finally, an answer. "OK. I hear what you're saying, Graham. And I'm not in a hurry to roll over for these…" He paused, running through the various possible words. Finding nothing suitable that he could use, he carried on. "So we'll wait out the ten days at least. I'll talk to the trustees."

"Thank you, Dec."

"Right. But no promises, mind. And be careful. These people – there were people like them back in Derry, during the Troubles. People who can make dead bodies disappear can do the same to live ones. I wouldn't want you to disappear, Graham."

"Don't worry about that. I've no plans to go up against them in person. I'm just going to dig a bit, that's all."

"OK then."

Declan hung up. A little abruptly, perhaps. He wasn't well pleased with me, and I couldn't blame him. My interference had seriously messed things up. Lonza, on the other hand, should be sending me a thank-you message.

I set about making more tea, and some toast to go with it.

Sam had been sitting quietly at the table, listening to one

side of the conversation and doing something on his laptop. I offered him a cup and a slice, but he declined. "I'm a coffee drinker, anyway."

"Heretic."

He grinned. "What did you mean by 'digging a bit', Dad? And just so as you know, before she left for work Mum gave me strict instructions not to let you do anything stupid or dangerous."

I raised an eyebrow. "That's rich, coming from the woman who got herself into the middle of the worst fire this town has ever experienced!"

"So what digging are you planning on?" he persisted.

"Honestly – I've no idea." I gave the toaster a careful inspection. It had been unreliable lately. If you left it to pop the bread out on its own you'd probably end up with a burnt offering. The trick was guessing how much time it needed and getting it out at the precise moment of perfection.

"Well, perhaps I can help a bit. I've been looking at that mobile Alison found."

"You've got something already?" Distracted, I missed my moment, and popped the toast out just after it had started turning from golden brown to black. Never mind, close enough. "That's impressive. And perhaps a little worrying that you know how to do it."

"Relax, Dad. It's not a big deal. Not for something like this, anyhow. A cheap pay-as-you-go doesn't carry much security, and with the right software..." He finished with an elaborate wave of his hand, a digital magician displaying his talents, and rotated the laptop so I could see the screen. It was displaying several boxes of information, all under a scrolling title, black on red: "HackerCrackerJax".

"And where did you find that sort of software?" I asked suspiciously.

"Oh, someone I hung out with for a while… he wrote some of this stuff, taught me a few tricks. Nothing to worry about, Dad."

There's nothing more guaranteed to make a father worry than when his son says "Nothing to worry about". Perhaps daughters as well, though I have no experience of that. But the time when I could push Sam for answers was long gone. I made mental notes, filed the information under "Son, Dubious History of", and returned to the main point.

"Security or not, I'm surprised you got anything out of it at all. It looked pretty smashed up."

"The screen was fragged, the casing cracked, and the battery's probably still under the wheelie bin, but that apart it wasn't in bad condition. The SIM card and the internal memory were still intact, and they were the bits we wanted. But, having said that, I wouldn't get too excited. There wasn't much on them."

"Anything at all would be more than we've got now."

"True. OK, so, let me show you. Here…" He highlighted a box, expanded it to full screen. "Numbers in the memory. Only two, you'll notice, both mobiles. And here…" – flicking to another box – "Call history. Not long. Three incoming calls, four texts, all from the second number on the list. The last call was yesterday. See the time?"

"I didn't take much notice of times yesterday. It got a bit blurry. But I take it that would have been about the time of the – ah – incident?"

"Yes. Near as I can tell. I didn't check my watch either. But it fits. You said he'd been on his phone just before he fell?"

"Yes. I heard it ring and he answered it. Telling someone where he was. And then Leather Jacket turned up just after it happened." I took a bite of toast, but it had gone cold. "That number is probably his mobile, then."

Sam nodded agreement. "And the other one could be for Lonza. My guess would be that when he came over from the States to run this scam, Leather Jacket bought a few cheap mobiles just for communications between the team. Something they could dispose of easily when they were done, nothing incriminating on them like old numbers, or photos. Burners, they call them."

"Yes, I'm familiar with the term. I watch TV, you know."

"Just one of the kids, aren't you, Dad?" He grinned. "But the point is, they're not supposed to use these for anything but basic comms. So the texts only say things like 'Downstairs, 10 min' and 'Be ready in 5'." He frowned. "Though this one's a bit puzzling. Answer to the first text – 'Can't find the stick'. Then there's a reply which says 'Come without it'."

I scratched my chin. "The stick? Adi's walking stick, perhaps? When were these sent?"

"Saturday. Oh, look at the time. That was while we were at the wedding reception."

"Yes. Not long before I went for a walk. And saw Adi – as I thought – in the bar, without his stick."

"Yes, that fits!"

I sat back and sipped my tea. "I'm wondering why they were there at all. You'd think they'd want to keep their fake Adi undercover for as long as possible."

"Dry run, maybe? Sort of dress rehearsal. Practise the accent, how to look English. Only the stick was misplaced. They probably didn't think that would matter. They certainly wouldn't have expected to be seen by Adi's oldest and closest friend!"

"No, I suppose not. But anywhere round here you could bump into someone who'd recognize Adi. Heck, anywhere in Britain, for that matter."

"Perhaps they didn't realize how big a star Adi was, especially in these parts. Or perhaps they did, and thought that being recognized by a fan would be a good test. They wouldn't need the stick for that – not when he was sitting at the bar – and they could always spin a story about getting some new surgery on his knee."

I turned the idea over in my mind. "They did leave in a hurry when it was clear that I'd recognized him."

"Job done. They'd proved that he could pass for Adi, didn't want anyone getting into conversation with him, so time to leave."

"Right. It could have been that. But does it get us any further? It still looks like a dead end."

"Perhaps not completely dead. I think our boy broke the rules… see here, Dad? There was one outgoing call, made to a US number. I don't think he was supposed to do that."

"Ah!" I put down my cup. "If we can find out whose that number is –"

"Way ahead of you." Sam opened another tab. "The number is for this place – the Harding Friemand Star Talent Agency."

The website showed a picture of a middle-aged man with a cheesy grin pasted over a fake tan. Underneath was an equally cheesy strapline: "I will turn your talent into stardust!" As Sam scrolled down, there was a list of exciting job opportunities in film, TV, commercials, modelling, and voice-overs.

"I don't think he's keeping his promises," Sam commented. "I've been all through his list of 'stars' and there's not a name I recognize. But there was this…"

He brought up a page of thumbnail pictures. Men and women of various ages, smiling or frowning or just staring into the camera. Whatever they thought would catch someone's attention, I supposed.

"Third row down, two across. That's him, isn't it?"

He looked younger, with thicker, darker hair and no moustache. A thinner face as well. But the resemblance was still clear.

"That's him. With a bit of make-up and hair dye – yes, that's Fake Adi."

The name under the photograph was "Jimmy Wayland". I read it out loud and felt a sense of relief, a lightening.

I didn't know Jimmy Wayland. The man I saw die wasn't my friend Adi. It was a stranger, an American actor from California.

Of course, it was still a tragic death, and mingled with the relief was a backwash of guilt for not caring more about this person. His life had been just as valuable as anyone's.

But it wasn't Adi I'd failed to save, and knowing that released something in me that I hadn't been fully aware of until it went. Now it had gone, I couldn't quite identify it. Grief? Sorrow? Dread?

But it was gone, and I felt myself breathing more easily.

"Dad?"

"It's OK, Sam. Just – well, it wasn't Adi, that's all. Do we know anything about this person? Jimmy Wayland?"

"Not much. He's got a few acting credits – as an extra in some films, a bit part in a TV show I've never heard of,

112

some commercials. Nothing more recent than last year. Not a Hollywood A-lister, for sure. There's nothing else on this site. I've Googled his name. He's on a few social media sites, the usual things, but there's nothing that tells us about his links with Lonza."

"I think we can work that out for ourselves. Here's an actor struggling for work who looks a bit like Adi, and here's an opportunity to give this scam some extra credibility. I wonder if he had any idea what he was getting himself into?"

"I doubt it. It's all too easy to get sucked into something dodgy, especially if you're a bit hard up and can't afford to be picky about jobs." Sam saw my look, and sighed. "Yes, Dad, I'm talking from experience. But it's all history now, and I'll tell you about it another time, OK?"

I could see that there was no point in trying to push it further. Another note for my mental file.

"Anyway, does this help us much?" Sam moved the conversation on. "Knowing who the fake Adi really was?"

"It helps me. But I don't suppose it gets us any closer to exposing this scam."

"We could go to the police?"

"And say what? Here's a person who looks a bit like Adi Varney and who fell off a building yesterday, then vanished?"

"Right. Still a bit thin. All the same…"

I sighed. "You don't let things go, do you?"

He flashed me a Sam Smile. "I can't help it. Genetics, Dad."

I snorted. "All the same *what*, then?"

"I would have thought that having a person like Rocco Lonza in the country would be of interest to somebody. There's probably an entire police unit tracking people like him. Chances are, they already know he's here. But do they know what he's up to? It might be worth passing on a bit of information – without going into all the details, of course. Anonymously, even. Just to make sure he's on their radar."

"You might be right. But who would you contact? You can't just drop by the local nick and ask to speak to their secret intelligence unit or whatever."

"I'll see if I can find out who to talk to."

"Alison, you mean? Would a CSI have access to that sort of information?"

He shrugged. "I can try. In the meantime, what do we do now?"

I shook my head. "I'm all out of ideas. We need a change of pace. A different perspective, perhaps. Shall we go and get some fresh air?"

"Go where, exactly? Bearing in mind I've had my instructions from Mum."

"Nowhere dangerous, I promise. Just a quick trip into the past."

CHAPTER 8

"When I was a kid, we didn't have a
TV, there were no computer games, so
we climbed trees, read books, or played
football. I didn't like heights and I hated
reading, so I mostly played football. Good
call, as it turned out."

Adi Varney, TV interview

We took the same route as we had the previous day, but
instead of taking the turning up towards the sports
centre, carried on south until coming off onto a small country
lane, which wound through some trees and eventually into
a rather exclusive little suburb of large detached houses, set
well back in their own grounds. Some were so far back that
they were invisible from the road.

"This was all open fields when I was a kid," I
commented. "Go a bit further south and west of here and
you're in Castle Vale."

A side road led to a quiet little car park with a sign
announcing that it gave access to the "Quarry Spur
Walkway".

"Walkway? Why can't they just call it a footpath?" I
wondered aloud.

"And what's 'Quarry Spur'?" Sam asked as we got out of the car.

"Oh, I know that one!" We walked over to the edge of the car park and through a gap in the fence. Beyond, a strip of grassy land ran away and out of sight to the left and right of us. About ten feet wide and rimmed with trees and bushes, it had a gravelled pathway running down the centre of it. "Here's the history lesson. Back in the late 1700s – before Delford Mills was built – there was a quarry just west of here, near a village called Burrowdell. With all the building that was going on, there was a good market for its product, but transporting it was expensive. So the owners invested in a canal – all the rage at the time – and built a link from the quarry to join the main canal over to the east."

"That's the one that runs through town?"

"Yes. The Central Navigation. Goes across the north of the town, then swings southwards just past the Castle. The Quarry Spur meets it along that stretch. Or did. As you can see, it's no longer a canal; just the memory of one."

We walked along the path, heading west. It was a bright day, sunshine filtering through the leaves and spattering over the grass. Birds whistling at each other, and a faint, indefinable scent of something sweet from someone's garden. The best of British summertime.

I didn't recognize anything, but there was something familiar about the atmosphere all the same, and a pressure started to build in my chest.

After a hundred yards or so we came out of the wooded area, and the northerly view opened up on our left.

"See that hill, Sam? Those buildings right on the top of it – that's the sports centre. Between here and there, where all those nice semis are now, was The Dingles. Don't ask me where that name came from, but everyone called it that. Rows and rows of terraced housing. Me and Adi lived on Hoskin's Street, which ran almost all the way up to the hill. Adi was number 45, about halfway up, next to Burrows' Corner Shop."

It was vivid in my mind. Old Mr Burrows, a round little man, always in shirtsleeves but with a bow tie that all the kids made fun of. Except when we were in the shop buying sweets, of course.

"Where did you live, Dad?"

"Number 82. Down near the bottom end. The street ended two houses further along, and then it was just a bit of wasteland, and the canal."

The wasteland was still there. The soil was poor stuff and full of stones, no use for agriculture. But no one had built on it either, which surprised me. It had been a very long time since I'd been this way, and I was surprised to find that some things hadn't changed at all.

The tightness in my chest increased. *Not my heart*, I said to myself firmly. *That's fixed. It's just memories.*

The path took a long, gentle curve to the right. On our left, a rough pathway cut through the waste ground, meandering through the scrubby bushes. Dry and dusty now, I remembered it being all mud and puddles most of the year. My school shoes were regularly caked with it.

"That could even be the same path we used when we came down here," I said, half to myself.

"They let you play by the canal?"

"Oh yes. By the canal or sometimes in it! That was forbidden, but it still happened often enough, by accident or design. And all over the wasteland and the fields as well. No such thing as an adventure playground in those days. Not much 'health and safety' either. You came home from school, had your tea, and went out to play. Often didn't get back until it got dark. It didn't bother our parents much it was pretty much what they'd done, after all."

Ahead of us, the ground rose. The incline was sharp enough that rough wooden steps had been installed to make the climb easier.

"The Lock," I explained. "It had a name, I suppose, but it was the only lock on the Quarry Spur, except at the end where it joins the Central. So we just called it the Lock."

The massive old lock gates with their great black timbers had long gone. So had the crumbling brickwork and the rusty metal of the winding gear.

Instead, at the top of the stairs the path continued on, with a wooden bench offering a rest for the weary. Next to it, a timber post held a metal plaque.

"So they kept that." I stared at it from a distance, then went and sat on the bench. My chest felt very tight now. Perhaps it was my heart. *That would be ironic*, I thought.

Sam came over and read the sign out loud. "In memory of Benjamin James Crowley and David Michael Deeson, who died on or near this spot as a result of a terrible accident, 19 May 1979. May their souls find eternal rest in the Grace of God."

He sat beside me. "That was Uncle David?"

"Yes. They put the plaque up before the canal was closed and filled in. By the towpath then, of course. I hadn't realized that they'd kept it. If I had, I'd have asked them to change it. Ben Crowley didn't die as a result of the accident. His death was the cause of it."

As a reporter, I'd had to learn when to ask questions and when to keep quiet and let people talk. Sam seemed to have a natural instinct for it, and said nothing as I struggled to find the words. Struggled to get them out against the pressure in my chest. Which wasn't my heart, I realized. It was grief.

"Actually, there were several causes. By themselves, they would have been small things. But they all came together. Nowadays, we'd call it a perfect storm."

A small brown dog ran past, then came back and sniffed at our legs. I reached down to give it a stroke and it licked my hand. The owner came past, called his dog away, and gave us a nod as he carried on down the steps. He looked to be about my age. I wondered if he'd lived round here then. If he remembered.

Probably not.

"The first thing that went wrong was the canal itself. And the lock gates in particular. It wasn't a good time for canals in general; they were run by the government through British Waterways, and of course there was never enough money to do everything that needed doing. What there was went mostly to the main canal routes. The Quarry Spur was well down the list, and it showed. Towpath overgrown, banks crumbling, the metalwork on the lock gates was rusting and the woodwork was rotting. In the lock chamber, the brickwork was cracked and some of the masonry had fallen out altogether."

"Why didn't they just close it down?" asked Sam.

"They wanted to. That was the plan. But there was a problem with that – it was still in use. Must have been one of the last commercial barges in operation. The *Madeline*, it was called. We just called it the *Maddy*. It had a one-man crew, and that was old Ben Crowley."

"Him on the plaque?"

"Yes. Old Ben had been working the canals all his life, and he was in his eighties by then, with no plans for retirement. He had a contract to shift aggregate from Burrowdell Quarry to a cement factory about twenty miles away, on the Central. And when British Waterways tried to shut him down, a newspaper heard about it and ran an article on how the government was destroying a way of life, etc."

"The power of the press."

"Exactly. Governments are very sensitive to bad publicity, so the plans were put on hold and old Ben and the *Maddy* carried on as before."

I looked around, overlaying the view I saw with an older one. The canal full of water, the old barge chugging down towards the lock with a trail of diesel fumes behind it. Ben at the tiller, with his pipe in his mouth, leaving its own fumes, almost as strong as the engine, touching his cap in acknowledgement as we ran alongside, waving, easily keeping up with the *Maddy*'s slow progress.

"But of course, they weren't going to spend any money on a canal they were going to close," Sam said.

I shook my head. "No. They weren't and they didn't."

"So what else went wrong?"

"Well, Ben wasn't the only person on the canal. The canal leisure industry wasn't anything like it is today, but there were a few private boats using it. On this particular day, there was a little cabin cruiser coming down from moorings near the quarry. It had just been sold to someone from Birmingham, who had taken a couple of his mates along to help him bring it home.

"Trouble was, they didn't know much about boats, or canals. And particularly about locks. It probably didn't help that they'd had a few beers each by the time they reached that point. Apparently they had some trouble getting the lock doors open – well, they were in poor condition, as I said – but one of them managed to fall in while they were doing it. He climbed out OK, no doubt a little sobered by the experience, but then they crunched their boat against the side of the lock, smashed up the gunnel – no fenders out, of course. And rammed the lower lock gates as well."

"Sounds like a comedy act."

"Yes. Except these idiots were a major contributing factor in what happened next. Because they then had even more trouble emptying the lock out and opening the lower gates to get out again. Perhaps because of the damage they'd caused. But in any case, they decided they couldn't be bothered to shut them again. Or perhaps they were just unaware of proper canal etiquette. Either way, they sailed off with the lower gates wide open and the paddles up."

I got up off the bench and went back to the stairs, looking down.

"The next factor in the tragedy was us. Me, Adi, and… my brother."

Sam came to stand beside me, and I pointed. "We were down there. About fifty yards or so from the lock."

"Did you come a lot?"

"I did. Adi not so much. He'd always rather be doing something football-related – playing, practising, reading about it. But even he couldn't be playing football all the time. And that particular Saturday, for some reason there was no one around. None of the usual kids we played with, that is. I don't know why. Sick, or away for the day, or helping their parents with something. Either way, it was just me and

Adi, with David tagging along behind. Couldn't get much of a game going with just us, especially as I was never any good. Davy was actually better, and Adi was 'coaching' him, showing him some moves. Ways to tackle or dodge a tackle, I think. Whatever, it was winding me up. I was feeling pushed out by my little brother. Or I think that was it – it's hard to remember exactly what I felt. But for that reason or another, I wanted to give football a break, so I suggested we go down to the canal. 'Down the Spur' is what we used to say. 'The Canal' or 'the Cut' was what we called the Central Navigation.

"Adi wasn't keen. He had a big match coming up – his youth team were in a regional cup final the next day. So he wanted to practise. But – as I pointed out – there wasn't much practice to be had. And I told him about my raft."

"You had a raft?"

"Built it myself, out of scrap wood and plastic barrels. A lot of stuff got dumped in the wasteland below our street, and a bit of imagination could always make something out of it. In this case, a raft. Not the most seaworthy craft, as you might imagine, but I could paddle up and down the canal on it.

"I hadn't told anyone else about it. Adi could be quite scathing about anything he wasn't interested in – so anything that wasn't football or at least sport of some sort – and I didn't want to share it with Davy. But I took the risk and this was one of the rare occasions when Adi was open to something different. The downside was that of course Davy wanted to come as well. I tried to dissuade him, but Adi took his side. He always did. So the three of us came down together."

I paused for a moment. *It was a long time ago*, I reminded myself. It was strange how the memories had dulled with age but the emotions remained sharp.

"I had the raft in bushes a bit further down. We pulled it out, got it in the water, and me and Adi started paddling it up towards the lock, with Davy following us along the bank. I hadn't been sure if it would take the two of us, I'd only used it on my own before, and the water was splashing through the planks, but it held together. Our jeans were soaked, but that wasn't a problem. It was a warm day, very warm for the time of year – about like it is now, I think – and we knew that they'd dry off before we got home.

"Of course, Davy wanted a go. I said he was too young, but he said he could swim as well as I could, and Adi told me to let him have a turn. So we pulled into the bank just below the lock – and I swapped places with my brother.

"He took a while to get settled. First he wanted to stand up, but the whole thing started rocking, so then he sat down. And complained that his bum was wet, so he had to get up and kneel… While all that was going on, I heard this sound in the distance, getting louder. An old diesel engine, which had to be the *Maddy*, coming down from the quarry.

"I told Adi, 'Better get the raft out of the water till she's past. Old Ben gave me a rollicking when he saw me on the water with it.'

"But Adi would have none of it. 'What's it to do with him, anyway? Not his canal! And in any case, he'll be ages getting through the locks. 'Specially as someone left the gates open!'

"And the noise was getting closer, and louder, and while I was arguing with Adi I was thinking, somewhere in the back of my mind, that Ben should have throttled back by now, getting ready to moor up while he opened the lock gates.

"What we didn't know was that Ben wasn't at the tiller."

Sam gave me a puzzled look. "So who was driving?"

"Nobody. That was the point. That was the last link in the chain."

I walked back up the path. "This, where we're standing – this was about twenty foot deep. The upper gates would have been about... here."

Sam stood next to me and we looked up the path together.

"There was a sort of basin here, space for boats to moor up while they waited for the lock. Then – you can see where the path runs – it's a straight stretch for over a mile before the next bend. Straight and quite wide. Ben used to use that to nip down into the cabin, pour himself a cup of tea, something like that. Never more than a minute, and he had a bit of rope that he'd slip over the tiller to keep it straight. There was rarely any other traffic – he'd have seen if there was anything coming out of the lock – and if the wind was light the *Maddy* would keep on as straight as a ruler for as long as it took him.

"At the inquest, several people testified that they'd often seen the barge running along, apparently unmanned. Then Ben would stick his head up out of the cabin and wave, so all was well."

"But not this time?"

"No." I closed my eyes, listening for that put-put-put growing steadily louder. "Ben hadn't been to a doctor in twenty years, it seemed, so nobody knew he had a heart condition. He probably didn't even realize it himself. But it caught up with him all of a sudden that day. He slipped the rope over the tiller, went down into the cabin, and never came back."

"Oh. Oh, crap."

"Yes. Exactly."

"It hit the lock?"

"Dead on. There was no wind at all that day, nothing to push the Maddy off course. I suppose that was another factor… She ran straight and true. Not fast, of course. Three miles an hour, perhaps three and a half, flat out. But she was carrying a full load, about thirty tons of aggregate, and that's a lot of momentum.

"One lock gate just disintegrated. Came apart. The other one was ripped out of the lock wall. In fact, a lot of the wall came with it. And all that water, all the water in the mooring basin and in the canal behind – it all surged through, carrying the barge with it."

"And the lower gates were open."

I nodded. "The pressure of the water should have pushed them shut. They're designed that way. But the poor maintenance and the earlier damage prevented that. One side did swing across, restricting the flow, but the Maddy hit it like a thirty foot javelin with the force of all that water behind her. The gate was carried away. Then she grounded on the sill, stuck halfway through and prevented the other gate from closing."

"And you were just below the lock when this happened." It wasn't a question.

"Yes."

We walked back again, down the steps and along the path.

"About here." I stopped and looked round. We were about forty feet from the steps, from where the lock had been.

"There was this noise. This incredible crashing sound. Not just one crash, it went on and on, a tearing and grating…

so loud, and it didn't stop. But it was drowned out by the water rushing through. A roar. That's what I remember. A crash and a roar.

"I was standing on the bank, holding a line to the raft, and I looked up and saw a huge wave coming towards us. Like a wall of water, muddy brown and frothing. I suppose – I suppose at the time I must have seen the *Maddy* smashing through the lower gates, but all I can remember – all I ever remembered – was seeing that water coming towards me.

"There was a tree..." I looked around. "Perhaps this one?" I walked over and touched the bark. *Some sort of birch? I'm not well informed on trees.* "Of course, it was smaller then. But the branches were across the towpath and hanging down near the bank. Just close enough to reach.

"I don't remember grabbing a branch. I don't remember grabbing Adi with the other hand. I can't remember anything of that moment – except how incredibly strong the water was. The wave spread out across the lower basin, so it had lost some of its power when it reached us, but it still dragged me so hard that my arms felt like they were coming out of their sockets. But I hung on. I don't know how. I just did.

"And it went on and on. So much water... but finally it eased off. And I was standing again, up to my knees in it but standing. I had hold of the branch in one hand, and Adi in the other. He was kneeling in the water, soaking wet of course. He was looking at me... I didn't understand his look. Why he looked at me like that.

"Then he said, 'Where's Davy? Where's your brother?'"

I stopped then and took some deep breaths. My cheeks were wet. I fumbled out a tissue and wiped my face.

Sam said nothing. Just looked at me, and looked around, and back at me.

"They found him about a mile down the canal. Along with bits of the raft. I…"

After a few minutes of silence, we began to walk back along the path.

"I really don't remember much about what happened after that. I'm told that when we got back home, it was Adi who did the talking. I was in shock, I suppose. He told them what had happened. My mother… poor woman, she somehow managed to cope with it. For a while. Called the police. The ambulance as well. They took us to hospital for checks, kept me in overnight, I'm told. I don't remember.

"Adi, though, he managed better. He went home that day. Next day he played in the match. Played a blinder, apparently. Scored a hat-trick, won the game and the cup for his team. There was a scout there from The Vale, and they'd signed him up by the end of the week. He was playing for them when the new season started, and he never looked back."

We reached the car, got in, and sat in silence for a while before I started the engine and began to reverse out of the parking space.

"What about you, Dad? I mean – a thing like that – how did you cope?"

I put the gear back into neutral and thought about it. "I don't know. I – we – just did. Somehow. The church was a big help. They supported us a lot. Shared our grief. I don't remember much about that time, but there was always someone to talk to when we needed to talk and that made a difference.

"That's when I started writing things. Someone told me to write down what had happened. I did that several times. Then I started writing other things. I tried stories and poems, but I didn't have the knack for that. So I wrote about things I saw, things that happened around me, and so on.

"Life moved on and we moved on with it. There was the inquest, of course, and the full story came out – all the things that had gone wrong, everything that had contributed to what had happened. That helped as well, in a way, though I don't know why. Perhaps just understanding it better.

"There was the funeral, of course. Adi came to that. He'd been at the inquest, but the funeral was the first time we'd spoken since it happened. He told me about the match, and his hat-trick, and signing for The Vale. I told him I was glad for him. I suppose I was. Anyhow, I wrote up what he'd told me and showed it to my mum. She showed it to the minister, Rev. Higgins, thinking he might put it in the church magazine. Instead, he sent it in to the local paper."

"*The Echo*?"

"The same. They printed it, and that was the biggest thrill of my life. For the first time since the accident, I felt happy, and I knew then what I wanted to do with my life.

"Adi was happy about it as well. He came round to see me, and asked if I was going to write some more about him. Well, of course I was. And we were mates again, just as we always had been. Closer than ever, perhaps."

I put the car into gear and drove on.

"Did you ever talk about that day?" Sam said, after we'd driven a mile or two and were coming back into town.

CHAPTER 8

I shook my head. "No. We never did."
Though actually we did once. Only once.

CHAPTER 9

"A draw wouldn't have been enough. A draw would have put us in the play-offs for promotion, and that's not something I need to happen just now."

Adi Varney, post-match interview after scoring the goal that secured promotion to the Premier League for The Vale

"I've had a thought," Sam said as we turned into our street. "Lonza and Fake Adi…"

"Wayland."

"Yes. Him. And this other man – the Leather Jacket one – they must have had some sort of base, somewhere they were staying while they set this up."

"I suppose so. I'd assumed that that was the hotel."

"Could have been. But we were thinking earlier that they might just have been using that to give Wayland some practice at being Adi. Sort of a dry run, let him practise the accent with the locals. So perhaps they had somewhere else?"

We reached the house and I turned into the drive. "Somewhere they could take a body to as well," I said. "I've been wondering about that. You can't dump a corpse just anywhere. Not without attracting some attention, anyway."

"Right. And obviously not that office building."

"No. Too busy, too obvious. And in any case, they arrived there from somewhere else. A car journey away."

We got out of the car and went round the back of the house.

"Lonza might have other properties – or his company might. I'll get in touch with Rich Hargreaves. He used to be on *The Echo*, went on to do research for the BBC business reports. He knows how to find out about things like that."

I put the key into the door lock, and as I did so, and the door swung open.

"That was careless of me. I thought I'd locked it."

Sam looked at the door and looked at me. "I thought you had. I'm pretty certain you did."

"Your mum must have come home early then." I stepped through the door. "Sandy?" I called. "Are you in?"

"No sir, I don't think she is."

A male voice, American accent. I didn't recognize it.

Entering through our back door brings you into a utility area, with a washing machine and tumble dryer. On the right, it opens out into the kitchen. No door, so nothing to stop us seeing the man sitting at our kitchen table, like a neighbour who'd dropped round for a cuppa. Except that instead of one of our bright and cheerful mugs, he was holding a large black pistol. Decidedly not cheerful, especially as it was pointed at me, with nothing to stop him seeing me either.

"Please step inside, sir," he said into the silence our shock had left. "Both of you, if you don't mind."

He had that polite but firm tone of voice often used by the police when giving orders to members of the public. The pistol gave some extra authority to it. We obeyed. In a distant part of my mind I heard Brodie whining in the other room, upset at being left out of the proceedings, and found time to be relieved that he seemed unhurt. He wasn't much good as a guard dog, though.

I finally found my voice. "Who the…"

He waved the gun. "I'm sorry, sir. No questions. This is what's going to happen. You will place your mobiles on the table here. And then you are going to go back out of the door. I will be with you. The pistol will be concealed, since we don't wish to trouble your neighbours, but it will still be pointing at you. You will get back in your car. Front seats. I will get in the back. You will drive off. I will direct you. Is that clear to you both?"

Sam and I looked at each other. There wasn't much room for discussion.

"Yes," I said. Sam nodded.

"Good. Please understand that I do not wish to cause you any harm, but neither will I hesitate to use this weapon if necessary. So let's stay calm, take things nice and easy, OK?"

He stood up, and came round the table towards us. A tall, broad-shouldered young man in a dark coat. Light brown hair, close-cropped in a military style, over a square face and an expression of earnest sincerity that clashed somewhat with the pistol. He looked like someone who was very keen to do us the favour of not shooting us.

"Your mobiles, please?"

He dumped them into a kitchen drawer. The pistol and his hand disappeared into his coat pocket, though I had no doubt that he was keeping his promise to point it in our direction. He was very believable.

Back into the car, just as he had instructed, and we were reversing out of the drive while I was still struggling to grasp that we'd been kidnapped. The facts were clear enough, but the relevant emotions were taking time to catch up. Shock does that, I suppose.

At his direction we drove for about a mile, before pulling into a large car park behind a pub. The pub I recognized as the Huntsman", an old pile of red brick that had closed down the previous month. The car park was almost deserted, apart from a small collection of supermarket trolleys that had been dumped there, and a black van parked in the far corner under some trees.

We drove over to it.

"Please exit your vehicle, sir, lock it, and put the keys on the roof." We complied, and he motioned us back with a wave of the pistol while he collected them.

"Now step over to the rear door of the van." He pulled out his own keys as we did so, and unlocked the doors remotely.

"Open the door and climb in." He watched as we did so, the pistol once again clearly in sight and not wavering from us. "I would advise that you sit down, for your own safety. We'll be travelling a spell."

The interior was short on amenities. No seats, for example. No windows – not even looking into the cab. And no light, we discovered, as the door slammed shut behind us.

The cab door opened, then closed, and the engine started.

"I don't suppose there's any point in trying the door," I said into the darkness. "It'll be locked."

"There's not even a handle on the inside."

"You noticed that? I didn't even think to look."

"Getting out was the first thing I thought of. But it doesn't seem likely to happen just yet."

The van reversed, turning as it did so. On the bare metal, even a low-speed manoeuvre sent us sliding across the floor. It was going to be a very uncomfortable journey, I realized.

That was confirmed as the van moved forward, then turned out of the car park, sending us bumping into the walls and each other.

"Sorry, Sam."

"Not your fault, Dad."

"I mean for getting you into this."

"Not your fault either. We didn't go looking for this – it came to us!"

The van braked quite sharply, bashing us into the front bulkhead. I grunted, and Sam used a word I'm sure he never learned from us.

I used a few choice words myself during that journey. My watch – fortunately illuminated – told us the trip lasted about half an hour, but it felt longer. When we finally stopped and the doors opened again, I felt bruised, sick, and disorientated. Perhaps that was the intention. Either way, I also suffered from loss of dignity because I needed Sam's help to climb out again.

We were standing in an enclosed yard, with high brick walls all round and a closed wooden gateway, so no clues as to where we were. Our chauffeur stood off to the side, pistol in hand, watching dispassionately as we stood blinking in the sunlight.

When he was satisfied that we could manage to walk and see where we were going, he motioned towards a door.

"Enter the building, sir."

The door was a blank sheet of unpainted wood, flanked by boarded windows. It didn't look like somewhere we wanted to enter.

"Now." The gun was raised, pointed in our direction. Just a reminder.

Sam pushed open the door and we went inside.

There was a long corridor, dimly lit, with grimy walls, and broken black and white tiles underfoot.

"Straight down to the end, and through the door."

Another wooden door, but this one had a bit more class. Varnished oak, it looked like – peeling, but still solid. With a brass handle that could use some polish. It was again Sam who opened it, and we went through into a large old-fashioned sitting room. Large, but so over-furnished that it felt cramped. Big sofas and armchairs, small tables, and several chests of drawers, all ornate but shabby and smelling of dust and old fabric. Dull brass ornaments covered the top surfaces, dark oil paintings of severe gentlemen and gloomy landscapes covered the walls.

It gave the impression of a well-stocked but abandoned antique shop. The tall windows on the far wall had their curtains drawn, which made the room dim in spite of the bright sunlight outside, and amid the clutter I failed at first to see the man sitting over to one side.

But I knew his voice at once.

"Hello again, Graham. Been a while, hasn't it?"

I turned to the sound.

"Adi? *Adi*?"

"Oh, yes. It certainly is."

As my eyes adjusted, I made him out more clearly. He was sitting back on one of the sofas, regarding me with the expression of sly amusement that he had always greeted me with. He had shaved his moustache and grown his hair out longer; he was not, of course, wearing his trademark jacket

135

and the stick he cradled in his hands was plain wood, without the brass handle he had preferred.

"And this is your lad Sam, isn't it?" Adi continued. "Well, you've grown up a bit, haven't you? Hear you've been travelling around a bit."

Sam shrugged. "I had itchy feet. How are you, Uncle Adi?"

Adi laughed. Adi's laugh always had a particular richness to it that made it stand out from other laughs. He could be laughing with you or at you, but you always wanted to join in with him.

"Well, I'm not too bad at the moment, Sam, thanks for asking. Been better, perhaps, but certainly been worse. And much better for seeing your dad again."

I was in shock, I think. Part of me was standing back, open-mouthed, listening to this conversation with my old pal who'd just had us kidnapped at gunpoint.

The other part, which was just going with the flow, said, "And I'm glad to see you, Adi! Where on earth have you been all this time? We'd completely lost track of you!"

Then the more rational segment of my psyche took control of my mouth, and I added, "But if you were so keen to see me, why the heck couldn't you just come round the house? Or phone me up and tell me where to meet you, if that was too much trouble." I nodded at the kidnapper. "What's all this about, eh?"

"Ah, yes." Adi shook his head. "I am sorry about that. But believe me, it was necessary. I did tell my associate to avoid hurting you, but I'm having to be very careful about people knowing I'm here." He waved at a seat. "You don't have to stand there looking like a wet weekend, Graham. Sit down, for goodness' sake. Sorry I can't offer you much in the way of refreshments, but Casey makes a decent cup of coffee. Oh, apologies, I've forgotten the proper British way of doing things. Introductions first, eh? Graham, Sam – this is Casey; Casey, this is my oldest and best friend, Graham, and his son Sam."

Casey inclined his head in our direction. The pistol was no longer visible, but I doubted it was far away.

"We have met," I told him. "Sort of. He was making himself at home in our kitchen. Him and his gun." I took the offered seat and Sam sat next to me.

"Like I said, I'm sorry about that." Adi sounded impatient. He didn't like going back over things he considered dealt with. "Casey was acting on my instructions. I needed to get you here quickly and quietly, and that was the best way to do it. I couldn't risk a phone call. I can't risk being seen and perhaps recognized – and as you know, there's a lot of people who might recognize me. Any word that I'm here would get around, and that is not something I need to happen just now."

Somehow, it was the phrasing that struck me before the words. "Not something I need to happen" was a use of words as much part of the Adi Varney legend as the jacket had been. It had regularly come out in team briefings, in numerous interviews and private conversations. And somewhere inside of me, something that I hadn't been aware of relaxed and acknowledged that this really was Adi.

Much more Adi than Jimmy Wayland had ever managed to be.

I shook my head. "OK, it's just – I'm still struggling with it really being you this time. I mean, last time I saw you – it wasn't you. And…"

"What's that supposed to mean?"

"Well, there's this American lawyer, by the name of Lonza, who's been pressuring Declan and the trustees to give up the sports centre. He's told them that he's had your authority to take over control, and to back that up he had some actor made up to look like you."

"He did what?" Adi's eyes narrowed. "That slimy piece of…"

He cut himself off, shaking his head. Adi had always had a fine command of English profanity, but I'd trained him out of it over the years. "Not good for your image," I'd explained, and that had convinced him to take control. I was glad to see that it was holding.

"I knew he was capable of some devious tricks, but I hadn't anticipated that one," he continued.

"You know Lonza?"

He chuckled. "Oh, yes. Me and Rocco Lonza have had a lot to do with each other in recent years… but tell me more about this actor. You've seen him? How much of a likeness is there? Could he fool Declan, do you think?"

I took a deep breath. "He did look very like you. Fooled me the first time I saw him. But he's not involved any more. He – had an accident."

Adi leaned forward. "What sort of an accident?"

"The fatal sort. He fell off a building."

"Oh? Well, that's a thing!" He leaned back again, and a smile came across his face. "How sad for him – and for Rocco!"

"It wasn't a smiling matter, Adi. I saw it happen. His name was Jimmy Wayland, and it wasn't a death I'd wish on anyone."

In my mind, the screaming face receded, falling...

"I'm sure it wasn't, Graham, but here's one of the tough facts of life: you take money from someone like Lonza, you take the risk that comes with it. You say you saw it?"

"Yes. I was trying to talk to him at the time."

"Bit of a shocker for you as well, I suppose. Sorry about that. But how come it's not been on the news? I'd have thought that a corpse looking like me would have rated at least a local mention." Adi sounded as if his pride was hurt.

"It never happened, officially. I called an ambulance, of course – but by the time it arrived the body had gone. There's a big man following Lonza around. Wears a black leather jacket. He turned up just after it happened, and I presume he whisked it away."

"Big man in a leather jacket, eh?" Adi exchanged a glance with Casey. "That'll be Handy Jack."

"Handy Jack?"

"Just my name for him. Jack Crail – Go-to Jack, he's known as in certain circles, since he's a good man to go to to make things happen. Especially things involving broken limbs or damaged property."

"Or disappearing bodies?" Sam suggested.

"Exactly. A handy man to have around, as I said! And for the past few years he's been Lonza's personal bodyguard and full-time fixer."

"How come you know so much about Lonza and his associates?" I asked, with a trace of suspicion.

"Well now, that's a long story. And actually, it's all to do with why I needed to speak to you, Graham. But we're going to need some refreshments to get through it. Casey, would you mind getting that coffee?"

"I'd prefer tea," I said.

"Well, of course you would. Still a bit of a tea snob, eh, Graham? I didn't expect that to change! But to be honest, you'd be better with the coffee. Americans don't understand tea. We make it in a pot – they make it in a harbour!"

I laughed along with him. "Adi, I told you that one about thirty years ago! And I had to explain it – you'd never heard of the Boston Tea Party!"

"Well, you always did know a lot of useless information."

We laughed again, and the moment of banter brought back the old days, all the shared jokes and the long conversations about life, the universe, and football. But mostly about football.

"There's beer in the fridge if you'd rather have that," said Casey, not sounding amused, and bringing us back to the present.

"OK, beers all round then," Adi agreed as Sam and I nodded.

"I'm surprised this place even has a fridge," Sam commented as Casey left the room. "Looks more like one of those 'living museum' places."

Adi glanced round as if seeing the room for the first time. "Yes, it is a bit of a dump. All this clutter – that all came with the house. The kitchen's better… I bought this place years ago. Some old lady died here, no relatives, needed some doing up, so I thought it might be a good investment. And a quiet little hidey-hole, somewhere to escape to. Did have a bit of work done on it, but then I left before it got very far. So Casey and I are just camping out here for a while."

"You could have gone home, Adi," I said. "Karen and the girls – they miss you. You could work something out."

He frowned. "Yes, well, like I told you, I've got to keep a low profile at the moment. As far as Lonza knows, I'm dead, and I don't want him to find out otherwise."

I raised an eyebrow. "Well, that explains why he brought in a double. I was thinking that he must feel pretty sure the real you wouldn't show up."

"So how did you get involved with him in the first place?" Sam asked.

"It was… 2009. You remember I took the family over to the States for a holiday? New York, Disney World, Las Vegas – all the big places."

I nodded. "You took a couple of months at it. Longest holiday you'd ever had."

He shrugged. "Karen was nagging at me to take a proper break, spend time with the girls. And we finished the season in a good place, so I reckoned I'd earned a bit of time off. Besides, I was curious about how football was taking off over there. Soccer, I should say. I had the idea that there must be some good talent waiting to be recruited, a pretty much untapped resource."

"So mixing business and pleasure, then?"

Adi winked. "As always, Graham. As always… Anyhow, while I was over there I met this guy Lonza. Slick lawyer type, not someone I'd take to, but he was interested in the business side of sport in general and gave me some talk about the money potential in US soccer. He got as far as suggesting that if I moved over there, he had a project in mind that we could work on together.

"Of course, at the time I wasn't ready to make a move like that, and I told him so. And that would have been the end of it…"

Casey came back into the room with a cluster of opened beer bottles on a tray. Budweisers, of course. I'm not a great beer drinker, but when I do I prefer a local ale. Still, this was no time to be picky. I accepted mine without comment.

"So why wasn't that the end of it?" Sam prompted.

Adi took a sip from his bottle and continued. "Well, things change, don't they? That was 2009 and I was committed to staying with The Vale for the rest of my career. The following year I had a different point of view."

"We've talked to a few people about that," Sam said. "No one understands why you did it."

"Don't they?" Adi met my eyes and for a long moment we stared at each other. "Someone understands very well, Sam. But perhaps they prefer not to say."

He took another drink, without breaking eye contact with me. "But the point is that when I did decide to leave The Vale, Lonza's offer came to mind. It sounded good. So I got in touch and asked if it was still on.

"And of course it was. I flew over there a few days later. Lonza had contacts, he knew how to sort out visas and work permits and so on. He took me out to California – top hotel, all the perks – and set out his scheme. He wanted to start up a brand new team, and he wanted me to manage it."

"Yes," I broke in. "We heard about that. California Strike All-Stars, wasn't it?"

Adi looked irritated. "Superstars. California Strike Superstars. The CSS, I called it for shorthand. Well, you should have heard of it. I worked my butt off to get the name out there, to make it happen."

I smiled to myself at the Americanism. Adi hadn't quite acquired the accent, but he'd made a start on the phrasing.

"So what happened? We heard you'd got a pretty good team together – even beat Real Madrid in a friendly! – but then everything went quiet."

Adi said nothing for a moment. He just glared. At me, I thought, and I was taken aback by the venom in his expression, but then I decided, *No, that's not directed my way*.

"Well, it was a scam, wasn't it?" He grinned suddenly. The old Adi, the irrepressible Adi who hated to lose but never accepted defeat as final, just a detour on the way to the next win. "Right from the start, Lonza was playing me. And I have to say, he did a good job. Everything looked right. He could talk the talk, he had all the names, all the contacts. The money was in place, he told me, but what he needed was the expertise, the knowledge of the game. And I was the one to provide that. Ex-England international, successful manager, someone with a track record of success – we were the Dream Team, and together we'd make CSS the biggest sensation in football history. Of course, he was telling me what I wanted to hear."

Adi paused to take another drink. "Hated this stuff when I first went out there. But it grows on you. America grows on you. The size... the big thinking, big talking, go-for-it attitude. And Lonza had all the trappings in place. The hotels and the press conferences, the cars and the parties and the girls..."

"Didn't you ever think about *your* girls, Adi? And your wife?"

He jabbed a finger at me. "Don't go there, Graham, all right? You know I never shared your puritanical outlook. What was between me and Karen was over, long before I left. I did my duty by her, I saw her set up OK."

"They missed you," I said quietly. "They loved you, Adi. They still do."

"They'll get over it. Things change, people change; you've got to move on. We all have to learn that lesson, Graham, even you – so don't get all judgmental on me. I put up with that holier-than-thou attitude for years, but not any more – you getting me?"

I opened my mouth, then shut it again. This was getting us nowhere. Arguing with Adi rarely achieved anything. I made a conscious effort to sit back and relax, and after a moment Adi continued.

"For a long time, things were good. I was travelling all over, meeting people, talking it up. And the team was coming together. I got some good people in to build round – you remember Hans Van Hoorn, don't you? Solid player, not as fast as he had been when he played for Holland, but he knew how to read a game. And José Santos – he went back to Brazil after he finished with Inter. I tracked him down coaching some low-budget youth team, but he still had the skills and he jumped at the chance to get back into real football."

"Yes, we heard. What you were doing got noticed."

"Of course it did. That was the point. Lonza's point, particularly. The more publicity, the more credibility – the more money coming in. He had all sorts of people wanting to invest in this big new team. As I was building the team, he was selling it, and the money came rolling in.

"The problem was, we weren't actually seeing much of it. Oh, he was still providing the stuff for show. There was a new strip, some top designer Lonza conned into putting his name to it. We made a big thing out of that. And the parties were non-stop.

"But when I pushed for some actual progress, he backed off. Not the time, things not quite in place, need a bit more patience, Adi. He had talked about a brand-new, purpose-built stadium that was going to be built in Los Angeles, or Sacramento... but there were problems, building regulations, not the right site, not the right time. So perhaps it would be San Francisco, or San Diego... then he was talking about smaller places, maybe Fresno, which after all was pretty central for California. Or Bakersfield, which wasn't that far off. Or perhaps somewhere else. Never happened, of course. It was never going to.

"Still, I was pretty happy and doing OK. I wanted to bring in some bigger names, but Lonza pushed for me to get some local talent. So I spent a year or more scouting out the soccer teams in California, going round the colleges and schools. And you know what, Graham? I found some serious talent there. There were some kids with decent skills, and a few who could be up there with the best, given the right coaching and the right opportunities."

"You were always good at that stuff, Adi. You could see talent in places no one else thought of looking."

"True." Adi grinned. "What was that you wrote once? 'Adi Varney could sniff out a rose in a dungheap.' That was after I found Johnnie Muldoon languishing down in the Fourth Division and got Dandy Dan to give him a trial. He saved two penalties in that game."

"That was just the first draft that I showed you. The editor reworded it. Probably for the best."

"It worked for me. Never mind. The thing was, I put together a team with some real potential. Started training, arranged a few friendlies with local sides – college teams, mostly, but a few pro clubs. And we did OK. Nothing phenomenal, but it was coming together.

"But it was all on a game-by-game basis. I couldn't get Lonza to come up with proper contracts for these boys, or even a regular training venue. He had the same old excuses, and they were starting to sound a bit tired. And by then I'd found out a bit more about him."

"Like he's some sort of Mafia money-man?" Sam put in. He had been sitting on the sofa, sipping his Bud and idly playing with the knick-knacks that covered the table next to him.

"Oh, you found out about that, did you?"

"Wasn't difficult. Seems he has a bit of a reputation in the States." I gave him a steady look. "How long was it before you cottoned on?"

"Yes. Well, OK, I knew he was a bit dodgy from the start. But so what if some of the money he was using was a bit dirty? There always has been some of that floating round in sport. If he was using the CSS to launder some cash, that wasn't my problem. But I started to wonder what else he was into. And yes, I should have looked into it a bit more from the start."

"So what else was he into?" I wondered.

Adi shrugged. "Lots of stuff. Anything where there was money to be made. But his speciality was exchanging cash for promises. He'd launch a project with a lot of razzmatazz, give it a big build-up. He'd use money from some of his dodgy friends to do that – they'd make donations to his scheme like legitimate investors – then all of a sudden the whole thing would collapse. The Mafia or whoever he was working for would get their money back, freshly laundered with a good bit of interest on top. Lonza would skim off his own cut, and all the real investors were left high and dry. Sometimes bankrupt."

"And that was what he was doing with California Strike?" Sam asked. He'd picked up a paperweight, a sort of brass and glass thing with a serpent wrapped round a globe, and was tracing the line of the serpent's body as he spoke.

"Yes, that was the plan." Adi finished his beer, then rolled the empty bottle between his hands. "What I didn't find out till later was just how I fitted into the plan. I should have dug some more.

"Lonza's MO was to handle things from behind the scenes, while someone else did the upfront stuff. Usually someone with a bit of a name, a bit of credibility in that particular business. Like me. Then, when the scheme tanked and Lonza slipped out the back with a bag of cash, the poor dope who had fronted things was left to try to explain things to the creditors – and the cops. Very often, they'd done some time as a result. But Lonza was clean, and so was the money."

"You should have got out then, Adi," I said.

Sam had put the globe down and had picked up a small brass pyramid, which he was turning over in his hands. I was starting to find it a bit annoying.

Adi shrugged. "Maybe. But as you know, I don't like to lose, Graham. And besides, I still thought I could make it work. The original plan – what I'd thought was the plan – that was still good. I knew that we could really make something out of CSS. There was no need for dirty dealing. Given a bit more investment, a bit more opportunity, we could have a successful team that was also a serious business proposition.

I just needed something to convince Lonza and the other investors of that. And I saw a way."

He paused, and looked pointedly at Sam. "Like the ornaments, do you?"

"Oh, sorry, Uncle Adi." Sam hurriedly put the pyramid back on the table.

"No, keep it if you want. It's just some junk the previous owner left behind. She was a bit of a hoarder."

"Oh, cool. Thanks." Sam stuffed it into a pocket.

"Real Madrid?" I suggested, trying to get Adi back on track. He turned his attention back my way.

"Exactly. I got to hear that they were doing an off-season tour of the West Coast – bit of a holiday for them really, but they'd keep in practice and get some publicity by playing a few exhibition matches. So I got in touch. I knew a few people who knew some people, and yes, they were open to it. So I put it to Lonza.

"To my surprise, he was really keen on the idea. Backed me to the hilt. Promised to hire a big stadium, even let me get players on a short contract to train them properly. And I thought I'd done it. That things were going ahead properly at last, and CSS was on its way up.

"But what I didn't know was that Lonza was having a bit of trouble of his own. He'd got greedy, skimmed off more than his share, and his bosses were starting to get a bit suspicious. Plus all the legitimate investors were wondering when they were going to see a return.

"I'd given him the answer. Get CSS playing a big match, something really high-profile. Like a big European team. And then make sure that we lost, and lost big. Then he could go around to everyone who was asking for money and tell them that it had all gone; that Adi Varney had talked big but he couldn't deliver and he'd spent all the investments on a crap team that was going nowhere."

Adi contemplated the empty bottle sadly. "I'd given him his escape route, and my head on a platter along with it."

"But you didn't lose," I pointed out. "In fact, you took them down 5–2! It was sports headline news everywhere."

He looked up at me and his expression was classic Adi Varney. A huge grin with a slightly feral edge. There was nothing that made Adi happier than winning – unless it was winning big.

"That we did, Graham. That we did."

CHAPTER 10

"Everybody says that football is 'a game of two halves'. But not everyone plans their strategy with that in mind. Adi, however, always does."

Graham Deeson, match report in *The Echo*

It was good to see Adi looking happy, but there was obviously more to tell, and I didn't think that this was going to be "happy ever after". I started to point out the most obvious fly in the ointment.

"But Lonza…"

Adi cut me off with a wave of his stick. "Sure, Lonza thought he had it sorted. The fix was in. Not through me, of course. I was the patsy, the fall guy. And I guess he knew that I'd never agree to throw a match anyway. But the evening before the game, Hans Van Hoorn came to have a quiet word with me. Seems that Handy Jack had been round to see him, and had made him an offer. If Hans saw to it that the CSS lost to Real, and preferably lost big, then he'd get to go back home with a significant cash-in-hand bonus. Now Hans is a straight arrow, not a dishonest bone in his body, and he told Jack straight out that he'd have nothing to do with it. Jack just shrugged, and told him that if he didn't he'd go home with two broken legs, at a minimum."

"Carrot and stick," I commented.

"Carrot and baseball bat most likely," Adi said. "That being Jack's tool of choice. So Hans said yes, but first chance he got he slipped off to see me.

"Of course, I knew straight away that Lonza wouldn't be putting all his rotten eggs into one basket. If he'd had a go at Hans, then he'd probably also had a word with José Santos – and from what I knew of José, he wasn't above taking a backhander. And there were a couple of the others who I thought would be especially vulnerable to that sort of pressure. So Hans and I put our heads together, had a bit of a think, and came up with a plan.

"We'd hired a big stadium – the home ground for LA Galaxy – and Lonza had laid everything on to make a big spectacle of it. Cheerleaders, fireworks, a marching band – the whole kit and caboodle. The stadium was packed, the TV cameras were there, and Lonza had booked himself a big corporate box, where he planned to sit and watch me go down the pan while he raked in some big bucks.

"Of course, I didn't need for that to happen. So just before the players went out, I changed the starting line-up. I pulled Hans out, and made sure that all those I had suspicions about were in."

Sam frowned. "Wasn't that the wrong way to go about it? I'd have thought that you'd pull Santos and anyone else you didn't trust."

Adi gave him a sly look. "And let Lonza know that I was on to him? No, he wasn't going to find that out until it was too late to stop it. After all, football is a game of two halves, as your dad often said."

I winced. "You know I always tried to avoid clichés, Adi. I don't think I ever used that one. Well, rarely at any rate."

"A cliché perhaps, but a truth as well. And something I was going to teach Lonza all about." Adi finally put down his bottle so he could use his hands to illustrate the moves of the game. "So, first half, Madrid started well right from the kick-off. They pushed their forwards through the centre…" (he jabbed his left hand forward) "… crossed the ball in from the right…" (wave of his right hand) "… and the centre-forward hammered it in" (punching with his left). "We were 1–0 down in the first minute.

"I was proud of those lads, though. A shock like that can knock all the confidence out of a team, even an experienced one, but these lads had some character. They picked themselves up and got back into the game. Well, some of them did. It was soon pretty clear who was pulling their weight and who was coasting. Or worse, who was deliberately playing to lose. Santos, for one. Every pass he made went astray, a lot of them were gifts to the opposition. Madrid kept piling on the pressure, but our lads hung on in spite of it. Still, without all the team on the same side there was only one way it was going to go. Five minutes before half-time, Madrid put another one in our net."

"Tough one. But you've pulled it back from worse than that," I commentated. "Remember that cup tie against QPR? 4–1 down at half-time and you still came out on top!"

Adi laughed. "Yeah, 5–4 it finished and I knocked in the winner in injury time. That was a classic, wasn't it? And that's the story I told them in the changing rooms. Of course, they all came off looking pretty dejected. But I knew how to deal with that."

I nodded. Adi's team talks were legendary. It was said that he'd reduced men to tears on occasion, though I never actually witnessed that – but I had seen him fire up a losing team to go out and play like champions.

"What did you do about Santos?" Sam asked, focusing on the practical.

"Oh, I pulled him out, of course. Him and a couple of others. They didn't like it. Santos was furious, but I just told him to disappear back to the backwater I'd found him in."

"Harsh," said Sam, raising an eyebrow. "If he'd been threatened the way Hans was."

"Maybe. But nobody plays to lose on my team. No ifs, no buts, no excuses. Has it ever been different, Graham?"

I shook my head. "Not on your watch, Adi. Not on your team."

"That's right. So after half-time, the team went out without the losers." Adi was sitting forward on his seat now. "Madrid had the kick-off, but they were pretty relaxed about it. It was obvious that they thought this one was sorted. I was glad to see that. Nothing better in an opponent than complacency. But the way they were just kicking it around, like it was just a warm-up for a training session, that was annoying as well.

"Then they got a bit too careless, and fumbled a pass. One of my lads picked it up, passed to Hans, who knocked it back into our half." Adi was gesturing again, but now he'd picked up his stick and was waving it to add even more emphasis to his words.

"Madrid weren't too bothered by that, as it looked like Hans was playing defensive, just doing his best to keep possession and not concede any more goals. So they went after it, but in no great hurry. They didn't expect it to be going anywhere.

"The thing was, though, the ball had gone to a particular person, a lad named Johnson Delgardo. Now Johnson was a solid lad in defence, not fast but powerful. And he had a huge kick on him, one of the strongest I'd ever seen. What's more, he was accurate with it as well. And this was a play that we'd worked out in training and practised a bit, so he knew what to do.

"He kept the ball until he saw that Madrid had taken the bait and were coming down the field towards him. Then he sent it back up, huge long kick well into their half."

A long wave of the stick described the arc of the ball.

"And at first it looked like he'd panicked and just kicked it anywhere. Out into open space. But then Mickey Cratz comes out of nowhere and picks it up.

"Mickey's one of the lads I've just brought on at half-fit. Thing is, he's not really match-fit. I haven't had enough time to train him up properly, and he doesn't have the stamina for a full ninety minutes. But when he's fresh, he's one of the fastest lads I've ever had on a team. And he can take the ball with him as well.

"So before Madrid know what's happening, he's away with it, heading for goal. They're all over the place, out of position, he's past the defenders with only the goalie to beat.

"Mickey hasn't got a fantastic shot on him, so I've told him to play to his strengths. 'Don't go for anything fancy,' I told him. 'Go in fast, get in close, and tap it over the line.'

154

Which is exactly what he did – swerved off to the side, pulled the goalie out of position, then back the other way, right round him, side-footed it into the net from five yards out!

"Some of the Madrid players were shouting that it was offside – which was ridiculous, they'd had players between Mickey and the goal when he got the ball. They just hadn't been fast enough to intercept him. It did give me a worried moment though, because I couldn't be sure that Lonza hadn't got to the referee as well. But he obviously hadn't, because the goal stood, no problem."

"I'd have thought that the ref was the first person Lonza would have gone for," said Sam.

"Yeah, well, it was a possibility. But this guy was on the level, Major League referee. It would have been a lot riskier for Lonza to nobble him than it was to work on his own team members. More expensive as well!"

"So you were 2–1 now?" I prompted.

"Yes, back in the game, and those Spanish lads are lining up for the kick-off still scratching their heads and wondering what the heck happened." Adi laughed. "Their faces! And I just wish I could have seen Lonza's. Even better, I wish I could have seen him a few minutes later when we scored again! Johnson this time, and I was really glad he got one in – he deserved it, he's a hard worker. Free kick, thirty or forty yards out, curved it perfectly, top right-hand corner of the net.

"Of course, I knew Lonza wouldn't just take that. So I wasn't surprised when Handy Jack storms into the dugout with a face like an angry pit bull, telling me to pull Hans off and send Santos back out.

"I told him that that wasn't going to happen, and he starts getting nasty about it. I mean, physically nasty. Time was when I'd have had a go at him myself, but I'm not up to that so much nowadays. So I'd taken a few precautions.

"While I was out scouting, I'd come across a tall young man – just eighteen, but four inches over six feet, and agile with it. Vincent Tansen, one of the best lads in the air I've ever come across, and pretty good with his feet as well. Of course, I'd snapped him up and he was one of the ones I'd put out against Madrid.

"While I was getting to know Vincent, I also met his cousin. Who, as it happens, was ex-military. What particular branch of the military he never actually said, but I gathered he'd been involved in some interesting operations that the public never got to hear of, in places that the US weren't officially involved in, doing things that never actually happened according to the records, which didn't exist anyway…"

"Yes, OK, I've got the idea," I told him. "Casey, I presume."

"Let me tell the story, Graham." Adi frowned. "You get a few articles published and you think you've got all the answers!"

I grinned. "Sorry." Same old argument.

"The point is that this cousin – yes, OK, Casey – had now moved into the private sector and was looking for employment. So I asked him to come along to the match, watch Vincent make his début against Real Madrid, and to even things up a bit if Handy Jack got a bit too handy. So when Jack took a step too close to me, fists all ready to go, Casey just stands up, steps between us, and looks him straight in the face.

"Well, I can tell you I've felt tension in a dugout before, but never anything like that. You could just about hear the air crackling between them.

156

"Then Jack takes a step back, and pulls back his jacket. Of course he's – what's the term you use, Casey? Packing heat?"

"He had a concealed firearm," Casey said. "Specifically a Ruger SP-101 357 Magnum revolver."

"OK, whatever. But Casey was also wearing a jacket, and he also pulled it back, and he had a gun as well."

"Sounds just like the Wild West," Sam observed.

"Yeah, I know." Adi looked grim. "But when it actually happens, right in front of you, you're not thinking of *The Good, The Bad and The Ugly*. You're just thinking that people could die and hoping that you won't be one of them."

"It was never going to come to that," Casey said. "Only amateurs and film directors would start a firefight in those circumstances."

"Yes, well, I didn't have your professional insight." Adi was gripping his stick very tightly, I noticed. Clear evidence of how taut the situation must have been at the time, if the mere memory could get him so wound up.

"But he backed down?" I asked.

Adi nodded. "Seemed at the time like they were staring each other out for ten minutes or more. Of course, it was only a few seconds. Then there was a big cheer went up in the stadium – we'd scored another. Nice goal as well – Hans floated it in from a corner kick and Vincent slipped between two defenders, out-jumped them both, and just flicked it past the goalie and into a top corner. Beautifully done. Of course, none of us in the dugout saw it, which was annoying, especially for Casey, who had come to see his cousin."

"I caught it on replay later," Casey told us.

"It was a while before I got to see it. But at the time, the really important thing was that Jack just turned and left without another word."

"He was thinking that TV would be zooming in on the dugout," Casey explained. "They always do after something like that; they want to get the reactions. He didn't want to be caught on camera, and he'd already figured out that he wasn't getting anywhere."

"Whatever. The point being, he'd gone, we were winning, and there was nothing Lonza could do about it. Nothing Real Madrid could do either!" Adi relaxed his grip on the stick and sat back, grinning. "We put two more past them before full-time! The whole stadium was on its feet when the final whistle went. People were going wild, it was like we'd won the World Cup or something. I went out onto the pitch, hugging those lads as they came off, and they lifted me up on their shoulders and took me all round the stadium. Best moment of my life, Graham. Best moment ever."

I saw the look in his eyes, the hunger. That was what Adi lived for. That adulation, that success – that victory. Nothing mattered more to him than winning. But...

"But you still had Lonza to deal with," I pointed out.

"Well, yes." Adi sat back, shaking his head. He held his stick up in front of him, examining the top of it minutely. He would do that with his old brass-headed stick, I remembered. When he didn't want to meet my eyes.

"See, I thought that I could talk him round," he said. "I had it all planned out. I knew what I was going to say. CSS had won, and won big. We were on the map, we were ready

CHAPTER 10

to rock-and-roll… All Lonza had to do was get behind it, make good on his promises, and he'd get back everything he'd invested and more besides. It was all pretty clear to me. I thought he'd see it my way. So as soon as the lads put me down, I went up to his box."

"I did advise against that," Casey said.

"Yes. OK, yes, you did." Adi clearly didn't like to be reminded of it. "But I took some precautions, OK? I told the lads to go home, celebrate, wait for a call. Hans – we both thought it would be best if he stayed out of the way for a while, so he went straight to the airport from the stadium, still wet from the showers, and was on the next plane home. I said I'd be calling him back in a week or two. Santos of course was already gone. He hadn't waited for the final whistle."

"And you went to see Lonza," I stated. "I take it he wasn't that impressed by your arguments?"

"He never even heard them. I stepped into the box – he was standing there, looking at me, with Handy Jack next to him. I opened my mouth and Jack just stepped forward and hit me in the gut. I mean, really hit. It drove all the breath out of me, doubled me up, and dropped me to the floor. And as I'm lying there, curled up and gasping, Lonza walks over and kicks me. Which showed how mad he was as he never did any of the rough stuff himself – that was what Jack was for. But he made an exception in this case."

"Where was Casey?" I asked.

Adi shook his head. "He wasn't there. Not his fault. I told him to make sure Hans and the other lads got out OK, but I wasn't really expecting any trouble. And, like I said, I was pretty sure that now we'd shown what we could do, Lonza could be talked round."

"People like Lonza, they don't talk to people who've screwed them over. Not without a gun to their heads."

We all looked at Sam. He glanced round. "Just what I've heard," he added, but I hadn't liked the assured way he'd assessed Lonza's character. I didn't like the way Casey nodded slowly, looking as though he was reappraising Sam.

"So when did you get to be such an expert?" Adi challenged him. He didn't like the implied criticism, even though he'd pretty much admitted his mistake.

Sam shrugged.

"Guess you learned a few life-lessons on your travels," Adi continued. "You'll have to tell us more about those sometime."

"What happened after that?" I asked, wanting to move the conversation on. "I take it Lonza didn't just leave it there?"

"No. No, he didn't." Adi sat back, stony-faced. "Jack put cable ties round my hands and feet – I couldn't do anything to stop him – and carried me out like a sack of spuds. Dumped me in the trunk – the boot, that is – of Lonza's car and off we went. And you think you had a rough trip coming here? Believe me, you don't know the half of it. Hours, I was trussed up in there, breathing fumes and still aching from that punch. But I didn't want it to stop, either, because I was pretty sure that when we got to where we were going, I'd be made to dig a hole, then shot and dropped in it. Or maybe not even shot first." He cast a look at Sam. "Ever had an experience like that in your travels?"

"No, nothing like that," Sam admitted.

That gave Adi his smile back. "Thought not. Not many people do – not and live to tell the story afterwards! Still, it was a pretty close thing. When they finally pulled me out

Lonza was standing there with a gun in his hand, and from the look he was giving me, he wanted to use it. But he held off, and instead had Jack cut off the cable ties and (since I was too stiff and cramped to walk) carry me inside.

"It turned out that we were somewhere out in the desert. The Mojave, about 250 miles from LA – but I didn't know that then. All I knew was that we were in this sort of ranch-house in the middle of nowhere – nothing but sand and rock and scrub. Bleakest place I've ever been in. They didn't even bother locking me up; there was nowhere for me to go.

"Lonza and Handy Jack went off again after a day or two. They had guards round the place – especially round the garage – but I was free to wander off into the desert and die, which would save Jack the job of killing me himself when he got back. The only reason I was still breathing at all was that Lonza thought he might be able to salvage the situation, and he might have a use for me in doing that. Like, perhaps, as a sacrificial goat – that's how Jack explained it to me.

"There was no mobile signal out there, of course. There was some sort of satellite communications set up, but that was as well locked and guarded as the garage. So I sat around and waited."

Adi put down his stick, picked up his empty bottle again, and waved it at Casey. "Any more of these in the fridge? Talking about that place makes me feel dry. Heck, just thinking about it does that!"

"Sure. Anyone else?"

"No thanks," said Sam, and I shook my head.

"Thanks, Casey." Adi leaned forward as Casey went out of the room. "He's so military, he likes following orders!"

"He doesn't look like someone who'd follow any orders he didn't like," I observed.

"Well, I certainly wouldn't care to push him," Adi agreed. "But he's got a well-developed sense of loyalty, and that was my best hope while I was stuck out in the desert. Only hope, actually. I'd only asked him to cover my back at the game, but I thought that when I disappeared he might extend that to finding out where I'd gone."

Casey came back with the beer.

"I was just telling them how you were looking for me," Adi said.

Casey nodded, though his expression gave nothing away. He wasn't a man who showed much emotion at all, I'd noticed. "I was tracking Lonza. I had no idea where he'd stashed you, but I expected him to lead me there eventually."

"But it took a while. Lonza didn't come back again for several months, by which time I was almost ready to try walking out anyway. If I'd had any idea which direction to go in, I might have done. But then he flew in – helicopter – and sat me down for a little talk."

"Sounds cosy," I suggested.

"Not really. Keep in mind that Jack was standing behind me the whole time, and doing a good job of being threatening without actually saying anything."

Adi took a couple of drinks from his bottle. "Lonza's point was that I'd cost him a great deal of money and also a certain loss of reputation. I'd made him look bad with people he needed to look good to. And the only way to repair that was to pay them off, with interest.

"I did try and suggest that getting CSS back together would be a viable way of doing that, but then Jack clouted me

162

on the side of the head – not too hard, just enough to let me know that this was a one-way conversation. So I shut up and let Lonza carry on.

"It turned out that he was quite interested in some of my assets back here in the UK – specifically, in the sports centre. I was a bit surprised by that, since he'd never seemed the sort to involve himself with charities, except as a scam. But then he caught me up on the news from home – about Delford Mills going up in flames."

"Sandy was in that fire," I said.

"What? Really? Heck, I didn't know that. How did that happen? I take it she got out OK?"

"It's a long story. She had some nasty burns, but she's recovered."

"Oh. Well, I haven't caught up on all the news."

"Of course not. You've had your own troubles, Adi. But you were telling me about Lonza. I'm guessing that he realized the value of the sports centre had suddenly gone up, once they started getting serious about rebuilding the area and all the investment that would be going in."

"Worked that out already, did you?" Adi nodded. "Yes, that was his plan. He'd been looking at what assets I had that he could make some money out of, and when he found out about the Delford Mills Project, his eyes must have lit up. It was money almost in the bank, and a good bit of it, even if he stuck to legitimate transactions. A lot more if he ran a few scams – which with Lonza is pretty much a given. All he needed was control of the property – and since he had me, that wasn't a problem. He just needed me to sign it over to him, and he was back in business."

"And you did that?" I leaned forward. "You gave it to him?"

"What – like I had a choice?" Adi was frowning. "It was that or an unmarked grave in the desert, Graham! Would you have done something different?"

I shook my head. "No. I suppose not. But this means that Lonza has a real legal claim to the property! He's not just playing smoke and mirrors here; he's got documentation that can stand up in court."

"It's not that cut and dried. Don't forget how he got my signature. I'm pretty sure that a document signed under duress is legally null and void."

"Yes, maybe. But only if you can prove it."

"Of course that might be difficult. But I don't think Lonza would let it come to that. Quite apart from the sports centre, there's a lot of his dealings that he wouldn't want brought out in court. Which is probably why he went to all the trouble of bringing in someone to double for me – to try and head that off."

"Why didn't he just make *you* do it? That would have saved him a lot of trouble. Oh – didn't you say something about Lonza thinking that you're dead?"

"Oh, good, I'm glad you were listening, Graham. Yes, there's a bit more to the story yet. Like he said, Casey had been keeping an eye on Lonza, and when he flew out to his ranch, he tracked him there."

"How do you follow a helicopter?" I wondered aloud.

"Friend of a friend in Los Angeles ARTCC," Casey said laconically. "That's Air Route Traffic Control Center," he explained.

"Lonza didn't stop long, once he'd got my signature. He flew off again and left me wondering what would happen once he got his money back. Perhaps he'd forgive and forget, but it didn't really seem his style. So I was truly relieved when Casey showed up. Slipped in past the guards one night like a ninja and into my room."

"Cool!" said Sam, with a nod in Casey's direction.

Casey shook his head dismissively. "They weren't very alert."

"To be fair, all they had done for weeks was guard an old guy with a limp," Adi conceded. "They certainly weren't any problem for Casey. His biggest issue was waking me up without me making a noise. He had to put a hand over my mouth, which nearly triggered a heart attack.

"But once he'd calmed me down, we had a little discussion about what to do next. My instinct was just to get out of there as fast as possible – maybe set fire to the place on the way, just to yank Lonza's chain a little. But, as Casey pointed out, if I just escaped then Lonza would be on the lookout for me – and he had a lot of people who would help him with that. Much better if he thought I was out of the picture altogether."

"There are advantages to being dead," Sam put in. "But how did you pull it off?"

"Casey had that all worked out. He helped me sneak past the guards – not difficult, there were only two of them awake and they were playing cards on the front porch. I climbed out of a back window – ground floor, of course – and set off walking due north."

"You knew which way north was?" I asked. Adi had never had much interest in what he termed "Girl Scout stuff".

"Of course not! Casey did. He pointed at a landmark – amazing how far you can see at night in the desert with clear skies, moon, stars, and so on – and sent me on my way.

Then he went off on another route. I needed to leave traces – footprints and so on – but it had to look as though I'd gone off on my own."

Adi sighed and shook his head. "Back in the day, I could have done it at a run. But since the leg went, I'd got lazy. Half an hour of slogging through sand and scrub and I was about done – but the ranch was still in full view, like I'd hardly moved at all. So I had to keep on going. Finally cleared a ridge and got out of sight of the house, but the other side was still more of the same. Then the sun started coming up, and things got really tough.

"After a while, I dumped my jacket. My old tweed one that Dandy Dan gave me. You remember, Graham?"

"Of course."

"I didn't want to, but a tweed jacket in the desert? It wasn't working. And besides, we had to leave them a few clues."

"They must have found it," I said. "Your lookalike was wearing it when…"

"Oh, so it's ruined now, then. Covered in someone else's blood, I suppose. Ah, heck with it. Time I got a new one anyway."

"How far did you go?" asked Sam.

"I don't know for sure. Another mile or so, perhaps? Then I was on rocky ground, where footprints wouldn't show, and Casey was there. With his help, I managed to get a bit further.

"Finally, when he'd decided we'd gone far enough, Casey let me rest for a bit. But not long, because they'd be out looking for me by then. So, while I was trying to catch my breath, he started ripping off my clothes."

Adi stopped and laughed at my expression. "Relax,

Graham! It wasn't like that... I'm surprised at you, thinking such thoughts, churchgoing man like yourself!"

"I take it that these were to be more clues as to your disappearance?"

"Exactly. So the clothes came off, and then he got out a knife and got some of my blood on them. Had to be mine, just in case Lonza decided to get a DNA test. We weren't sure how far he'd go.

"Then we left my bloodstained clothes and my stick scattered amongst the rocks. The blood would attract some scavengers – buzzards and coyotes – and when Lonza's men finally arrived they would probably conclude that I'd passed out and been finished off by the local wildlife."

"What about bones?" asked Sam.

"Carried off somewhere. We hoped that was what they'd assume. It wasn't likely they'd make a long search. Why would they? They didn't know I'd had help.

"We carried on a bit further – and in case you're entertaining thoughts of me romping through the desert in my birthday suit, Graham, Casey had got some spare clothes for me. He also had a jeep not too far off, and a few hours later I was drinking cold beer in an air-conditioned motel room."

He raised his bottle to the memory and drank deeply.

"It must have worked – at least, Lonza never came looking for me. It took a while, but Casey got me out of the country and back here. We knew that Lonza would still be after the sports centre, and we worked out a way to get him to back off. But the problem was how to approach him – while still being dead, that is. And that, Graham, is where you come in."

"Me?"

"Yes, of course you. You don't think I got you out here just to have a chat and a beer, do you? Oh no, mate. You're going to help me out here. After all, that's what friends are for, isn't it?"

CHAPTER 11

"Don't be predictable. If you do the same thing the same way every time, they'll be ready for you. The other team, that is. Keep them guessing, always do something different."

Adi Varney, magazine article on "Football Strategy and Tactics", co-authored by Graham Deeson

It was less of a surprise than it might have been. Somehow, I'd known that Adi was leading up to something. Because I knew Adi.

And because I knew Adi, I was cautious in my response.

"What exactly did you want me to do?"

Adi knew me as well. His lips curled in what might have been a smile. "You don't sound too eager. I thought you'd have jumped at the chance to give a hand."

It wasn't the first time I'd felt Adi was backing me into a corner. "If I can, certainly." I smiled back at him. "As long as it's not illegal, immoral, or fattening."

Adi's smile broadened and became more genuine. "That's your dad, Sam – always the same caveats!"

"I taught him that word!" I said to Sam, who grinned at us.

"It's a bit late to worry about the 'fattening', Dad!" he said, and Adi laughed out loud.

"He's got you there, Graham."

I harrumphed. "Youngsters nowadays – no respect."

"Just what they said about us, wasn't it?" Adi dismissed that with a wave of his stick. "Look, Graham, all I need you to do is to deliver some documents."

"What documents? And who to?"

"These documents." He reached down beside the sofa he was sitting on, and picked up a large padded envelope: A4 size and apparently stuffed full. "These are the details of some properties and assets I have. Things like this house, other properties. Some of them overseas. And investments I've made in companies. Stuff I've bought over the years, but kept quiet about. It actually amounts to quite a bit when you total it up. I'm not sure how much – property prices change and so does the value of companies – but we're easily talking about several hundred thousand quid's worth altogether."

"As much as that? How did you put that together?"

He shrugged. "A bit here, a bit there. I was surprised myself when I counted it up. Good thing I left it all in safe storage over here, or Lonza would have got his grubby mitts on it already. But as it is, he doesn't know anything about it. So you can use it as a bargaining chip."

"I can use it?" I gave him a long stare. "OK, I think I see where this is going. You want me to offer this to Lonza in return for him backing off on the sports centre takeover."

"Oh, good. Not all the brain cells are dead then! Yes, Graham. That's the plan. You can tell him that I sent this stuff to you a while ago. Say it was before the Real Madrid match, and that I wanted you to keep it safe in case anything went wrong. He'll believe that."

I shook my head. "Look, Adi, this stuff may be worth a few hundred thousand, but that sports centre land, properly developed, that could be millions! There's no way that Lonza's going to go for it. Or if he does, he'll just take these documents, say thanks very much, and keep them as a bonus."

"Oh, come on, Graham. Do you think I'd make it that easy for him? This isn't the whole package. Just a taster. Enough so that he knows it's genuine. And the thing is, this is straightforward, no strings attached, easy profit. Whereas now he's lost his fake Adi, his play to take over the sports centre is open to challenge."

"He has your signa…" I started to say, but Adi talked over me.

"Just tell him that you've persuaded Declan and the trustees to take it to court. Tell him I must have been under duress when I signed. Anything like that. All you need to do is to show him that getting that land isn't going to be as easy as he'd hoped. But if he backs off on it, he can have this lot" – Adi waved the envelope at me – "for free. Trust me, he'll go for that. I know him. He won't run the risk of having his dirty tricks exposed in court. He's already got a lot of troubles; he doesn't want more."

He held the envelope out to me. I took it with some reluctance. It felt solid and quite heavy.

"Obviously, I can't go myself," Adi continued. "If Lonza knows I'm not dead – well, he'll do his best to rectify that!"

"Right. I get that. But this is the same man you want me to try to do a deal with? No doubt with Handy Jack standing next to him."

171

"Heck, Graham, man up!" Adi pushed himself to his feet and waved his stick in my direction. "Lonza's not going to do anything to you! One unknown American actor disappearing isn't a problem, but do you think he wants the police chasing up your disappearance? Anything happens to you, he'd probably have to skip the country and abandon his plans for the sports centre anyway!"

I was standing myself by now. "Well, that's good to know! I'm sure it'll be a comforting last thought before Handy Jack starts shovelling earth over me!"

"You owe me, Graham!" He was almost shouting now. "You owe me this!"

"Why? Because I saved your life thirty and something years ago?"

He held my gaze for another moment, then shrugged and turned away. "Well, if you won't do it for me, do it for the sports centre. That's something you used to believe in. The best thing I'd ever done, you said once. Well, it's all I've got left of a legacy now. Heck, The Vale's going down the pan; anything I ever did there is just a memory. But the sports centre, that's still good for something, still helping kids out. And Declan, he's a good man. He'll do a lot more there given the chance. Do you really want a shark like Rocco Lonza to get his hands on it? Do you, Graham? Because this is your chance to stop him."

He'd sat down again while he talked, sat looking at the top of his stick as though he was looking for the brass dog's head. He didn't meet my eyes.

"Up to you, Graham."

I took a deep breath. "Adi... I don't want it to be like this between us. I..."

"Are you going to do it or not?"

I looked at the package, looked at Adi. Shut my eyes and sent up a brief but wordless prayer.

"Yes," I told him. "I'll do it."

He nodded. Just once, and still without looking at me.

"I'll take you back to your car, then," said Casey. "If we're all done here?"

Adi nodded. "Yes. We're done." Then he glanced over to me. "If this all works out, Graham, then we're all square. And you won't be seeing me again."

"Doesn't have to be like this, Adi. We..."

He banged his stick on the floor. "That's it, Graham. Do this one little thing – then it's goodbye. Clear?" He shifted his gaze to Sam. "And if you want to know why I left – ask your dad."

"This way, please, gentlemen," said Casey. He had slipped his hand casually into his pocket – not with any apparent intention of using the gun there, but just to remind us that he had it.

We took the hint, and left.

The trip back was as uncomfortable as before, but at least we didn't face the uncertainty of not knowing what would happen at the end of it. Nevertheless, I was once more feeling bruised and nauseous when Casey finally opened the doors and let us out again. We were parked in the same place we had left from, right next to my car.

He handed back our phones and the car keys. "I would suggest that you do not delay in contacting Mr Lonza," he said, in his menacingly polite military tone. "The sooner this matter is resolved the better."

He didn't wait for a reply, but got back into the van and drove off.

Sam took the little brass pyramid out of his pocket. "I thought this thing was going to punch a hole right through my leg when we took that sharp bend," he said, glaring at it.

"Well, why did you take it anyway? Just a bit of tat."

"Yes, I know, but I thought we might want to know where Adi's holed up. Especially since he went to so much trouble to hide that information."

I looked at him with raised eyebrows. "And how, pray tell, is a little brass knick-knack going to tell you that? Does it have some sort of esoteric properties that will guide you along the ley lines? Is divining one of the skills you picked up in your travels?"

He laughed. "Of course not, Dad. I did try divining once but couldn't get the hang of it. But I do know where Adi is." He turned the pyramid over and looked at the base. "Mill House, River Lane, Corsten."

"What? Show me that!"

He held it up so that I could see the small label that had been stuck on the bottom of the pyramid, with the address neatly handwritten in dark blue ink.

"The original owner was a Mrs Horton-James," he said, referring back to the label. "Very meticulous woman, it appears. I bet she labelled every item in the house."

"That other ornament you were fiddling with – the globe – that had one as well?"

"Yes, but at some time it had been put down on a damp patch, and the ink had run. Almost illegible. So I had to find another. The tricky bit was checking the base without Casey seeing. He was standing right behind us. But I managed to keep it out of his line of sight, and Uncle Adi was too busy telling his story."

"But how did you know?"

"I didn't. But I could see that all that stuff wasn't Uncle Adi's, even before he told us. I thought it was worth a closer look. I doubt if Adi had ever given it a second glance."

"No, he wouldn't," I agreed. "Good thinking!"

I gave my son a long look. For someone who had been kidnapped at gunpoint, he was remarkably calm and obviously more capable of clear thinking than I was. It would never have occurred to me to check the ornaments for clues. I wondered again just what he'd been up to in his wanderings. The young man who had come back to us was not the lad who had left, and that put a twist in my guts.

He met my gaze guilelessly. "What?"

"Oh, nothing," I dissembled. "But I know where Corsten is – just a few miles away. Ten minutes' drive, maybe fifteen at the most. We were rattling around in the back of that van for half an hour, each way!"

"Just normal practice, Dad. He didn't want us to know how close Adi was."

"Normal practice for who?" I asked.

"Anyone who ever read a spy novel," he said with a grin. "So, are you going to phone Lonza, then? I've got those numbers from Wayland's phone – we could try one of them, perhaps? Might be quicker than trying to go through his office."

"That's a good idea," I agreed. "But first of all, there's something much more important we need to do."

"Oh? Like what?"

"Go home and have a cup of tea," I told him, and got in the car.

*

For every occasion, there is the right tea. Or so I've always believed. Earl Grey, for example, I consider ideal for social occasions – unless of course we're eating Chinese, in which case it has to be a green tea. But what on earth should one drink before talking to a senior member of an organized crime gang?

It would have to be the Irish Breakfast Tea, I decided. I had a special blend from a local merchant which was darker and stronger than my normal English Breakfast Tea, but smooth as well, and – unlike Sharkey's Navy Special – it didn't leave your mouth feeling furry. I normally kept it for special occasions, and this definitely qualified.

I prepared a pot and left it to brew, keeping an eye on my watch.

"You'd better get started before Mum comes home," said Sam, watching the process.

"She's working late tonight," I told him. "Some event at the library." She had told me what it was, but it had slipped my mind. The day had been quite full-on. "Perhaps it's just as well. I think this whole situation is going to be easier to explain after the event."

Sam smiled. "Good luck with that, Dad. Is that tea ready yet?"

It took two cups before I was ready to face the next stage.

"Right. Let's have that number, then."

Sam had his laptop up, and swung it round so I could read the screen. "That top one," he pointed out. "That's the one that was never actually contacted, so I'm surmising that, if the other one belongs to Handy Jack, then this one is probably Lonza. Of course, they might have ditched the phones when Wayland was killed, in which case we'll have to try getting him through his office."

I took a deep breath and dialled.

The ringtone sounded. And again. And again...

After about six rings, I was expecting an answering service. After eight, I was beginning to think that no one was going to answer, and allowed myself a cautious amount of relief.

At ten rings, it was answered.

"Who is this?" An American accent, a surprisingly cultured voice with a rough edge to it.

"Mr Lonza?" I asked.

"Who is this?" he asked again.

"My name is Graham Deeson. I'm an old friend of Adi Varney. I have something of his that you might be interested in." It was all I could do not to gabble the words out. Now he had answered, I was afraid he'd hang up again before I could capture his interest.

"What something?" The rough edge, I thought, was suspicion, and it was getting stronger.

"Some papers... information about certain assets of his. Property, shares, that sort of thing. If you're Lonza, that is."

There was a longer pause, perhaps some muffled words in the background. I imagined Lonza holding his hand over the phone while he talked to someone. Probably Handy Jack.

"OK, I'm Lonza."

"Right. Good. Well, I understand that you worked with Adi over in the States."

"Who says so?" The suspicion was thick enough to curdle.

"He did. I got a letter from him, a little while ago. Along with these papers. He said he was setting up a football – soccer – team for someone called Rocco Lonza. But he was a bit worried about how things were going and so he wanted me to hold on to these things for him. He said that they were worth a lot – hundreds of thousands. And he was right – I've checked.

"But then it all went quiet. Didn't hear anything else from Adi. Instead, you turn up here, with someone made up to look like Adi, even wearing Adi's jacket. And at the same time someone starts to try to take over Adi's sports centre. Turns out that that someone is you."

"I get it now. You're that guy who's been following us around."

"Not following. Our paths have crossed, no fault of mine."

"No? And Jimmy Wayland falling off a roof? You saying you had nothing to do with that?"

"No! That was an accident. I was just trying to talk to him."

"Yeah, sure. Listen, Mr Deeson – you were seen. One of my guys was there and he can testify that you were up there with Jimmy and you pushed him over the edge."

"No! That is absolutely not true!" Somehow, Lonza had wrested the initiative away from me and gone on the offensive.

I felt a light touch on my hand. My mobile was on speaker and Sam was listening; now he reached over and tapped the mute button.

"He's just trying to rattle you, Dad. You know he can't go to the police with this story. Don't forget it was Jack that took the body!"

I nodded, and unmuted the phone.

"You still there, Deeson? Because…"

I interrupted him. "Enough games. Wayland fell, he wasn't

pushed. Your man got rid of the body, because obviously you couldn't cope with the publicity a dead Adi Varney would generate, especially not a *fake* dead Adi Varney. You were going to use him to pressure the sports centre trustees to give up without a fight and hand over the property, which could be worth millions once the Delford Mills Project gets under way.

"The fact that you had a fake Adi with a genuine Adi jacket – believe me, I know it well – means that something bad has happened to the real Adi. So now I've got all his assets, and you've got a fight on your hands – because I've talked to the trustees, and they're not giving in without one. Especially as we've now got the resources to do it properly – take you to court, here and in the States if necessary – you personally, Mr Lonza, as well as your company. We'll press for your prosecution for the kidnap and murder of Adi Varney, and I'll give evidence about the fake Adi. We'll block every attempt you make to take control of the sports centre, and whatever signatures you might have from him we'll contest. We'll allege that they were obtained under duress. We'll dig into your past history, Mr Lonza, and expose it – in the courts, in the papers, on TV – and Adi's money will fund it all!"

I looked over at Sam as I finished my little tirade, and he gave me a big grin and a thumbs up.

"Or," I added into the silence from the other end of the line, "we can make a deal."

The silence was shorter than I expected. "Let me take a guess at this. I back off from the sports centre takeover, you hand over Varney's assets – right?"

He was quick on the uptake, but I suppose that would be necessary in his business. "In a nutshell," I confirmed. "Or, to put it another way, several hundred thousand – sterling, that is – upfront, no strings attached. Or see you in court, and all over the news as well."

"You should be careful who you threaten, Deeson. You think I'm some lightweight who'll just fold with a bit of tough talk? There's a lot of guys who've thought they could take me down – in a court or out of it! Only, they tend to change their minds after a while."

I'd been threatened before, of course. Occupational hazard – some people just don't like the press, especially when we tell uncomfortable truths about them. Lonza was much more polite than most of them – and much more convincing. What he implied was more frightening than anything he might have said.

But I couldn't back down now.

"I'm not talking threats, Mr Lonza. I'm not looking to start a war. I'm just offering a deal, that's all. Something you want for something I want. And you get a bonus: no bad publicity, no court challenge, and – here's an extra – if anyone should happen to be investigating Adi's disappearance, I won't give them the other information he sent me. The stuff about what was really going on with California Strike Superstars; about what he was afraid would happen to him. And your part in it."

"That's a lie. CSS was a legitimate business venture as far as I was concerned, and I lost a lot of money on it. Whatever Varney told you – and I'm not convinced he told you anything – I had nothing to do with it, and nothing to do with him disappearing."

"Then you'll have no problem with me going public with all this."

After years of interviewing people, I was sensitive to the subtle nuances of silence. There are silences that give nothing away, and there are silences that speak volumes. Lonza's silence was that of a man reluctantly accepting he couldn't take the risk.

"OK, I'll take a look at these documents." He spoke as though he was doing us a favour, but that was just to save face. We both knew he'd been outmanoeuvred. "If they're what you say, maybe we can do a deal."

"Thank you, Mr Lonza," I said humbly. It was in my best interest to help him save face, I decided.

"Merstan House. It's in some place called Priory Green. You know it?"

"Certainly."

"On the main street, at the end of the village. You go past a bar called the Priest Hole and it's about five houses along on the left."

"No problem. I'll find it."

"An hour from now. Be alone and don't even think about doing anything stupid like wearing a wire."

"A wire? Oh, right. No recording or anything like that. Fine by me."

"OK." He hung up abruptly.

I sat back and looked at my hands, which were shaking. I suppose that was a reasonable reaction to negotiating with Mafia bosses.

"You all right, Dad?"

"Yes. Just thinking that I've used up more adrenaline in the last few days than in the past five years."

He grinned. "You should get out more."

"I'm not saying it's a good thing."

"Don't knock it, Dad. Good cardio exercise, gets the blood pumping. And you did OK. We've got what we wanted."

"What Adi wanted. Thanks, anyway." I glanced at my watch. "Plenty of time to get there. I'll put the kettle on again. Hey, do you want to know something funny?"

He gave me a suspicious look. "Are you going to tell a dad joke?"

"No. And what's wrong with dad jokes anyway? Never mind. It's just this address Lonza gave us. Priory Green is just a few miles from Corsten. Adi and Lonza are practically neighbours!"

*

Merstan House was an elegant, three-storey Georgian building, set back only a short way from the road but screened off behind high railings and thick shrubbery. Through the gates we could see a gravelled parking space and a glossy white front door.

I looked across at Sam, who was driving. "You really shouldn't be here. Lonza did say 'come alone'." I was very glad he was with me, and simultaneously worried that I was risking him as well as myself.

"We've had this discussion, Dad. No way was I going to let you come here on your own."

"Did I ever tell you how much you're like your mum?"

"Yes. I have her hair."

"That wasn't what I meant. As you know full well. And did you really need to bring that?" I nodded at the back seat.

Sam glanced over at the cricket bat he'd taken out of my office. "I find it reassuring."

"Yes, well, just bear in mind that that's a serious collector's item. It's signed by every member of the last English team to win the Ashes. So don't damage it!"

Sam gave me one of his trademark grins. "I'd have preferred a baseball bat, but you haven't got one. Don't worry, it's only there to make me feel more secure." He indicated the gate. "Shall we do this?"

We'd parked on the opposite side of the street to take a look. Sam put the car in gear, and pulled over to face the gates – which immediately swung open.

"We're expected!" he said. "How polite."

There were no cars in front of the house, but the gravelled area continued round the back, presumably leading to the garages. Sam, however, parked near the front door, manoeuvring carefully to face the gate. By the time he'd finished, the front door was open and a man was walking towards us.

I'd expected Handy Jack, but this was someone new to me. A short, compact figure in a nondescript grey suit, his most noticeable feature was badly pockmarked skin. I opened the door and got out as he approached.

"Deeson." A deep, gravelly voice. "You were told to come alone."

"My father has a heart condition." Sam stood up and leaned on the inside of the open door. "I drive him."

"You stay in the car." The tone of voice left no room for negotiation. "This way, Deeson."

Sam shrugged, and got back behind the wheel. "I'll be waiting here, then."

"It shouldn't take long," I told him. I leaned back into the car to pick up Adi's package from the dashboard, and followed my guide in through the front door.

The hallway was nicely decorated and furnished in keeping with the exterior, but I had no time to stop and admire. It led to a wide flight of stairs, with a landing halfway up that gave you a choice of directions, left or right, both leading to a wide mezzanine with doorways off it in all directions. We went right, along a corridor, and through a door. *First floor, rear,* I thought to myself.

The room had the same feel as the hallway, all very period, apart from the large modern desk with two computer monitors on it. Lonza was sitting behind it, fingers on a keyboard and eyes on the screens.

He barely glanced up when I came in, so I stood in the middle of the room and looked around. The tall windows behind him had their curtains pulled back, allowing in a lot of late afternoon sunshine and leaving Lonza partially silhouetted from my point of view.

The pockmarked man stood on my right, but level with the desk. Handy Jack, complete with leather jacket, stepped out of the shadows by a window and stood next to Lonza. He barely spared me a glance, and appeared to be staring at whatever Lonza had up on the computer.

This, of course, was pure showmanship, as was the sunlight in my eyes. All standard tactics to make me feel on edge and intimidated.

However, the same sunlight would have been reflecting off the monitors and making them difficult to read. If Lonza had really been interested in what was on them, he would have drawn the curtains.

I wondered how long he planned to play this game. I could have just tossed the package onto the desk, but there was no point in upsetting him unnecessarily. I could let him have his fun.

So I waited, and Lonza pretended to be too busy for me for about five minutes, before he finally glanced up at me again, then looked at his watch to let me know how little time he had to spare for me.

"So. Deeson." He leaned forward over the desk, and fixed me with a stare. "Well, you've got some nerve, I'll say that for you. I didn't think you'd actually show."

I held up the package. "This is what you asked for." I didn't want to engage in conversation.

"It had better be. If you're messing me around, Deeson..." He left that hanging, I suppose to let my imagination fill in the unpleasant details.

Jack came round the desk, and approached me, hand outstretched for the package but eyes very firmly on me, and a face like granite.

"I saw you up there with Jimmy Wayland," he said softly. "I'm holding you responsible for what happened to him. Jimmy was a friend of mine."

Another attempt to intimidate. I was starting to lose patience. And also I didn't want them to think I was a complete pushover.

"Jimmy Wayland was a bottom-of-the-rung actor who looked a bit like Adi Varney." I used the same tone as he had. "So you hired him to give your scam a bit of credibility. He fell off that roof because he was too scared of you to talk to me. And by the way, where did you put your friend, Jack? In a hole in the back garden?"

Jack's eyes narrowed and I wondered if I'd pushed him too far. But then Pockface gave a little cough. "Perhaps Mr Lonza should take a look at that package?"

I wondered who he was. Not just another bit of muscle – his suggestion had sounded almost like an order.

Jack looked at Pockface and nodded. He snatched the envelope out of my hand, then turned away and dumped it on the desk in front of Lonza. Who picked it up in one hand, and had a knife in the other. Not a paper knife. Something with a thick ugly-looking blade, serrated down one edge.

He pointed it at me, and laughed. "You know, I see a lot of guys like you, Deeson. Little guys, who think they've got what it takes for the big time. Your pal Adi, he was another one like that."

This, I decided, was more than just another attempt to intimidate me. This sounded more like Lonza building himself up.

"Well, you know what? Punks like you and Varney, they come and go. And me, I hardly notice them. Few weeks' time, I'll be back in the States, doing serious deals with real players, and this – this was just a vacation, just a little time out, and I'll be struggling to remember your name or your face."

He paused, but I couldn't think of anything worth saying, so after a moment he carried on.

"You think you're pulling off some big deal here? Saving your precious sports centre, your Adi Varney memorial thing? Well, whatever you think you've got here, it's barely worth my time. Might cover my travel expenses, that's all. And Varney was just another little man with big ideas. He got what was coming to him and, sports centre or not, he's not even history now. Not worth remembering." He jabbed the knife in my direction again. "And neither are you, Deeson. Neither are you."

I shrugged. "Look, Lonza, I don't care about being remembered. Certainly not by you. And as for Adi, he'll be better remembered and better thought about in this town than you will be anywhere."

CHAPTER 11

Lonza's lips curled back in a snarl. "You little –"

Then Pockface coughed again, and Lonza shot a look in his direction. His expression didn't change – if anything he looked even angrier – but he turned his attention to the envelope.

"OK, then," he said. "Let's just see what you've got. If it's anything."

It occurred to me, too late, that I had no idea what I'd got. I'd taken Adi's word for it. Perhaps I should have checked it before I got myself into a confrontation with a Mafia boss and his two henchmen.

Lonza slipped the knife under the flap. It was very sharp. The thick paper fell apart easily under the blade. And then there was a brilliant light, and a blast of heat and pressure that flung me backwards, and a noise so loud that I could barely hear it.

CHAPTER 12

"Don't think about it. Thinking is
overrated. Just do it."

**Adi Varney, speech at a local school
sports day**

I was on the floor. I didn't know how I'd got there. I couldn't
remember falling over. Something had hit my head, I
thought. My ears were still ringing, there was an acrid smell,
and the room looked hazy. I wondered if I was losing my
eyesight. Perhaps I was finally having that big heart attack.

*But the stents were supposed to have stopped that happening,
weren't they?* I got to my feet. I was shaking. *Perhaps I should
lie down again?*

There was no sign of Lonza. His desk had been cleared
– the monitors were lying on the floor in front of it, glass
smashed, but he'd disappeared. Behind the desk, the curtains
were flapping in a gentle breeze that was blowing in where the
windowpanes had been, dispersing the haziness like smoke.
Which, of course, it was, I realized.

Handy Jack was on the floor at the side of the desk. He wasn't
moving, and the side of his face that I could see was bloody.

On the other side of the room, Pockface had got to his
knees. He was looking at me, and fumbling under his jacket

with one hand. The muddled thought came to me that he was looking for a wallet. I couldn't understand why.

"What…" I tried to say, but I still couldn't hear very well, so I wasn't sure if anything was coming out. All I could hear was a sort of shrieking noise, like very bad tinnitus. Some sort of alarm, I realized. "What?" I said louder.

Behind me, the door burst open. I turned to look and saw a man standing there. He had a gun – it looked like a sub-machine gun or an assault rifle. He was looking round the room with an expression of shock, the gun muzzle following his gaze. Until both gaze and muzzle settled on me, and he stepped forward, his expression hardening.

"I don't know what happened," I started to say. Tried to say.

Then a cricket bat swung up behind him and connected neatly with his skull just above his right ear. Even partially deafened, I could hear the solid "thunk!" it made. The gunman collapsed sideways, and Sam was standing behind him, following through with the swing as if he'd just put one over the slips and away for six.

"Dad!" I heard him calling faintly. "This way!"

I staggered towards him. "We need to get help!" I still wasn't sure if I was actually saying anything.

I probably was, because he answered. "No, we're getting out!" he shouted in my ear. Then he looked past me. "Down!"

He jumped forward, pushing me aside, and hurled the bat across the room. Following its trajectory, I saw it slam into Pockface. He'd managed to get to his feet, and had found what he'd been looking for under his jacket. Not a wallet, a pistol. The bat impacted his hand, knocking the gun out of it and sending him staggering back against the wall.

"Run!" Sam shouted, grabbing me by the shoulder and half dragging me out of the door.

I did my best to run. Difficult, because my legs didn't seem to be working properly, but with Sam's help I staggered along the corridor and, clinging to the banister, half slid down the stairs.

There was a man lying on the floor, halfway through a side doorway. There was a pistol lying next to him.

"Did you…" I began.

"Not now, Dad!" Sam pushed me towards the front door. "Open it and get to the car. I'm right behind you." He scooped up the gun in passing and, as I tottered towards the exit, ran past me and into a room on the left. Inside it I could see a bank of CCTV monitors. I recognized the drive and our car.

"Where are you going?" I shouted.

"Opening the gate!" I'd lost sight of him – he was behind the door. Ignoring his instructions I started to follow, but then he burst back out. "Got it. Come on!" On one of the screens I could see the outside gates starting to open, and behind me, on the stairs, there was a loud bang, and chips flew out of the tiled floor near my feet.

Pockface was on the landing, gun in hand, and aiming it at me. Sam stepped between us, pointing his pistol and shooting a rapid volley. Pockface ducked or fell behind the banister, and Sam dragged me to the front door.

"Get it open!" he shouted, holding his aim on the stairs.

I fumbled with the lock. Just a standard Yale, fortunately, and the door opened easily as soon as I turned the knob. I ran out.

The car was still where we'd left it. Sam, after backing out of the door with his gun still pointing inside, turned and ran past me, opening the doors, sliding in and starting the engine, all apparently in one movement. I followed, less gracefully but almost as quickly, and we were moving before I could get the door shut. Sam accelerated in a spray of gravel, not bothering to check the road before he shot through the gates, turning and flooring the pedal as he did.

We hurtled down the road leaving rubber smoking on the road. A van coming the other way blared its horn. I saw the driver's mouth open as he shouted at us. Probably something rude but I didn't hear, didn't much care, and in any case Sam had us on the right side of the road – just – by the time we passed it. Then we were racing clear of the village and out into open country.

He slowed down a bit after a mile or two, and gave me a look. To my surprise he was smiling.

"More fun than the average day, eh Dad?"

"Fun…" I shook my head. "Fun used to be a day at the park with a ride on the miniature railway! What – what happened?"

"You tell me. You were inside." He gave me a concerned glance. "Are you OK? Only you've got blood on your face."

I put a hand to my forehead, which felt sticky. When I pulled my hands away, my fingers were red. "Oh. I think that might have happened when the letter exploded." I was noticing the pain now as well. "I don't think it's deep." I pulled a packet of wet wipes out of the glovebox. I kept them for wiping marks off the dashboard, but they worked pretty well on my face.

"But the bullet missed you, didn't it?"

"What bullet?" I remembered chips flying out of the floor tiles. "Wait a minute – he was shooting at me!"

"Yes. Well, us. Good thing I picked that gun up. I don't think he was expecting me to shoot back."

"You shot him?"

"No, I just shot at him. I'm fairly sure I missed."

"Sam – where did you learn to do that?"

"Shoot a gun? Anyone can shoot a gun, Dad. You just point it and pull the trigger."

"Yes, but you looked like you'd done it before."

"Oh, somebody I met somewhere gave me a few lessons… but you still haven't told me what happened."

I rubbed my head, trying to think. "Well, I'm not sure. I met Lonza… and the other bloke, Handy Jack, was there as well. And the one who was shooting at us. We were talking, then Lonza opened the envelope and – I suppose there was an explosion or something."

"There was definitely an explosion," Sam confirmed. "I heard it outside in the car. Sounds like it must have been a letter bomb."

"A letter bomb? You mean – in that envelope Adi gave me?"

He looked across at me. "Yes. Of course – what did you think?"

"I don't know. A gas leak, perhaps."

"That was no gas leak, Dad. A detonation like that, from a package that size – we're talking military-grade high explosive. No amateur weedkiller and sugar sort of device – that was some sort of plastic, I'd guess. C4 or similar."

I shook my head. "Are you saying that Adi gave me a – a bomb?"

"That's right."

"But – but this is Adi, Sam. I mean – what does Adi know about bombs?"

"Not much, perhaps, but I think Casey probably knows quite a lot. And he managed to bring a gun into the country, or got it when he was over here, neither of which is as easy as people imagine – so I suppose he'd have known how to get the makings for a little bomb."

He slowed down and pulled over into a lay-by. It was one of those that had a small kiosk parked up more or less permanently. A faded sign announced that this was "Mama's Snack Bar".

"Cup of tea, Dad?" Sam asked. "I'm told that it's ideal for all situations."

I nodded. "I taught you well. At least about tea."

My only son was showing a lot of knowledge about all sorts of things that I had definitely not taught him. But that was a discussion for another time. While he went over to Mama's Snack Bar, I sat back, closed my eyes, and tried to get my brain working.

Ten minutes later we were sipping at a weak grey liquid in plastic cups. I missed Sharkey's Naval Brew, but it was a beggars and choosers situation. And the water might perhaps have caught sight of a teabag at some point in the past, so better than nothing. It may even have helped – my head was starting to clear.

"How did you manage to get in?" I asked after a few minutes of silent imbibing. "The front door was locked."

"Yes. But the windows were no match for a cricket bat. And after I heard that explosion, I wasn't going to hang around outside, was I?"

"So you smashed your way in – and him on the hallway floor presumably tried to stop you?"

"He must have been in the security office opposite. I'm assuming there were two of them. One went upstairs to find out what had happened, the other either saw me on CCTV or heard the glass going in. Anyhow, he was coming into the room through the door just as I was coming in through the window. What was left of it."

"Sam, he had a gun!"

"Ah, but I had a cricket bat! Also the advantage of surprise, in that he wasn't expecting me to throw it at him. He caught it very nicely on the forehead. I was in a hurry, though, because I didn't know what had happened to you, so I didn't stop to collect his gun, which I should have. But I just grabbed my bat…"

"My bat."

"I recovered the bat, and came up the stairs. There was still some smoke drifting out into the corridor, so I knew which way to go, and I turned up just in time."

"Yes. Full marks for timing. I think – that one in the doorway, he was going to shoot me."

"I think he was, Dad. Well, I changed his mind for him."

"Hmm. You did that. I just hope you didn't kill him, that's all."

"No, I used the flat, not the edge. He should be OK. Well, apart from a bit of concussion." He looked directly at me. "And I wasn't going to let him hurt my old man, was I?"

I met his gaze. "I do appreciate it. I just hope that I haven't got you into trouble." I thought about what I'd just said, and laughed bitterly. "Trouble! Bombs, gunfights, breaking and entering – we're already up to our necks in it. We've got to go to the police now, Sam. Before they come to us."

"Ah. That reminds me. I need to send a message." Sam dug into his pocket and brought out a mobile. Not his normal one. This looked like a pretty basic model. He took the back off and slipped a battery into it.

"Sam – what phone is that?"

"It's my burner, Dad." He gave me a grin. "All the rage now, you know. I thought, if Lonza's got one, I'll have one as well." He started tapping on the keypad.

"Why do you need a burner, Sam?"

"You remember that conversation we had? Where you agreed we should let someone know about Lonza?"

"Did I?"

"Yes. So I did. I got a number from a contact of mine…"

"Just a minute – what number? What contact?"

"Just someone I ran into while I was travelling."

I held his gaze.

"Do you really want to know, Dad?"

I nodded. "Yes, Sam, I really want to know. Because when my son left home he was a bright, cheerful, slightly cocky but basically pretty normal sort of lad. And when he comes back he looks much the same, but he knows far too much about guns and explosives, and has contact numbers for mysterious people that normal people don't even know exist. So yes, I want to know about these people you ran into while you were travelling."

He shrugged. "OK, then. Short version. While I was in Africa, I got recruited to drive a truck. Just a simple job: pick it up, drop it off, don't ask any questions. Obviously a bit dodgy, but I was too naive to worry about it and too short of money to care. Except that I found out I was transporting a load of poached ivory. I wasn't keen on that sort of work, so I turned the whole lot over to the police.

"They passed it on to a specialist unit who dealt with that sort of thing. And then it got passed back to me, and they told me to carry on as before – though this time, of course, they were tracking the ivory.

"I ended up working for them for nearly a year, tracking the smuggling routes all the way to China. And along the way, I learned a few skills.

"My contact was a senior officer in that unit. He was the one who recruited me. Somebody who's been around a bit, and he knows other people who do similar things in other countries. So he was able to put me in touch with someone over here who likes to keep track of people like Lonza. I used a burner, though, because I didn't necessarily want to get too involved. But it seems like we've moved beyond that stage."

He finished the text, hesitated, then put the burner back in his pocket with the battery still in place.

"When she hears this," I said slowly, "your mum…"

"… is going to freak," he finished for me. Not the words I would have used, but accurate enough. "Why do you think I wasn't talking about it? She was bad enough when she thought I was just wandering around."

"Humm. Well, I'll find a way to mention it. When the time's right. But – getting back to here and now – what did you tell this friend of a friend?"

"Just the bare bones of it. Lonza's location, bomb, shots fired. Enough to point them in the right direction."

"Did you mention the cricket bat?"

"Didn't seem important."

"Only, you left it behind."

Sam gave me an irritated look. "Yes, well, sorry and all, but I was busy at the time. Do you want to go back for it?"

"No. But I did mention that it's a collector's item?"

"I know, OK? I didn't think you cared that much about collecting memorabilia, anyway."

"You're missing the point. The thing is, Sam, there are not that many like it around – and there's a few people who know I've got it."

"Ah. So it can be traced back to you, you mean? Right. I admit that hadn't occurred to me. But it doesn't change anything. Not at the moment, anyway. We still can't go and get it."

"True."

"So where do we go? Back home?"

I thought about it. The idea was attractive: I was ready for a proper cup of tea and a nap, and Sandy would be home eventually. And how would that conversation go? "How was your day, dear? Sam and I have had an interesting time. Met Adi, would you believe? He gave me a bomb... Oh, and I found out something interesting about Sam as well."

I wasn't ready for that. Not until I could at least answer all the questions.

"No," I decided. "Not home. Corsten."

Sam turned and stared at me. "Corsten? To see Adi? Do you really think that's a good idea, Dad? Bearing in mind that he just tried to blow you up."

"The bomb was meant for Lonza, not me. I think."

"So you were just collateral? Does that make it OK? What sort of mate sends his oldest friend off with a bomb anyway?"

I met his gaze. "I don't know. That's why I need to go and talk to him."

Sam turned away, stared out of the windscreen for a moment.

"If it was your friend, would you just leave it at that?" I asked. "Or would you want to... discuss it?"

After a moment, Sam nodded. "Fair enough. Let's do that." He started up and pulled out of the lay-by.

From where we were, the direct route to Corsten led through some narrow lanes and typical English countryside. Gently rolling hills, woods and copses, green fields studded with cattle, old grey churches, and picturesque little cottages. Nothing dramatic, but in the late afternoon sunshine, nothing could be more peaceful and calming.

The contrast with the rest of the day was so intense that it seemed unreal. Those things couldn't possibly have happened.

We found ourselves stuck behind a tractor belching black diesel fumes, which added some balance to the perfect scenery. Slowed to a crawl, Sam took the opportunity to resume conversation.

"Dad, I've been meaning to ask – what did Adi mean? The last thing he said to me, to ask you why he left?"

"Oh. That."

"Thing is, Dad, I thought you must know more about that than you're saying. Every time the subject comes up, you go quiet."

"Do I? Well, yes. I do. Thing is I… I suppose I feel guilty about it. Sort of."

"It's a good day for revealing secrets."

"Right." And actually, that wasn't a bad idea. I needed to tell someone. I'd been holding on to it for too long.

I closed my eyes, shut out the summer afternoon, and thought back to a slightly dingy bar several years ago.

"Adi and I used to meet up every Thursday night at the Empress, an old pub near the Castle. A run-down place, but it was convenient. We'd have a couple of drinks and talk things over. Football things, that is. How last Saturday's game went, how the next one might go, who was playing well, who wasn't performing. That sort of stuff. Adi used me as a sort of sounding board, to bounce ideas and opinions off – especially the ones he couldn't talk to anyone else about. I soaked it up, and made a note of things I could use when I was writing up the next game.

"We'd had that routine going for years. But this particular time, Adi turned up a bit late and very morose. The Vale had had a bad run recently – in the last five games they'd drawn four and lost one. Which wasn't a complete disaster, but for Adi, going that long without a win was close to it.

"Turned out it was more than that, though. 'Did you hear?' he said as soon as he saw me. No preliminaries like 'Hello, Graham'.

"'Did I hear what?'

"'Desmond Farcourt has been named European Manager of the Year!'

"'Ah, that,' I said. Of course I'd heard about it. It was my job to hear about things like that. But I was hoping that Adi hadn't."

"Desmond Farcourt? I've heard that name," Sam put in. The tractor turned into a farmyard, but the narrow lanes didn't allow for much acceleration. Sam moved up a gear, but had to drop down again as we came to a steep climbing turn.

"You should have done. One of the big names in European football, and a contemporary of Adi's. They both got their first England caps in the same year – same game, in fact – but apart from that they were chalk and cheese. Different social backgrounds, different approaches to the game, different all round. Adi couldn't stand him. Said he was a rich kid who was all about publicity and nothing about skill. Des Farcourt called Adi a kick-and-rush leg-hacker who'd never really got out of the slums."

"Ouch."

"Yes, and it went downhill from there. Got to the point where they couldn't play on the same team together, so they were both dropped from the England squad at one point. Which didn't exactly pour oil on the water, as you can imagine."

"But Adi got back in, didn't he?"

"Eventually. Des was a bit older than him, and retired early – at the top of his game, mind, but Adi called him a quitter. However, that gave Adi the chance to get back in the England squad, which he did just in time for that friendly with Sweden and the end of his playing career.

"They both moved into management. Adi at The Vale, of course. Des went into Europe, though – he'd always had good contacts there, had played a season on loan to one of the big clubs. He started in Italy, did well, moved to France, and did even better. So, eventually, European Manager of the Year."

The road levelled out on top of a ridge, with sunlit fields falling away to either side, a chequerboard of deep green with patches of brilliant yellow oilseed rape. Sam accelerated.

"I can see how that would have upset Adi."

"More than just upset. I didn't realize it at first, but he was angry – deep-down furious. I found out later that he'd already had a few to drink, up in the club bar with Johnnie Muldoon. He could hold his booze pretty well, it took a lot to make him really drunk, but alcohol chipped away at his inhibitions.

"It wasn't unusual for him to have a moan about how well someone else was doing. I could usually cheer him up by reminding him of all he'd done, so that was the tactic I followed this time.

"'European Manager of the Year?' I said. 'What's that, Adi, compared with what you've done here? You've built The

Vale up from nothing – your playing, your managing – and everyone knows it. There's not a club in the world that owes more to one man, and not a town in the world that knows who its hero is like this town does. Heck, the whole country knows it. There isn't a team in the UK that doesn't wish they had an Adi Varney! European Manager of the Year – that's nothing. You, you're a legend, Adi!'

"But it wasn't working. Adi was just staring into his glass. Glaring, actually, and I wasn't sure that he'd even heard me. Then he started swearing. Of course, Adi always did have a fine command of the vernacular, but he usually kept it under control, especially in public. And with me. But this time, he just let it all out.

"In amongst the bad language, what he was saying was that The Vale was a nothing little team, the town was a dead-end nowhere place, and nothing he'd ever done here meant anything at all.

"I tried to calm him down. Fortunately, the place was pretty quiet, and there was nobody too close, but all the same, people were looking. And if it got out that Adi Varney had bad-mouthed his own team and his town – well, that would make a few headlines that I wouldn't like to read. But he didn't care. He just went on about what he could have done and who he could have been if he hadn't been 'shackled' – his word – to this place and this team. Only he put it more colourfully: the town was the bottom of the sewer and the team was what floated in it. More or less."

"Ouch! That was a bit strong," said Sam.

"You should have heard the original. But he hadn't finished. He'd told me more than once about all the offers he'd had from other teams, both as a player and a manager.

Heck, he told everyone. He was quite proud about how many people had wanted him – and that he'd turned them all down to stay with The Vale. In the early days, he'd even had to fight his own manager, who thought that the transfer fee would have been worth more than Adi himself. But he was always ready to tell anyone who'd listen that he was a local lad, through and through.

"Well, now he was putting a different slant on it. He was telling me that if he'd taken up some of those offers, it was him who would be European Manager of the Year, and it would have been him who did this and that… Anything he'd achieved with The Vale, he would have done ten times more and ten times better if he'd left.

"I was starting to get annoyed with his ranting. But all the same, I should have thought a bit more before I answered him.

"'Well, why didn't you go, then?' I asked. 'There was nothing stopping you!'

"People had said that to him in the past, and that's when he'd stop and smile and come out with his line about being a local boy. But not this time. Instead he turned and glared at me.

"'You know why I didn't go!' he said (with expletives). 'How could I, after Davy?'

"And I just looked at him for a moment. I was stunned. 'Davy?' I asked him. 'What's Davy got to do with it?'

"'Davy's got everything to do with it!' he told me. 'You left him and saved me! So how could I leave? With you always telling everybody that The Vale needed me, that the town needed me? *You* needed me. You built your little career on me. Adi Varney, the local boy, your best pal – that's what made you, Graham. I made you! I reckon you knew just what you were doing when you grabbed me and let your brother go! Well, it worked out all right, didn't it? You got what you wanted, you got your sports page and your headlines. You saved me and I've paid and paid ever since. I'm still paying for it; still paying what I owe you for your brother!'

"He'd said often enough before that I'd built my career on his – but always as a joke. I thought it was a joke. But in any case, there was a lot of truth in it and I'd never denied that. Knowing Adi, having the inside track on the local golden boy, had certainly been a big help. But I'd never known before that he resented it. And I'd never heard this stuff about Davy."

Sam shook his head. "So – Adi had it in his head that you'd deliberately chosen to save him and let your brother go?" He braked as we came off the ridge and began descending through woods on the other side.

"Yes. That's exactly what he thought. That's what he'd been thinking for the past thirty-something years. That's why he'd stayed with The Vale – not because he was committed to his roots, but because he felt he owed me for my brother, and because I wanted him to stay.

"But I only worked that out afterwards. At the time, I just didn't get it. It was too much to take on board all at once. I just sat there gaping at him, until I finally found my voice. And then I said the stupidest thing I've ever said.

"'That's not how it was, Adi,' I told him. 'I didn't know who it was I grabbed. I didn't know it was you and not Davy until afterwards.'

"It took a while for that to sink in. I could see the look in his eyes change.

"'You're telling me that it was an accident? That you would have saved Davy if you could have? That you would have saved him and let me go?'

"'No, not like that,' I told him. 'I didn't have chance to decide. I just caught hold of someone.'

"Adi wasn't shouting any more. He was whispering if anything, and he'd even stopped swearing.

"'And you never told me? All these years, you let me think you chose me over your brother?'

"I tried to tell him I hadn't known that he thought that, that; I'd never deliberately deceived him. But it was too late. He wasn't listening any more. Instead he just got up and started for the door. I went after him. Followed him outside.

"'Adi, wait. Let me explain!' I said, but he ignored me. So I grabbed him by the shoulder, and he turned round and laid into me with his stick."

"That brass-handled one?"

"The very same. Hit me right above the eye with the first blow, and I didn't remember much about things after that. But he must have gone on hitting me, because when I came round in hospital I had multiple bruises all over."

I shook my head, thinking about it. Thinking about waking up and realizing what Adi had done to me. Trying to understand why.

"I always knew that Adi had a temper. He'd never let it go at me before. Verbally, perhaps, but never like that. But what I told him – I think I kicked away the foundations of his life. I suppose that must have hurt. I suppose that would spark anyone's temper…

"The police wanted to know who'd done it. I told them that I hadn't seen them properly. And I told your mum the same thing. Which I'm not proud about. But I just couldn't bring myself to tell anyone. Not what Adi had done, not what he had said… I just couldn't do it, Sam."

We drove on in silence for a few minutes. The road was still descending, coming down from the ridge through thick woodland. It was very dark in the shadows after the bright sunlight.

"So what did you do, Dad?" Sam asked.

"I sent him messages. I thought that if I could just talk to him when he was a bit calmer, we could get it all sorted out. But he didn't answer.

"I hoped to catch up with him at the next Vale game, but I was still in hospital. That knock on the head had them worried. I was having trouble with my eyesight for a while. So I sent him more messages. Left some with other people as well, saying I was sorry I'd have to miss it but I hoped it went well and that we could talk again afterwards. I hoped that if it went well, he'd cool down, get in touch, and we could put things right.

"It did go well, in fact – 2–1 against the league leaders. I watched it on TV, in the hospital. And I watched Adi announce that he was leaving, and I watched that interview in the car park afterwards.

"I couldn't believe it. I sat with my phone in my hand, just staring at it. For hours. Expecting him to call. Expecting him to visit. When Sandy came to see me, she took the phone off me, but I was still waiting for him. For days.

"I never saw him again. Not until today, that is."

We were coming into a village now. Corsten. Not quite the sleepy little village that I'd imagined. Someone had built a big housing estate round the original centre: streets of identical semis that managed to look both modern and shabby at the same time.

There was a shopping area as well, with a supermarket, a charity shop, and a full range of fast-food and takeaway places.

The old village was tucked away behind all this, a leftover from the past. Village green, village pub, parish church, all looking a bit out of place and bewildered by the new neighbours. A side road off the green took us past a row of cottages, beyond the end of which was a detached building in an overgrown garden. Two storeys, old and looking a bit shabby, verging on dilapidated at the edges. A barely legible wooden sign by the broken gate read Mill House.

It had probably been a long time since an actual mill had stood here, but when Sam turned off the engine we could hear the river gushing and splashing somewhere in the background. A side road – well, more of a track – went down past the house, presumably leading to the yard where Casey had taken us before.

My phone rang as we sat looking at the house. I pulled it out, wondering if it was Sandra, wondering what I would say if it was. I had no idea how to even begin to tell her about my day.

But the screen was showing me Declan. I certainly wasn't going to try explaining things to him just now, so I declined the call. When it rang again I switched it off. I didn't want any interruptions when I talked to Adi.

"Dad, this could be dangerous," Sam said.

"Trust me, I won't be accepting any more packages."

I got out, pushed aside the remains of the gate, and marched up to the front door.

CHAPTER 13

"Adi isn't all that bothered about the
money. He likes it, of course – who doesn't?
– but the important thing for him is that
he's from the back streets of nowhere, and
everybody knows his name."

Karen Varney, TV interview

There was no bell, but there was a very tarnished brass knocker. I lifted it, but on the first bang the door swung open.

"Unlocked?" Sam said from behind me. "That's strange. I'd have expected Casey at least to be more security conscious."

"Adi?" I called out. There was no answer. "Adi?" I tried again, louder. "Anybody home? It's Graham and Sam. We need to talk."

The silence persisted. Sam and I looked at each other, and then Sam took out the pistol he'd taken from Lonza's house. I didn't like the way he did that so naturally.

"Just precautionary," he said, and pushed past me to enter first.

The corridor beyond was similar to the one at the back, except that someone had made a start on cleaning it up. Same black and white tiles, but the broken ones had been removed.

There had been pictures on the walls here, but they'd been taken down and stacked at the end, leaving their shadows on the faded wallpaper. It still smelt of damp and musty neglect.

Sam tried a door on the left, looked in.

"Kitchen," he said. "Empty."

He went to another door, further down and on the opposite side, and pushed it open.

"Oh," he said, and suddenly his alert state seemed to go up a notch. He raised the gun to a ready position and dropped into a crouch.

"Get down and stay here!"

He dived through the door.

"Sam?" I asked. I was crouching down, as I'd been told. "Sam – what's going on?"

He came back out, standing upright, gun still in hand but not pointing anywhere. There was a peculiar expression on his face.

"It's clear," he said. "But it's not nice."

"Why? Is anyone there?"

"Casey is. Sort of."

I stepped past him and into the cluttered living room where we'd met with Adi. It was much the same as it had been then, except that Casey was sitting on the sofa where Adi had been. Actually, it was more reclining than sitting. He was slumped back, with his legs stretched out and his arms draped loosely down by his sides. He was wearing a red T-shirt with white sleeves, and for a moment I thought he'd put on an Arsenal strip.

But then I saw that he was staring sightlessly into nowhere, and I saw the holes in his chest, and realized that the red was blood.

"Casey?" I asked, pointlessly. I walked over to him, thinking I should take his pulse or something, but it was clearly a waste of time. There were at least three entry marks that I could see, grouped tightly round his heart, and blood had soaked into the fabric underneath him and spread beyond his body. Which suggested that the holes went all the way through.

"Don't touch anything," Sam warned me. "This is a crime scene. We don't want to mess it up. We'd better get outside."

"Yes." I stepped back. "No. Not yet. We need to find Adi."

"OK. Let's go carefully."

We checked the ground floor first. From the looks of it, Adi and Casey had been camping out in rooms at the back – there were two camp beds set up with sleeping bags. We found the door to the backyard – the van was parked there, but no one was in it.

The first floor looked as though it hadn't been used in years. The roof was starting to leak in places, plaster had come down from the ceiling in several rooms, and mould was growing on the walls and the old bits of furniture still left in place. A lot of the rooms were empty, though – probably cleared for renovation work that had never happened.

There was no sign of Adi.

We went back out into the sunshine, back to the car, where I sat on the bonnet and rested my head in my hands. Too much happening, too quickly. Too much death. This wasn't my world.

"Where is he? And who did this?" I asked the obvious questions.

"I should think that whoever killed Casey has taken Adi as well." Sam had put the gun away, but he was keeping his hand very close to it, and from the way he was constantly looking around, he was still on alert.

"Yes, but who? I would have said Lonza, but even if he survived that explosion…"

"I doubt that," Sam put in.

"So do I, and even if he did, he'd be in no condition to come looking for payback. Some of his men, though. Handy Jack? Though he was right next to Lonza when it went off."

Sam shook his head. "Not him, then. Perhaps the other bloke – the one with the pockmarked face. He was moving around when we left. And shooting. I don't think the ones I hit with the bat will be doing much of anything for a while."

"There might have been others. Perhaps not in the house."

"Yes, perhaps. But it still doesn't explain how they found this place so fast. Adi and Casey had kept a very low profile – and Casey was professional. He wouldn't have stayed here if he thought there was a chance it had been compromised."

"I don't know, Sam." I rubbed my forehead, closed my eyes. It had been an exhausting day. "Could it have been your mysterious friends?"

"No. Not like this, anyway. If they wanted Adi and Casey out of the way – and after that explosion, they might well – they'd have been much more discreet about it, and they wouldn't have left a mess."

"Discreet? What does that mean?" I asked suspiciously.

"Well, they could just have had them arrested. More than enough grounds. But in any case, I doubt if they could have done this. I didn't tell them about Adi or where Adi was. They might well find out, but not this fast."

"Somebody else, then."

"A new player in the game?" Sam suggested.

"Yes. Perhaps. After all, there's a lot of money involved here. If someone else is involved I bet they're after the same thing as Lonza – getting control of the sports centre. Which is why they've taken Adi."

"He should be all right then. For now at least."

"For now. But we've got to find him, Sam."

"I don't know how we can, though. We don't have the resources. Time to phone a friend, I think. Or text them."

Sam took out his burner and started pressing buttons.

"Wait a minute," I said, and he stopped, giving me an expectant look. "Perhaps it's time to make this official? Go to the police? The normal police, that is. We've got a body to show them this time – and your friends are a bit of an unknown quantity. We don't know when they might respond."

Sam frowned and scratched his chin. "You do have a point. But the thing is, I've already brought them in on this. We can't just say, 'Thanks, but we've changed our minds.' They're involved, whatever. Not keeping them informed would be a bad move. Might make them think we're playing games with them – and these sorts of people don't like playing games!"

I put my hands on my head, closed my eyes. I was so out of my depth here.

"I could tell them what happened and ask them if we should call the police?" Sam suggested.

"Right," I agreed. "Do that. No – tell them that we're going to call the police. In five minutes. That gives them time to respond if they want to."

Sam opened his mouth as if to say something more, then just shrugged, nodded, and went back to tapping at the keypad.

I switched my phone on again, wondering if Sandy had called. Or even Adi perhaps? There were several missed calls, but they were all from Declan. And some texts. I opened the first one.

"Call me! Urgent!" I didn't know what his idea of urgent was, but I doubted it counted for much compared to my day.

"Well, that's done," Sam said. "I've given them the address and told them about Casey."

His phone buzzed.

"That was quick." He checked the screen, then showed it to me.

"MATTER IN HAND. DO NOT CALL POLICE. GO HOME. YOU WILL BE CONTACTED IF NECESSARY."

"Well, we got a reaction at least," I commented.

"Mention of dead bodies often does that. So do we go home?"

I hesitated. "I suppose that would be the sensible thing to do."

"Only – I've been thinking. Would Adi go to Karen?"

I shrugged. "Perhaps. If he had nowhere else to go. Or he might be hiding out at the Castle."

Sam nodded. "Yes, maybe. But what I was thinking, Dad, was that if someone had taken him, someone who wanted to put pressure on him, then…"

His voice trailed off, as if reluctant to make the connection, but I could see where he was going.

"Oh no," I whispered. "These people – they'd do that, wouldn't they? Threaten Karen. Or Adrienne – she's still living at home."

Sam nodded. "Perhaps we'd better go there first, then."

"Right. And let's hope your friends are on the ball."

We got back into the car, and Sam used the side track to help turn round in the narrow lane. He put his foot down as he headed back towards the green.

"Go right at the bottom," I told him. "Up to the top of the hill, then right again. It's signposted from there."

My phone buzzed again. "Declan, I'll talk to you when I'm ready," I said pointlessly, then checked the text message anyway, and my blood froze.

"Graham – Adi's been here and he's NOT A FAKE! What's going on? CALL ME NOW!"

"What is it, Dad?"

I flashed the screen at him. He gave it a glance as he tore round the green and onto the road out.

"Well, now things are just getting weirder," he said. "Why would he go to Declan's?"

"I'll find out."

I fumbled with the buttons until I had Declan's number, and called. He answered it at once.

"Graham! 'Bout time – where the heck have you been?"

"Busy. Long story, but very busy. What's this about Adi?"

"You said he was a fake! Well, I don't know what you've been drinking or smoking, boyo, but he's been here and I can tell you for certain he's one hundred per cent the genuine Adi!"

"I know. There was a fake, but yes, there's a real one around as well!"

"You knew?" Declan sounded halfway between fury and tears. "Why didn't you say something, then? Why didn't you tell me, Graham?"

"I've only just found out myself. Well, not long ago. Where is he now?"

"Adi? He's gone to the sports centre, I think. He took my keys anyway. And here's the thing, Graham: he told me he's closing it down. Has closed it. Effective immediately. I'm not to go back, no one's allowed up there. Except you. He told me to call you, and tell you to meet him there, soon as. You and Sam, he said."

"Did he now? Well, I'm on my way to see him anyway, and we'll have some words. Find out what's going on."

"I'm not sure that's a good idea, Graham. He's not alone. There's a couple of hard-looking lads with him, so there is, and they mean business."

The phone was on speaker, so Sam could hear. We exchanged glances. "What did these hard lads look like, Dec?"

"Well, there was a big one, bald with a little goatee beard. Silly little thing, but no one's likely to tell him that. Then there was another one, with some sort of marks all over his face. He didn't say much, but the way he looked at me wasn't nice. Might have been one out in the car as well."

"OK, Declan. Just hang tight. I'll go and talk to him, find out what's going on. I'm sure we can sort this."

I hung up and looked at Sam. "Pockface."

He nodded. "I didn't see a big bald guy with a beard. Could have been somewhere else at the time, I suppose."

"Yes. If we assume that Jack, Lonza and the two you batted are out of the picture, then there might only be those two and perhaps one other, the driver."

"Or there might be others that we don't know about. And we'd better expect them to be armed."

"Right."

"But you're still going there. In spite of that text."

214

I thought about it. Of course, it didn't make any sense. But...

"It's Adi, Sam. He might be in trouble. I can't just let him disappear again. Not without talking to him. Or at least trying to."

What I couldn't say, what I couldn't put into words, was what Adi had meant to me for so many years; how deeply my life had been wrapped up with his. How much I'd invested in him. My friend. My best friend ever. I hadn't even realized how much that mattered.

Not until he'd walked away from me. I couldn't let him do it again.

"Right then." Sam wasn't going to try and talk me out of it, I realized.

"You're not going, though," I added. "It doesn't make sense for both of us to just walk in there. Someone needs to stay clear, be ready to call in the cavalry if things go really bad."

"If?"

I glanced across at him and realized that I'd never seen him looking so grim. It changed him completely, the relaxed and cheerful young man I'd gotten to know was suddenly a much darker and somehow older person.

"Dad, the last time we went into a house we found a dead body and the time before that a bomb went off. I don't want to sound pessimistic, but there is a bit of a pattern developing here. This isn't about *if* things go bad; it's just about how bad things are going to get."

"All the more reason for you to keep at a distance. And keep in touch with those friends of yours. Perhaps you can persuade them to do more than send texts."

"I had hoped for something more," Sam admitted. "But, to be fair, I'm an unknown source. They're probably still checking up on me."

"They need to get a move on."

The traffic built up as we headed back into town. There was a lane closed on one of the main approach roads, thanks to a couple of cars that had had a bit of a bump. Time ticked on while we crawled past the scene. Finally we were able to get onto the Queensway and the pace picked up. All the same, it was getting late by the time we pulled up in a street not far from the sports centre – 7 p.m. by the dashboard clock. Still a lot of daylight left, but I suddenly realized I was starving. I couldn't remember when I'd last eaten. I could have done with a cup of tea at least.

Later, I promised myself.

"I'll call you before I go in," I said to Sam. "Then I'll leave the phone on. You should be able to hear everything."

He raised an eyebrow. "And of course they won't suspect a thing, unless they saw the same film you got the idea from."

"Oh, I'm not going to hide it. I want them to know someone's listening in. But if we get cut off, find a panic button and hit it hard."

He gave me an approving look. "Good thinking, Dad. But you do realize that if things go pear-shaped, I won't be close enough to help?"

"You won't be close enough to get caught up in it, that's the point. And, as long as they know that, then things won't kick off."

"You hope."

"I'm just going to talk, that's all. Do you have any better ideas?"

216

He shook his head. "No. But I'm going to contact my friends again and see if they've got their act together yet. And if you're not out again in half an hour from now" – he indicated the clock – "I'm going to call the police anyway and get them here in a hurry."

"How will you manage that?"

"I'll report gunshots. If need be, I'll make sure that there *are* gunshots." He tapped his pocket significantly. "They'll come, don't worry."

"Right. Thanks."

I got out of the car and looked back in at him. "I knew you'd have been changed by all that travelling, Sam. I didn't have a clue how much."

"Yeah. It surprises me as well," he said, with that familiar grin back in place. "Clock's ticking, Dad, and you've got a bit of a walk!"

I nodded, and started off down the street.

It wasn't as far as Sam had suggested. Just down the street and I was in sight of the playing fields. Turn right, a short distance down the boundary road, and I was at the gates.

I phoned Sam. "I'm here. Just going in."

"Right."

It was one of those glorious, golden summer evenings, with the heat just starting to go out of the sun so that I could feel the stored warmth from the day beating up at me from the paving. Behind me, the houses had doors and windows open to catch the breeze, while kids played in the gardens.

Some were going up and down the street on bikes and scooters. Not as many playing out as I remembered from when we were kids, but then we didn't have gardens.

The playing fields were deserted, though. There used to be something going on all the time; if not an organized match then at least some lads having a kick about. But there wasn't as much as a dog walker patrolling the perimeter.

When I got closer I could see why. The gates were locked, and a notice had been printed out, stuck in a plastic sleeve, and taped to the frame.

SPORTS CENTRE CLOSED

NO ACCESS

TRESPASSERS 'WILL' BE PROSECUTED

"Adi," I said to myself, "you never did learn how to use quotation marks."

I went to the pedestrian gate at the side. It was also locked, with a padlock fitted through a sliding bar. It was supposed to stop the bar moving, but it had always had a fault. Reaching through and wiggling it around a little I was able to take the whole bar off, leaving it dangling from the padlock and the gate swinging open.

Declan had never got round to having that fixed properly. Probably because he rarely bothered to lock the gates anyway. He always wanted it to be open and available for use at any time.

I walked down the road towards the car park and the buildings. On my left I could see the ugly scar of the Delford Mills Project, with the yellow dots of construction machinery scattered around. Not moving now, but ready to get back into action next morning, working to finally erase the eyesore and bring some prosperity back to the area.

Money was coming in, and so were the sharks, eager to get a share of it. This whole thing with the sports centre was just the start of the feeding frenzy, I realized.

I could see the office windows. Someone was looking out, watching me approach. Then the blinds were brought down. *So it's to be a private meeting*, I thought to myself.

As I neared the door it swung open and someone stepped out. The big bald man that Declan had described. He hadn't mentioned the black suit, with the jacket hanging open just enough to show a gun butt. Perhaps the jacket had been kept buttoned up when Dec had seen it. But he was right about the goatee – it did look ridiculous.

"Place is closed. Can't you read?" he growled. American accent. I'd wondered if they'd hired local muscle to replace their imported goons, but it seemed they'd had some spares.

"Graham Deeson. I'm here to see Adi Varney."

"Let him in, Carlo," said someone inside. It sounded like Pockface.

The big man stepped aside, frowning. Not at me, particularly – I got the impression that he just met the whole world with a frown.

Inside, Pockface was leaning against a wall, facing me. He had some plasters on his forehead and hands, but otherwise seemed unharmed.

Adi was sitting behind Declan's desk, looking at me with a strange expression. It was as though he didn't know whether to be sad or happy.

"I told you he'd come," he said to Pockface. "It's the newshound instinct, I guess. He wants to get another Adi Varney story. Just like the old days, eh, Graham? But where's Sam?"

"Sam couldn't be with us in person. But he's listening in." My phone was in my hand. I held it up, half turned so that Pockface could see it as well. "Say 'hi', everyone."

Nobody said "hi". Adi narrowed his eyes and glared, but Pockface just gave a little smile and a nod.

"It doesn't make any difference," he said in his distinctive voice. "We can always find him if we want to."

I didn't like hearing that. I hoped Sam had taken note.

"Hello," I said to him. "We've met, but I don't think we were ever introduced?"

He shrugged. "Well, do forgive my manners, Mr Deeson. Ignacio D'Razzo." He indicated the seat in front of the desk. "Make yourself comfortable, why don't you?"

"Thanks." I sat down. D'Razzo stayed where he was, which meant that he was behind me and out of my line of vision. Which made me uncomfortable, but I didn't want to start an argument over seating arrangements. The big guy, Carlo, was standing off to the left, near the door, and just within my peripheral vision – which was also uncomfortable. There was no sign of the possible third man, which I didn't much like either. In fact, the whole situation was decidedly unpleasant.

"So how do you and Ignacio know each other?" I asked Adi. "Only, it seems a bit strange that the last time we met, you sent me over to his place with a bomb."

"The bomb was for Lonza," Adi said with a touch of asperity. "I didn't know that Mr D'Razzo was going to be there."

"You can call me Ignacio," said D'Razzo from behind me. "Since we're all being so friendly."

I got the impression that he was enjoying the situation. I wasn't, and Adi didn't look that pleased either.

"Ignacio is in the same line of business as Handy Jack. The late Handy Jack, that is. Only, whereas Jack was Second Division at best, Ignacio is more Premier League level. He works for a very important man in the States, and I'm very pleased that he came over here in person to help deal with this situation."

"This situation? I suppose by that you mean Lonza trying to steal the sports centre?"

"Yes, but there's a bit more to it than that. You remember I mentioned how, when I figured out what Lonza was up to, I took some precautions?"

"You got Casey in to watch your back."

"That was one of the precautions. But you know me, Graham. Never all my eggs in one basket, eh? I had a few other things going on. For example, I reached out to Ignacio's boss. Who is – or was! – also Lonza's boss, as it happened. I let him know what Lonza was really up to, and how we could cut him out to our mutual benefit. I thought that if I couldn't talk Lonza round to my point of view after the Madrid game, then we'd just manage without him altogether."

"So you went over his head."

"That was the idea. Only it didn't play out quite as I'd hoped, what with Lonza hiding me out in the desert after the game. But once Casey had rescued me, I got in touch again. Passed on what I'd heard from Lonza and renewed my offer – basically, 'Get Lonza off my back and help me launch California Strike properly, and you can take all the profit directly.' Legitimate profit, so it wouldn't need Lonza to launder it.

"I still hadn't got an answer, though, when we came over here. Which was disappointing. I'd hoped things would move faster."

"My boss likes to consider things carefully before he makes a decision," said Ignacio. "And we were taking a closer look at all of Lonza's deals. Turns out he'd been skimming off more than we'd realized. So I needed to come and have a conversation with him about that."

"Lonza knew that Ignacio was coming for him," Adi continued. "That's why he was pushing so hard to get the sports centre. It was his best chance to buy himself out of trouble. He was running out of time. But so was I. I couldn't let him get his hands on it. So Casey suggested some extreme measures."

"The bomb."

"Yes. Of course, I didn't know that Ignacio had already caught up with Lonza." He shrugged apologetically in that direction. "That was unfortunate. A breakdown in communications, I suppose you'd call it."

"Yeah, you could call it that," Ignacio agreed. "Crazy thing is that if you hadn't called when you did, Deeson, Lonza would already have been dead. We were kinda close to finishing our negotiations, you might say, and Rocco, he wasn't looking to come out of it too good." He chuckled. "You threw him a lifeline. A short one… He did his best to drive a bargain, but the truth is he'd have gone with any deal if he thought it was gonna buy him some time. I thought we'd go along with it, see if I could get a little extra out of it, cover expenses."

I remembered the way Lonza and Handy Jack had deferred to D'Razzo; the way his "suggestions" had guided the discussion. Well, that was explained, anyway. If I hadn't been so wound up myself, I would probably have felt the tension in the room. "So the whole thing was a waste of time?

What a mess." An image flashed across my mind – Handy Jack after the explosion. I was glad I hadn't been able to see Lonza. "And the bomb was Casey's idea?"

"He had the expertise to do it," Adi confirmed. "And the materials."

"But you hadn't told him about your other little arrangement with Ignacio and his boss?"

"Need-to-know basis, Graham. Just like managing a team, really. You tell people what's necessary to get the best performance out of them. Anything else just gets in the way."

I rubbed my forehead wearily. "Managing a team, Adi – what's the worst that happens? You lose a game, you have a bad season, you get relegated? This is a bit more serious. People have died. Lonza, Jack... that actor who was pretending to be you... and now Casey. It's not football, it's not a game."

"How did you know about Casey?" Adi said sharply, shooting a glance past me at Ignacio.

"We found your house, Adi. We went there. We saw him. His body, that is."

Behind me, Ignacio muttered something. It sounded like an obscenity. He wasn't enjoying himself so much now.

"That's a pity, Graham. I don't know how you found the place, but I'd rather you hadn't."

"Is that all you can say about it, Adi? Your friend's dead and you just wish I didn't know about it?"

Adi laughed. "You think Casey was a friend?"

"He rescued you from Lonza, didn't he?"

"Yes. But that wasn't for friendship. Casey was a mercenary, Graham. He was helping me because I promised him money. A lot of money, actually. Fifty per cent of what I could get from the sports centre, and a regular cut from the CSS income after that!" He shrugged. "Of course, that wasn't in the deal I'd made with Ignacio's boss. So I'm afraid Casey was in the way."

"And I was kinda upset about the bomb," added Ignacio. "Not that I'm weeping for Lonza or Jack, but I was in the room as well! Can't have it going round that someone took a shot at me and got away with it. I've got my reputation, you understand. Besides, I was planning my own thing for Lonza."

A lot of information was swirling around in my head. I grasped at something, trying to get things in order.

"So – let me get this straight, Adi. You did a deal with Ignacio, told him where Lonza was and where you were. But you didn't know he was there, so you sent the bomb to get rid of Lonza. After it went off, Ignacio knows right away that it must have been you who sent it, so he gets some of his lads…"

"Carlo and Donnie," put in Ignacio. Which confirmed that there was a third man. Somewhere. "They were already over at Adi's house, keeping an eye on things. After you and your son had left us so quickly, I told them to take out Casey and bring Adi to join me in town. I figured with things blowing up like that your police would be round pretty soon, so we had to move in a hurry."

"You went to Declan's, got the keys, and came here…" I stopped. I was missing something. I ran through what had been said. "But what did you mean about paying Casey fifty per cent of what you got for the sports centre?"

"Yes, I know; it was pretty steep. But what could I do? When he got me out of the desert he wanted to know how I was going to pay for his services, and that was the only thing I had to offer. I didn't have a good bargaining position, so when he asked for fifty per cent, I had to agree."

"Yes, but..." I felt unsteady, even though I was sitting down. As if something I'd thought was rock solid had started to move. "Adi, the whole point of stopping Lonza was to keep the sports centre going... wasn't it?"

Adi gave me a baffled look, then suddenly laughed. "Heck, Graham, did you think that this was what this was all about? Saving the sports centre? You really haven't got a clue, have you?"

"But – this place – it's your legacy. Your gift to the town, to the people, to all the fans..."

Adi rolled his eyes. "Graham, I don't give a rat's backside for the town, the fans, or the sodding sports centre! I need this place sold off. I need the money to get CSS back up and running! Didn't you get that? It wasn't Lonza's plan in the first place. I was always planning to sell it off. He just hijacked the idea from me."

CHAPTER 14

> "Keep your eye on the ball. That's all there
> is to it."
>
> **Adi Varney, at a press conference, when
> asked, "What's the most important rule
> in football?"**

I stared at him, aghast. "You can't mean that. I – OK, I understand you wanted to go and try something new in California. But this place – it's done so much good for so many people, so many kids…"

Adi shrugged. Baffled by his indifference, I glanced round, searching for inspiration, and my eye fell on an especially old and yellowed newspaper cutting in a worn wooden frame.

"Look," I said, pointing it out, and he glanced in that direction. "Do you remember that day, Adi? Of course you do." In the faded picture you could just about make out a younger Adi and younger Graham, flanking an elderly man in a clerical dog collar who was holding a large pair of scissors over a length of ribbon. "The opening of the Sports Hall – this building, Adi! That's Reverend Allen. The minister who did the funeral for Davy. He talked about that, about how you were rescued, and how your life and career were all a demonstration of giving back to the community…"

Adi snorted, and I realized I was going the wrong way with this. But nothing better occurred to me, so I ploughed on.

"He prayed for you, remember? He thanked God for you, Adi, and for your vision, and your skill, and –"

"Enough!" He slammed his stick down on the desk, breaking my flow. "Enough of that!" He leaned forward across the desk, indifference replaced by fury. "That was always one of the things I hated most about you: the way you were always trying to shove your religion down my throat! Always so damned holier-than-thou and righteous, always telling me where I was going wrong, like you were my conscience or something!"

I recoiled, physically moved back in my chair, in the face of his anger. I was shocked by it – even more by the words he used. Especially by one word. Hate.

"No," I said. "It wasn't like that at all, Adi. We talked about things, yes, and I gave you my opinion – but I didn't try to force anything on you…"

"Oh no? How many times did I hear, 'Adi, you can't do that, you shouldn't, you mustn't – you've got a position to uphold, you set an example, you should think of the team, you should think of Karen, you should think of your kids? Always telling me what I should be like, who I was supposed to be, and I was only there at all because of you and your little *brother*!" He spat the words at me.

"My brother who died, you mean?" I said, as calmly as I could. "My…"

"Your little pest of a brother, always following us around and hanging about and getting in the way and who shouldn't have even been there on the canal that day! But he had to come with us, and he had to get himself killed, and I've wasted my life trying to make up for that, because I thought you chose me over him and I owed you for it!"

I tried to speak, but Adi was in full flow now and shouted over me. "And I put up with it, with being stuck in this little hole of a place, with having you preach at me and tell me how I should be living, with all these community projects and charities that you pushed me into, and all the time watching you build your comfortable, boring little life on the back of my skill, my success, all the while knowing that I should be out there doing bigger things, better things, greater things, but I couldn't because of your stupid brother…"

He paused to draw breath, and I tried again to get a word in but he carried on.

"And it was all a lie, wasn't it, Graham? All a lie because you never meant to save me anyway. That was just an accident. So I've wasted my time, wasted myself – and now I've got one last chance to show the world what I can do and you want me to give it up for this poxy little charity that I only ever started in the first place because you wanted me to! Well, forget it!" He slammed his stick down on the desk again. "Forget it! This place, this town – and you – you've all had as much of me as you're getting! Now I'm taking something back, and neither you nor your religion nor your little brother is going to stop me!"

He finally ran out of words. But he was still glaring, panting with the force of his anger, and gripping his stick so tightly that it looked as though he was going to snap it between his fingers.

He wasn't the only angry one, though. What he'd said had hurt. The injustice of it, the cruelty of it – the stupidity and arrogance of it. I could feel my own temper rising.

"Do you know why I became a Christian, Adi? Did you ever understand that?" I was still keeping my voice calm, but I was shaking. "It was after Davy died. After that day down at the canal. We were never very religious before then, our family. But when we were grieving, when we were broken, the church was there for us. Reverend Allen" – I pointed at the newspaper cutting – "he was there for us. He spent time sharing our grief, sharing our tears. A lot of the church did. That's why we started going, because they were there for us when we needed them. But where were you, Adi? Where were you when I was ripping myself apart with grief – and with guilt, because I'd let my brother die and saved my friend? You were off playing football, Adi. That's where you were. The church people we hardly knew were there for us and my best friend whom I'd pulled out of the water was away playing games!"

"Now just…" he began, but I wasn't finished.

"Yes, I know, it was your big chance. And you took it, didn't you? Scored a hat-trick! Because you were always good with a ball, you were brilliant." I leaned towards him, stared him straight in the eye. "But that was the day after he died, wasn't it? Davy lying stone cold in the mortuary, me still in shock and nearly broken with grief, but *you* were out being brilliant. Because that's all you were any good at. Being brilliant at football. You were no good at being a friend. You were rubbish at caring about people. Left to yourself, you just used them and dropped them, failed them, let them down. Couldn't be bothered with anyone who wasn't helping your game, or listening to you talk about your game."

"Graham!" he snarled. But I wasn't about to stop now.

"You think I've held you back these past thirty-plus years? Well, I have, Adi. I held you back from alienating nearly everyone you knew with your single-minded, self-centred obsession with your own greatness. All those times I was being your conscience – I was helping you treat people with respect, with consideration, with dignity. You found it hard enough to get on with people anyway, but you never realized how much worse it would have been if I hadn't been there! Without me around, your marriage would have failed in the first year, because I had to tell you how to treat your wife properly. Without me you would never have made it as a manager, you wouldn't be the big name in this town, you wouldn't be the legend you are now. Because it's not just about football, Adi. That's what you never understood. I had to be there to show you how to be a decent human being, not just a good footballer.

"I believed in you, Adi. I believed you could be a better person, that you were a better person, really, and that I just needed to help that part of you come out. I had to believe it, for…" I broke off, took a breath, forced myself to resume, "… for Davy's sake."

I looked at Adi, looked him straight in the eye. "I was wrong, wasn't I? This is the real Adi Varney. It's all there ever was."

He met my gaze. And all I saw was indifference.

I sat back again. I was feeling very tired. There was so much more I wanted to say, but I didn't have the energy.

"So go on then, Adi. Sell this place off, take the money, go and live your dream. See how well you do without me. But just have a think about how you've got on since you left. How well that worked out for you. Because you may be brilliant at football, but you're useless at just about anything else, and when I'm not there to –"

Adi was still fast. Not on his feet, of course, but with his hands. I didn't even see him move before his stick smacked into my skull, sending me sprawling out of the chair, pain exploding through my head.

Then he got out of the chair, and came round to stand over me. I squinted up at him, barely able to focus through the throbbing pain.

"You did it again," I muttered.

"Yeah, well, you wouldn't shut up, would you? Never did know when to keep your mouth closed. Idiot. You should have been thinking instead of talking. Why do you suppose I wanted you here? Just to catch up on old times?"

I certainly wasn't thinking now. "I – don't know…"

He shook his head. Prodded me with the end of his stick. "All that stuff you know about, Graham. About Lonza and the bomb. It's a loose end, you see."

He leaned back against the desk and stared down at me. "Of course, the best thing would have been if that bomb had taken you out as well. I wanted Casey to make it more powerful, to be sure of that. But he said that was the biggest bang he could put into a package that size. And of course, we couldn't have you delivering anything too big. Lonza or Jack would have got suspicious."

"You wanted to kill me?" I was having trouble with the idea, and not just because of the blow to my head.

"Oh, so many times." The thought of doing so had gone a long way to restoring Adi's temper. Or perhaps it had been hitting me. Either way, he was smiling brightly. "Casey thought that if the bomb didn't get you, Lonza's guys would probably finish you off. Didn't think you'd get out of there so fast, but then we hadn't planned on Sam getting involved. Bit of a complication."

"But Sam – he could have been killed as well," I protested.

"Yes. Pity. I've got nothing against Sam. But it seems he's inherited your talent for poking his nose in." Adi looked away from me and spoke to Ignacio, who had been watching us with an expression of mild amusement. "Speaking of Sam, did Donnie find him yet?"

Donnie. Out looking for Sam. I looked over at the window, and realized why they'd drawn the blinds. So I wouldn't see Donnie leaving, heading out of the gate. They must have decided on that as soon as they saw me walking towards them alone.

My phone was on the floor somewhere. I'd dropped it when Adi hit me. "Sam!" I shouted, hoping it was in range of my voice and still connected. "Sam!"

"This what you're looking for?" asked Ignacio. He stepped past me and picked it up from the corner of the room. "Hey, Sam, you still there?" he said. "Only if you want to say goodbye to your pa, you'd better get over here in the next five minutes!"

He switched it off and tossed it back on the floor. "Donnie texted me," he said to Adi. "He found the car, but no one was in it. Guess Sam went for a walk, eh? Donnie's taking a look around, see if he can spot him. But – hey, Graham? Where's your boy gone?"

"Police," I said. "He's gone for the police."

"Yeah? Why didn't he just phone them?"

"Because he was still listening in on the conversation."

Ignacio laughed. "OK. Not a problem, anyhow. So he tells the police? His word against ours – and there'll be no other evidence, I promise you!" I tried to interrupt, but he waved me down. "And now you're going to say he's recording it. So what? We've got lawyers, and lawyers love things like that. They'll be all, 'When was it made? How was it made? Can you verify that?' The worst you can do is inconvenience us a little. And that's only if Donnie doesn't find him first. Don't forget we know where you live. We'll just go round after we've finished here." He paused, and scratched his chin thoughtfully. "Of course, your wife might be there. Seems a pity to get her involved. So perhaps you'd like to save her the unpleasantness and us the trouble, eh, Graham? Where's your boy gone?"

"You stay away from Sandra!" I snapped at him. "And if I were you, I'd be getting on your way. Sam will be on to the police now, after what he's heard, and they'll be all over this place in ten minutes."

"Ten minutes? Really? Your British police are as good as that?" He shook his head. "Well, I kinda doubt it. But it won't matter much. We've got things all prepared. Lots of places round here for hiding a few bodies. And I'll be like, 'Sorry, Officer, we haven't seen anyone, but feel free to look around.' And perhaps they will, but they won't find anything. Nice try, Deeson, but I'm way ahead of you."

I managed to pull myself back up into the chair. "They'll hear gunshots."

"Gunshots? Why would there be any gunshots? Show 'em, Carlo."

Big Carlo reached behind a filing cabinet and pulled out a cricket bat. Actually, my cricket bat. I could see the signatures across the face. And a chip of wood had been knocked out of one edge.

Ignacio continued. "Y'know, I've got a nickname back in the States. They call me 'The Poet'. Because I like to do things with a bit of style, see? A bit of poetry. Like one time, there was this guy who was into that big-game fishing thing. Had all these pictures round his place, of him standing next to the big dead fish. So I hung him off his rod, with his own line, just like one of his trophies! You remember that one, Carlo?"

"Sure do," said Carlo. "That was a good one."

"Right. But I'm always trying to do better. And I thought, 'What would be more poetic than to use your own cricket bat?' Well, I kinda like the idea, anyway."

I looked at Carlo, who for once wasn't frowning. I looked at Ignacio, who was positively smiling. And I looked at Adi, who looked back at me and shrugged, expressionless.

"So I had Carlo bring it along," Ignacio continued. "He's kinda into sports... ever played cricket, Carlo?"

The big man shook his head. "No, sir."

"Well, today's your chance to try it out." He gave me a wink. "See, I'm the Poet. I get the ideas, but Carlo's the guy who gets to – ah – execute them!" He sniggered. So did Carlo, though I wasn't sure if he'd got the joke. I didn't find it very funny myself, but they were enjoying themselves.

I looked round the room, desperately searching for a way out. And as I did so, my eyes flicked across the door at the far end, just in time to see the handle move.

I remembered then. I remembered Sam's story of how he'd spied on our meetings through that door.

"Stop!" I shouted. Because if Ignacio found Sam, he'd kill him. And he was my son, and any danger to him far outweighed the danger to me.

234

"It's a bit late for that, Graham," said Adi. "I thought you believed in heaven, anyway? You should be keen to be on your way."

He thought I'd been shouting at him, or Ignacio. Pleading for my life. He was liking it. I could see from his expression.

"But it's you I'm worried about, Adi. I've been looking out for you all these years. I can't just stop now."

The words were bubbling out of me almost without conscious thought. I didn't have time to think about what I was saying. I just had to keep talking, keep them looking at me, because the handle was still moving. Very slowly, but definitely moving.

"Nothing to worry about, Graham. I'll manage fine without you."

Adi stepped back a bit, letting Carlo come closer. He was hefting the bat, swinging it slightly and getting a feel for it. His eyes were targeting an area on the back of my skull.

"But, come on, mate, do you really think you can trust these people? How are they any different from Lonza?"

Adi sighed. "I thought I'd explained this, Graham. I'll put in the money from this place, and when CSS are up and running, Ignacio's boss gets paid off, with interest."

The door handle was all the way down.

I shook my head. "They aren't sports fans, Adi. Not soccer fans, anyhow. They're business people. And gangsters. Why would they let all that money go into something as risky as a soccer team when they can just cut their losses, take all the profit, and walk away? After all, Lonza didn't think it was worth a proper investment, did he? Why would they?"

"We did a deal," Adi said. But there was just a trace of uncertainty in his voice. Perhaps it was the old habit of listening to what I told him even when he didn't like it. Perhaps it was just that he was finally thinking past his own ambitions and considering what other people might want.

"Sure, you did a deal. What's that worth?"

Adi looked away from me and at Ignacio.

"You know, you shoulda listened better to your pal Graham. He really is smarter than you."

"We did a deal!" Adi said again.

"Yeah, about that." Ignacio sighed and casually pulled out his automatic. "See, I had a talk with the boss about that. And the truth is, Deeson's right: he's not really a sports fan. So, while we agreed that Lonza had got some big ideas and had to be taken down, that didn't mean he wasn't right about your soccer team. It sort of worked as a scam, but it's not really the kind of long-term investment we're looking for."

Adi had gone pale. Not with fear. Adi didn't really do fear, never had. It was anger that was rising in him – a greater anger than I'd ever seen in him before. Greater even than his anger at me had been.

Ignacio saw it as well, and stepped back to a safe distance, aiming his pistol at Adi as he did so.

"Don't get any smart ideas," he said sharply.

"Smart ideas?" Adi whispered. "You think you can back off from our deal, steal my money and just walk away? You think that's a smart idea?"

"Sure it is. We've got all the paperwork Lonza had cooked up, plus your friend Declan saw you and heard from you himself that the place is closing down. The deal will go through. You don't have to be around for it. After all, you've already disappeared once. Who's going to notice if you do it again?"

The door was open. Just a crack, so far. Would the hinges squeak? It didn't look as if Declan had done much maintenance lately, so they probably hadn't been oiled in a while. I had to keep them talking, had to make a noise, keep their attention.

"But you can't kill us here," I said, as loudly as I could without shouting. "You'd leave traces. Blood traces. The police can find them, you know. Even very small amounts they'll find. Kill us here and they'll know it was murder they'll be looking for you!"

Ignacio looked annoyed. "What d'ya take me for? An amateur? You think you're the first guys we've offed? Don't worry about it. Carlo's an expert – well, not with a cricket bat so much, but he knows how to hit someone so it don't make a mess – don't you, Carlo?"

Carlo was nodding and smiling. "Back of the neck, see?" he explained. "One hit, you're gone. It's real quick, and there ain't no blood. It's easier if you kneel down, though. Or I'll put you down. Whatever."

He was quite big enough to do it, even if we'd been a lot younger and stronger. As it was, he wasn't even going to be out of breath.

But the door was a quarter of the way open, and I hadn't heard any squeaks yet.

Ignacio and Carlo had their backs to it. Adi was facing that way, but he was focused on Ignacio, his fury rendering him blind to everything else. I could see his fingers twitching and I knew that he wasn't about to kneel down and quietly accept his fate.

Ignacio could see it as well, and he found it amusing. "Go on. Try something. Think I won't shoot you if I have to?

Or are you thinking it'll leave some blood, put the cops on to us? Not a problem. We know how to clean up a crime scene. Done it often enough before."

"Adi…" I said, and reached out to grab his sleeve. But he shrugged me off and continued to hold Ignacio's stare.

"Y'know, I was going to leave you for later, Adi. But I like this way better. You and your old pal – did I get the story right? He saved your life once? So now you get to die together. How poetic is that?" He began to laugh. A strange sort of laugh, nasal and surprisingly high-pitched. "And how about this – a soccer star killed with a cricket bat? Is that poetic or ironic, eh?"

And now the door was fully open, and Sam was standing there with pistol raised in a two-handed grip and aimed directly at Ignacio.

"Don't move, drop the weapon," he said.

Ignacio didn't move, though his expression changed to surprise, then chagrin. But he didn't drop the gun either. Carlo had frozen, cricket bat still in hand, though he'd gone back to frowning.

"Ah, so that's where your boy went," Ignacio said to me. "Nice move. But now here's the problem you've got. He's not a killer, or I'd be dead already. He's not a killer – but I am!"

Then several things happened simultaneously.

Ignacio swivelled and dropped to one knee, all in one fluid motion, bringing his gun to aim at Sam in the same moment.

Sam fired, the bullet going through the space where Ignacio's head had been, smashing into a filing cabinet behind me.

Adi launched himself forward with a wordless shriek of pure rage and brought his stick down on Ignacio.

Carlo dropped the bat and dragged a huge revolver out from under his jacket, turning towards Sam as he did so.

I did nothing, except to sit in the chair – and send up the fastest but sincerest prayer of my life.

Adi may have been intending to hit Ignacio's head, or his gun hand, but he missed both. Instead his stick crashed down across the gangster's shoulder. Perhaps he hadn't been sure what to aim for, but there was no doubting the fury behind it. The stick snapped in two and Ignacio was sent sprawling. His gun went off, but the bullet went wide, losing itself somewhere in the office furniture.

Carlo's big pistol, aimed at the storeroom door, boomed like a cannon – but Sam had moved, hurling himself down behind one of the secretaries' desks.

Ignacio was trying to roll over, but Adi was kneeling over him, raining blows on his head with the broken end of the stick and shouting obscenities.

Carlo fired again, putting a bullet in and through the desk Sam was hiding behind. The weapon was so powerful that the entire desk jerked backwards under the impact.

Magnum? I thought somewhere in the back of my mind. But I was finally moving – diving forward out of the chair, picking up the fallen cricket bat, and bringing it down on Carlo's gun hand just as he fired again. The bullet ripped up carpet and ricocheted away. Carlo roared, dropped the gun, and lashed out at me with his other hand while I was still trying to raise the bat for another blow.

He caught me on the chest, flinging me backwards against the chair I'd just got out of and toppling it over.

Ignacio was firing, twisting round as he did and Adi screamed, then stabbed downwards with the broken end of the stick. There was a sort of gurgling, choking noise and Ignacio stopped shooting. I was still holding the bat, but I had a pain shooting right through my chest and into my back and I thought, *My heart!*

Then Carlo loomed over me. He'd pulled out a knife, the blade flicked out as I watched, but there was another gunshot and Carlo staggered sideways into the desk, dropping the knife and clutching at his thigh. Blood was spurting out between his fingers, and at the end of the room Sam was standing up again, aiming carefully.

"NO, SAM," I shouted. "Don't shoot again!"

I forced myself upright and swung the bat, two-handed, across Carlo's head, and he collapsed.

"That's how you use a cricket bat," I told him. Whispered at him. I was having trouble catching my breath. "You weren't even holding it right," I added vindictively.

"Dad!" Sam was next to me, grabbing my arm. "Dad, are you all right?"

"I don't know," I told him, but the pain in my chest, though still bad, wasn't getting worse, and perhaps it was just the natural consequence of being punched by a gorilla. "You?"

"I'm fine. I'm OK."

"And Adi?" I turned to look.

Adi was sprawled on the floor, half draped over Ignacio's legs, not moving.

Neither was Ignacio. His face had taken a terrible battering from Adi's stick, but the final blow had been the fatal one. The broken end had been stabbed into his throat. It wasn't a pretty sight.

I didn't dwell on it. Instead I went to Adi, and with Sam's help turned him over. There was blood all over his front. Probably not all his, but at least one of Ignacio's bullets had gone into his stomach.

He was still breathing.

"Adi!" I said. "Adi! Sam – get help, get an ambulance."

"They're on their way, Dad." He held up the burner. "The 'friends'. I heard from them just before I went into the storeroom. They're coming."

"They need to hurry." I turned back to Adi.

His eyes were open, and he looked at me. "Gra... Graham..." he gasped. He reached up, clutched at me.

And suddenly it was thirty years ago. A wall of water was bearing down on us. The three of us: me on the bank, Adi and Davy on the raft, but all standing close together, staring at the huge wave...

I was grabbing on to a branch, not thinking about it, just hanging on, but reaching out with the other hand.

Reaching out for Davy.

But Adi was reaching for me, clutching at me, and then the water hit us.

"Adi..." I said. And grasped his hand, holding on to him as I had done then.

But the light was already fading from his eyes.

This time I couldn't save him.

"Dad?" said Sam. "Dad – I think he's gone."

"Yes. I know." I looked at him. "Where's that ambulance? Where are these people you've been contacting?"

He shrugged. "On their way. That's all I know. They should be..."

The door burst open.

A man stepped in – a smaller version of Carlo with an assault rifle instead of a pistol. His jaw dropped as he stepped inside and saw the carnage.

"What the..."

Then there was a sharp crack from somewhere outside and the man – Donnie, I assumed – grunted, stumbled forward, and fell.

"Looks like the cavalry finally arrived," Sam said.

"About time," I told him.

CHAPTER 15

"Write anything you like about me –
anything but the truth, Graham!"

**Adi Varney, in conversation with Graham
Deeson**

ADI VARNEY – A TRUE LEGEND
By Graham Deeson
19 May, 1979.
The great thing about that
day is that Adrian Varney
did not die.

Because he didn't die that day, on 20 May he
scored a hat-trick for Clayland's Youth Football
Club, which won them the Challenge Cup.

Because he scored a hat-trick, he was spotted
by a talent scout and recruited to the local pro club,
Delford Vale United.

Because he played for The Vale, they were
promoted three times in the next four seasons and
won the FA Cup twice, while Adi also got his first
England cap and scored his first international hat-
trick.

Because of that, when he was forced to retire due
to injury, he became the most successful manager

in The Vale's history. What's more, he was able to invest his time and fame into supporting a dozen local charities that helped thousands of people.

He was truly a local legend. Schools and working men's clubs and pubs and churches all across the city have memorials to him – plaques, photographs, signed scarves, and so on. People still talk about him with pride. He's still one of us.

All this because he didn't die that day.

All this because of me. The reason he didn't die was that I saved his life.

I sat looking at what I'd written, and ran my hand over the scar on my forehead. That gesture was getting to be a habit. The hospital had pulled a tiny bit of plastic out of the gash I had there, and it had healed quite well after that. As had the various other scratches, bruises, and minor injuries I'd accumulated since Rob and June's wedding.

The doctors had also checked my heart and pronounced it fully operational, but suggested that I should take it easy for a while. I had no arguments with that – not that Sandy would have allowed any.

So I'd spent most of the past few days in my office, writing almost non-stop. All the stories I'd been collecting over the years, all the quotes and anecdotes, all the highlights and lowlights of Adi's career – everything I'd been trying to put together for so long – suddenly poured out of me and onto the screen.

But I was having trouble with the beginning. I knew how the story went, but I wasn't sure where to start it. This was my latest attempt, and I'd been staring at it for over an hour. The problem was, although it was all true, it wasn't true enough. Or rather, it wasn't enough truth. Adi's story was incomplete without all the things I had recently learned about him.

I wasn't sure how to tell the complete story. I wasn't even sure I should. What would Karen and the girls think if I wrote it all down, put it out in public? What about Declan, Johnnie, Angie, and every other person who had known him, loved him, cheered for him? I thought back to the lad on the reception desk at the Stag, and his whole family. In my mind, they stood for the entire town.

Could I bear to tell them about the real Adi Varney?

Or could I tell them a lie? A nice, comforting lie, that made Adi out to be the hero and legend they'd always thought he was. That I'd always wanted him to be.

To tell a lie like that went against every principle I had as a Christian and a reporter. But so did hurting people, and the truth would hurt a lot of people. It was hurting me.

Sam came in. "Cup of tea, Dad?" He framed it as a question, but that was no more than a form of words: the tea was already made, in my favourite mug, which he placed on the desk next to me, before leaning over my shoulder to read the words on the screen. "You've settled on a title, then? And a way to start it off?"

"Yes. Maybe. I don't know. I'm still not sure about it."

"Perhaps you just need to give it more time. But – speaking of time – Mum said to remind you that our visitor is due any moment now."

Even as he spoke, the front doorbell rang, and Brodie howled. "And this time he's on time," I said. "For a change."

I took my mug with me as we went back through to the living room. Sandra was already there, ushering a man in. Grey hair, smart suit, the sort of face that would blend in with a crowd. He was carrying a long box, which seemed out of place – a briefcase would have seemed more appropriate for him.

Sandra gave me an anxious look. Contrary to expectations, she hadn't said one word of rebuke for what I'd got myself involved in – not even for getting Sam into it as well. But she wanted it to be over and in the past as soon as possible.

Which made at least two of us, if not three – I wasn't quite sure where Sam was on this.

Brodie, having sniffed the stranger cautiously and deemed him acceptable, was banished to the kitchen, while Sandra made introductions.

"Graham – Sam – this is Mr Smith. From the government."

"Oh yes?" I raised an eyebrow. "Which department?"

He gave me a bland smile, which I took to mean, "Don't ask silly questions." I thought of requesting some ID, but I was pretty certain that he could show me any sort of ID I might ask for.

"Would you like some tea, Mr Smith?" Sandra asked. "Or coffee?" The biscuits were already out.

"No, thank you, Mrs Deeson." Smith had a polite, well-practised smile. "I shan't be troubling you long. But as I said on the phone earlier, there are a few matters which we need to go over."

"Well, I'm sure you'll be here long enough to sit down at least," I said, and indicated our collection of sofas and armchairs. "Comfortable and well lived in," I think described them. Sandra had insisted on putting throws over the most well-lived-in items.

He smiled again and sat down. "Let's get straight to it, shall we? It has been decided, at a very high level, that it would be best for all if the recent events had not happened."

"You can say that again," I told him, with feeling.

He nodded. "I quite understand how you feel, Mr Deeson. But if I give you a little background information to put things into context, then I think you'll see what I mean."

"Please. I'd like to hear that. We all would."

"Yes. Well, the thing is, neither Rocco Lonza nor Ignacio D'Razzo – or, indeed, their, ah, 'support staff' – should have been in this country at all. Not without our knowledge, anyway. We have an arrangement, you see, with colleagues in various places, to let us know about the movements of people like that."

"Gangsters, you mean?"

"Yes, Mr Deeson. Gangsters, top-level criminals, terrorist suspects – any individuals likely to cause trouble, really. Unfortunately, in this case the arrangement seems to have broken down. Rather a worrying development, and obviously we will be looking into it. But the point is that these two people, rather significant people in the US criminal rankings, were in Britain without us being aware of it. I'm afraid that, as a result, when you initially contacted us" – he nodded at Sam – "your information was not accurately assessed."

"You didn't believe that Lonza was over here," Sam said. With his usual charming smile. I wasn't sure how much use it would be with Smith.

"Well, in view of our expectation of such intelligence being corroborated from other sources, there was a question mark, as you might say."

"Until the bomb went off," I said drily. I made no attempt to be charming.

Smith was unfazed. "Exactly so. Though I would point out that by then we had checked the references that your son had provided, and – given the very positive report from your friend down in Africa – we were already upgrading the matter somewhat. However, events rather got away from us, I'm afraid."

"I would say so," I agreed. "In fact, most of the events took place without you."

The professional imperturbability took a hit from that: Smith looked embarrassed for a moment.

"Yes, I have to admit that is the case. And we do owe you an apology. We should have been quicker off the mark. Unfortunately, we didn't have assets immediately available. A team was assembled and dispatched as soon as possible, but it took a little longer than we would have liked. However" – he recovered quickly – "we did at least arrive soon enough to neutralize the last gunman before he could cause any trouble."

I had a brief mental picture of Donnie falling forward onto his assault rifle. I had to admit, he could have caused a lot of trouble with that.

"Yes, and we do appreciate that very much," I conceded. "But it was a very close thing."

"It was. And I must say that, given the circumstances, you handled things very well. The outcome, whilst not the most desirable, could at any rate have been much worse."

"They could," said Sandra. "I might have lost my husband and my son." She couldn't quite keep the sharp edge from her voice.

Smith nodded. "As I said, we do apologize. However, I must make it clear that this apology, whilst quite sincerely meant, cannot be made officially."

"Because officially nothing happened?" Sam suggested.

"Exactly so. The degree of trouble that has already been caused could only be exacerbated by making these events public knowledge."

"Plus it would be very embarrassing for some people?" I suggested.

"Hmm, well, perhaps."

"Such as?"

"Well, Mr Deeson, here's the thing: in government circles there's often *talk* of embarrassment, but it is often very hard to pin it down to individuals. So I couldn't possibly say *who* is actually embarrassed. As a newspaperman, Mr Deeson, I'm sure you understand what I mean."

I reflected on that and saw his point. "So what non-embarrassing events did actually happen? Officially, that is."

"Ah. Well, it seems that Mr Lonza paid a brief visit to the UK to deal with some business matters here. However, he returned to the United States where he was unfortunate enough to be involved in a fatal car accident, along with an associate of his, one Jack Crail. I understand that, as a result of his visit, all the UK branches of his law firm will be suspending their operations and relocating elsewhere."

"I see. And Ignacio D'Razzo? The Poet, as he liked to call himself?"

Smith shrugged. "Who? There's no record of him ever entering the UK. It's possible that someone of that name died recently in some sort of gang warfare incident. There were several other casualties as well – some shootings, some involving a blunt instrument. But that all happened in America. Exactly where has yet to be decided, but that will be up to our friends over there to sort out."

"What about Casey?" I wondered.

"Believed to have gone to Mexico. Some parts of the country are very dangerous at the moment, with all the drug cartels." Smith shook his head, looking quite worried.

"And the actor?" Sam asked. "Jimmy Wayland?"

Smith's brow was furrowed, as if trying to recall a fragment of unimportant information. "Oh, he had a fall, I believe. Fatal. Somewhere in a remote part of California. After we dug him out of the back garden at Merstan House, that is. There's certainly no trace of him ever having been in the UK. Not even blood samples in a police station – thank you for letting us know about them, by the way."

I reflected on the sad irony of Jimmy Wayland's life. He'd lived as an actor, he'd died being someone else, and then even his death was turned into a fiction.

"Talking of Merstan House," Smith continued. "You may have heard reports of an explosion there. There were some rumours of a bomb, but it turned out to have been a gas explosion. Fortunately, no one was hurt."

"Well, that's a relief," I said, fingering my scar and carefully avoiding any sarcastic overtones. I hesitated for a moment, then plunged on. "But what… what about Adi?"

I felt Sandy's hand in mine, and gripped it tightly.

"Yes. Now that is a bit more of a problem, especially given your long friendship with him. And of course, Adi Varney is a great British hero. Particularly in this town, but he had fans and admirers all over the country." Smith met my gaze. "I remember seeing him at Wembley, in that last international game. The one that finished his playing career. I was impressed by his skill, of course, as we always were – but even more, I remember being amazed by the sheer raw courage of the man. And I say that as someone who sees a lot of courage. I'm not easily impressed, or amazed for that matter, but Adi Varney was something special."

"He was. He was... unique," I said quietly.

"Agreed. That being the case, we wanted to find some suitable way of bringing his story to a close, as it were. Unfortunately, that hasn't been easy. Especially given his long disappearance. But it now seems that he died as a result of a mugging. A street robbery that went wrong. It must have happened very shortly after that stunning victory over Real Madrid in California: his body was concealed and has only recently been found."

"A mugging?" Sandy shook her head. "You call that suitable? Didn't you think how it would be for his wife and kids to hear that? Can't you make it – I don't know, a heart attack or something?"

"They've got to explain the bullet wounds, Mum," Sam explained gently, and Smith nodded.

"Just so," he agreed. "And we can say that at least he died at a high point of his life, after pulling off a stunning and unexpected victory."

"He would have liked that," I agreed. "To go out on top. I think he would have preferred that to any, ah, alternative ending."

"Good. I'm glad you see it that way."

"What about Declan?" Sam asked. "He saw Adi!"

"We have had a word with Mr Healy. He now understands that the person he met whom he then believed to be Adi Varney was, in fact, an imposter – just as you had warned him. He has agreed that it would be better not to mention it."

I wondered how much Declan really understood. Certainly enough not to talk about it.

"The discovery of Mr Varney's body will be made public in the next day or so," Smith continued, "and I expect that there will be considerable media interest. I understand that you are something of an Adi Varney expert, Mr Deeson, and no doubt you will be contacted in regard to this. I hope I can rely on you to be discreet?"

I considered the alternative, of going public with my story of guns, gangsters, dodgy property deals, and multiple Adis, against the official account, which would no doubt be backed up by forensic evidence and eye-witness reports.

"I'll say nothing," I said. And while part of me was angry that the truth could so easily be suppressed, a much larger part was feeling the intense relief of a burden lifted, of a decision taken out of my hands, a responsibility no longer mine.

"You don't have to go that far. By all means talk to the press. Give them your memories of him, tell them your stories. Just avoid any mention of the past few days, that's all."

"Nothing much has happened recently anyway," I assured him.

"Good. And – sorry to pry, but I understand that you're writing a biography? I trust you won't put anything contradictory in it?"

"No."

"Excellent!" Smith beamed. "I'm glad we all understand each other."

"What about the sports centre?" Sam asked. "What will happen to that now?"

"Oh, yes. That. Well, of course I'm not privy to the contents of any will that Mr Varney might have left, but I presume that any property he owned will be inherited by his wife. What she does with that will be up to her, of course – I understand that the sports centre, or the land it stands on, could be worth quite a lot. But I think we can be confident that there will be no conflicting claims on it."

"Karen was always very proud of what Adi contributed to charity and community work," I said. "Especially the sports centre. I'm sure she'll want it to continue. We'll have to find a way to put it back on a better financial footing, though."

"Perhaps an Adi Varney legacy appeal of some sort," Smith suggested.

I smiled. "That would be… appropriate."

"Poetic, even," Sam said, with a grin.

I shook my head. "Let's not go there."

Smith stood up. "Well, if you do something like that, I'm sure that my department will make a contribution. Discreetly, of course, but the least we could do, under the circumstances. I think that's got everything settled, so I'll be on my way."

We all stood, and there was a round of formal handshaking. When Smith got to Sam, he paused for a moment.

"Your friend in Africa said that you had great potential for this line of work, and that seems to have been borne out by recent events. Would you be interested in doing this sort of thing on a more – ah – professional basis?"

Sandy caught her breath, and we exchanged glances. But Sam was already shaking his head.

"Thanks, Mr Smith, but no. I had a similar offer when I was in Africa, and turned it down then. It's not for me."

Smith raised an eyebrow. "May I ask why? Many young people would jump at such an opportunity."

"I know," Sam answered. "But... in that recent incident that never happened, if I'd been a professional I would have killed D'Razzo and the other man – Carlo – before they even knew I was there. However, like D'Razzo said, I'm not a killer. I don't want to be one."

Smith held his gaze, and behind the urbane exterior something much colder showed itself for a moment. "Yet if you had killed D'Razzo when you had the opportunity, Adi Varney would still be alive."

Sam met his gaze. "Even so." He looked at me. "Sorry, Dad."

I stood next to him, put my arm round him. "Don't be. Adi made his own choices. He created that situation, and he would have seen us both dead if things had gone his way. All the same, I would have saved him if I could have. But not at that price, Sam. Not to see you become another D'Razzo."

"I see." Smith nodded slowly. "Perhaps that is the wisest decision. There are plenty of people in the world who are willing to kill. Not so many who can choose not to when it comes to it."

Sandy came and stood with us. She put her arm round Sam from the other side, and rested her hand on my shoulder.

"I'm told that Sam got his looks from me. But he got wisdom from his father."

Smith smiled. "Yes, I can see that."

He turned to go, then stopped at the door. "Oh, nearly forgot – that package is for you. Is yours, in fact. A cricket bat, slightly used. We found it lying around somewhere." He smiled. "I'll see myself out."

CHAPTER 15

*

Later, I went back to the office. I took the bat out of the box and looked it over. There were several new dints and nicks in the woodwork, but the signatures were undamaged and it was still a serviceable piece of willow. Needed a little linseed oil on it, that was all.

I put it back in its place, turned my computer on, and looked at what I'd written earlier.

After a while I deleted it.

Then I deleted the other chapters of *A True Legend*. Afterwards I started going through the rest of the Adi files, deleting them one by one. All the documents. All the videos. All the images and photos.

All the truths. All the lies.

Carefully, systematically, one by one I erased them from existence.

Until, finally, I had only one left. A black-and-white picture of two teenagers, a younger boy, and a football.

Me frowning. Adi grinning. Davy looking on earnestly.

I left the picture on the screen and tried to pray for them. But my prayers turned into tears, and my tears became my prayer, as I wept for my brother and my friend.

CHAPTER 1

O ut of the last ten minutes of her life, Ruth Darnley spent five of them talking to me.

Is that significant? Or just coincidental? It feels significant, but I can't always trust feelings like that.

I'd just come out of court, and was standing on the back steps methodically checking my keys, my phone, my radio, and so on, when I heard her call my name from the corridor behind me.

"CSI Kepple?"

I turned round as she came out of the open doors. I was used to seeing her on the bench, and out of that context I didn't recognize her at first. A short, dark woman with a surprisingly gentle smile.

"Yes?" I asked cautiously. Then recognition kicked in and I hastily added, "Your Honour?"

She waved that away. "None of that, please. Ruth to my friends when I'm not in court. And you're Alison, right?" She put out a hand to shake. "There, that's the formalities over!"

I'd heard this about Ruth Darnley. In the courtroom, a stickler for protocol, very strong on upholding the dignity of the court. Outside it, friendly and approachable.

But still retaining a sense of authority and presence, I realized. I'm not a particularly tall woman, but I was looking down on her head. Yet at the same time I felt very much the inferior. It was confusing. Not knowing what to say, I said nothing.

She, however, had no such problem. "I'm glad I caught you, Alison. I wanted to say how much I appreciated your evidence. Not just today. You've given evidence before me on several occasions, and it's always excellent. Clear, factual, precise. So many people, even professionals, seem to feel the need to pad things out, but I've never had that from you."

I wasn't sure how to answer that. "I'm only there to say what I know. So that's what I say." *Did that sound rude?* I wondered. People think I'm rude, sometimes, though I don't mean to be. "Not much point in saying anything else." *Oh, heck, that did sound rude!* "I mean – I'm sorry – I…"

"No, no. You're absolutely right and I wish more people would think like that. It would make my job a lot easier!" She gave me a shrewd look. "You find it easier talking in court than outside of it, don't you?"

Not many get that. "There are rules, in court," I explained. "I know what I'm there for. It's defined. Outside, well – I…"

Ruth Darnley smiled. "Outside, the rules aren't clear and they're always changing."

"Yes," I agreed.

"Then stick to court rules, Alison. Be clear, concise, and accurate. People appreciate that more than you realize, and don't waste time on those who don't like it."

She held my gaze for a moment, and nodded as if she approved of what she saw. "I hope we can talk again, Alison. With more time. But I have to be going. If I can find my car in this mess!"

The main car park was being resurfaced. A yard at the rear of the courthouse, once intended for service access to the old boiler house, had been pressed into temporary car park duty, but even though it was supposedly restricted to court officials and police officers on court duty, it was totally inadequate. All the marked-out spaces had long since been filled, but vehicles had continued to drive in and park up wherever they could.

The situation was made worse by the lack of security. There were no actual human guards available to cover the gates – budget cuts had seen them replaced with CCTV and automatic barriers a year ago. And of course, the yard had neither. Just its own set of gates which, with the volume of traffic going in and out, had to be left open.

Which meant that anybody could drive in and take up space. And apparently had. The judge let out a word that I would have expected her to know but never to use.

"Looks like someone's blocked me in! That's my car, behind that rusty old Transit. I'm sure that shouldn't be here."

My CSI van was parked a short distance from Darnley's Mercedes – thankfully it seemed to be clear of obstructions. We walked in that direction together, while I considered her words, and my reaction. It seemed she was offering a friendship, which I suppose should have made me feel flattered, or even happy. Instead, it started my stomach churning with worry.

"It looks like they've left a note on my windscreen," the judge observed as we drew closer. "Good, I might be able to get out of here after all."

Something was bothering me, quite apart from the conversation. I glanced over towards the entrance. There had been someone standing there, watching us, when we came out. They weren't there now. But why should that bother me? There were people passing by all the time, often glancing in as they did so. I didn't understand why I felt uneasy about it, and not understanding made me feel worse.

We reached my van. "I have to go," I said.

"Yes, of course." Her attention was on her own car and the vehicle blocking it in. "Thank you again, Alison."

I opened the van and put my folder with all the court paperwork on the passenger seat. Ruth Darnley had reached her car and was reading a sheet of paper that had been placed under the wipers. She took out a mobile.

I went round to the side door and slid it open. I had a job to go to: a burglary on the north side of town. I'd checked all my kit was ready before I left the station, but I checked again anyway. I always do.

Fingerprint kit, camera bag, DNA recovery kit, all lined up in size order, just inside the door, just as I'd left them. I opened the camera bag, checked the camera, spare battery...

There was a thunderclap, the loudest I'd ever heard, and the van jerked sideways and flame poured round it, over it, even under it, licking up past my boots. The door sill hit my legs and I thought for a moment that the whole vehicle was going to fall over on top of me, but then it righted itself, rocking back on its suspension.

The flame was gone, but there was an acrid smell in the air, strong enough to have me coughing. And light – a colour of light that didn't belong.

I stepped out from behind the van, and saw flames climbing furiously into the air for twenty feet or more before turning into thick black smoke.

They were coming from Judge Darnley's Mercedes, or what was left of it. The car parked next to it was on fire as well. There was nothing visible of the van that had been blocking her in, though some of the burning wreckage could have been tyres.

In the midst of the flames, halfway through the Merc's windscreen, was a roughly human-shaped figure. It wasn't moving. It was never going to move again.

Behind me there was shouting, panicked screams. My radio had been turned off while I was in court; I clicked it on.

"9818 to Control."

"Control, go ahead."

"Explosion in the temporary car park at the courthouse. Several vehicles now on fire. At least one casualty, believed to be Judge Ruth Darnley. Fire service required ASAP."

There was a short pause. But Control Room staff are used to dealing with emergencies.

"9818, can you confirm the cause of the explosion?" A different voice, probably the Control Room manager cutting in. The 999 calls would already be starting.

"It appears to have been a vehicle that had been parked in front of Judge Darnley's car. A white Ford Transit, VRN unknown."

"Confirm your own status, 9818."

"I'm unharmed." I thought I was.

"Good. Do not approach the scene. Stay clear and keep other people clear. Is Judge Darnley visible to you? Does she appear injured?"

What did he think "casualty" meant? "She appears dead."

Long pause. "Stand by, 9818, Fire and Ambulance are on their way."

CHAPTER 1

I replaced my radio on its clip. Then went back into the van for my camera. I'm a CSI. We photograph things.

I started with wide shots of the general area, moved around for different angles, then zoomed in on details of burning wreckage. Especially Ruth Darnley's car. The flames had spread to other vehicles, it was hard to make out much even with the zoom, but there was still a human-shaped figure just visible through the conflagration.

I was still taking pictures when the fire service arrived. There were police officers there as well. They ushered me away, took the camera off me, led me over to some paramedics.

It was only then that I realized I was in pain from my legs, and that my eyes were aching from staring into the flames, and that my cheeks were wet with tears.

Also from Paul Trembling in Lion Fiction

PAUL TREMBLING

LOCAL POET

HE KILLED HER. BUT WHO WAS SHE?

978-1-78264-230-5

ROB SEATON KILLED A WOMAN.

Rob doesn't know Laney Grey. But when she steps out in front of his van and dies on impact, his life will never be the same.

He has to know who she was, why she chose to die, and why he had to be part of her death. To understand her, he must learn to read her poetry.

To know her, he must unravel the mysteries of her past. As Laney's dark secret starts to come to light, and Rob's innocence is questioned, he must learn the full truth.

But truth comes at a cost... Will Rob be the one who has to pay?

PAUL TREMBLING

LOCAL ARTIST

PERFECTING THE ART OF MURDER

978-1-78264-259-6

THE POLICE CALL CAME AT 4:00 AM.

A possible burglary that turns out to be a particularly nasty murder. Sandra Deeson, the Librarian who finds the bloodied body, is deeply shaken.

Then the nightmares begin... because what the police don't know is that this is not the first time she has found a corpse.

One of Sandra's colleagues is missing. The Police investigation starts and then stalls. There may be a clue in the painting someone left for Sandra — but the picture brings back memories she's tried to keep buried.

Two unidentified bodies, thirty years apart, and the only connection is Sandra herself. Last time, it cost her dearly. This time the price may be even steeper.

Christine Poulson

COLD,COLD HEART

SNOWBOUND WITH A STONE-COLD KILLER

978-1-78264-216-9

MIDWINTER IN ANTARCTICA.
SIX MONTHS OF DARKNESS ARE ABOUT TO BEGIN.

Scientist Katie Flanagan has an undeserved reputation
as a trouble-maker and her career has foundered. When
an accident creates an opening on a remote Antarctic
research base she seizes it, flying in on the last plane
before the subzero temperatures make it impossible to
leave.